# WITCHES

The fireball blasted John flesh with bits of burning metal. The pain scourged him.

It was time. He would have to risk transforming. The only alternative was death.

Blaze called upon the power of the Ghost Rider. It came with a sickening ease, shunting his thoughts and feelings off into a corner of his mind and replacing them with a single-minded need to enact justice on the wicked. Vengeance boiled the marrow of his bones, surging out of him with implacable fury. Flames burst from his collar and sleeves. His flesh faded away, exposing the smooth white surface of his grinning skull. Beneath him, flames ran along the sides of the classic Harley, twisting its shape into the familiar lines of his Hell Cycle. The wheels burst into fire as chrome twisted like liquid, rebuilding the powerful machine into something deadly: fire and vengeance on wheels.

## ALSO AVAILABLE

MARVEL UNTOLD

# GHOST RIDER IN: WITCHES UNLEASHED

## CARRIE HARRIS

ACONYTE

FOR MARVEL PUBLISHING

VP Production & Special Projects: Jeff Youngquist
Associate Editor, Special Projects: Caitlin O'Connell
Manager, Licensed Publishing: Jeremy West
VP, Licensed Publishing: Sven Larsen
SVP Print, Sales & Marketing: David Gabriel
Editor in Chief: C B Cebulski

Special Thanks to Jake Thomas

First published by Aconyte Books in 2021
ISBN 978 1 83908 100 2
Ebook ISBN 978 1 83908 101 9

Cover art by Fabio Listrani

Distributed in North America by Simon & Schuster Inc, New York, USA
Printed in the United States of America
9 8 7 6 5 4 3 2 1

**ACONYTE BOOKS**

*An imprint of Asmodee Entertainment Ltd*
Mercury House, Shipstones Business Centre
North Gate, Nottingham NG7 7FN, UK
*aconytebooks.com // twitter.com/aconytebooks*

*To Larry and Marian Rugg.*
*For motorcycle rides, biscuits and gravy,*
*and being the best bonus parents ever.*

# CHAPTER ONE

Johnny Blaze didn't notice the blood until it started flaking off. A deep red blotch circled the base of his pinkie, staining his wrist and streaking up the skin of his forearm. It was too much blood to be excused away, especially in the absence of any cuts. He'd been riding for hours in a plain white t-shirt, the gory mess advertising to every cop on the road, "I am a person of interest in the murder of Muriel Lefevre. Please pull me over. No need to be gentle about it, either." He couldn't decide which would be worse, going to jail for killing a woman who had already been dead when he'd met her, or telling the cops that her empty corpse had been possessed by Lucifer. Yes, that Lucifer, officer. They'd lock him up and throw away the key.

He crossed the state line into Georgia, sticking to the back roads. Not a lot of folks here to notice the dead woman's blood. But he had no water to wash up with, and rubbing at it with spit just smeared it around. He had to ride a good half-hour before he reached a gas station, his heart thumping all the while. Jails didn't bother him much, but he couldn't afford to waste time getting locked up, and he didn't like the idea of burning people who didn't deserve it. But somewhere deep inside him rested Zarathos, the spirit of the Ghost Rider, and it liked that idea just fine. It was almost eager, and that made him sicker than sending Muriel back to her grave had.

A dingy backroads gas station finally came into view, its lot choked with junker cars and tall weeds. He took a second to pull on his jacket despite the heat, then forced a whistle as he took the gas nozzle off the rusty machine. Places like this gave you a hard time if you tried to use the john without filling up, and he wanted to avoid attention. Just another road-weary biker in need of a piss and a fill up. Nothing to see here.

The numbers on the pump ticked up in excruciatingly slow motion. Johnny wiped sweat off his forehead and immediately regretted it. The last thing he needed was a bloody smear across his face.

An aging bell gave a desultory ding as a shiny SUV pulled up to the pump opposite him. A middle-aged mom in yoga pants got out, offering him a polite smile as she ran her card through the reader. He nodded back, whistling his tuneless song and feeling more than a little stupid about it.

The pump turned off with a bang that made him jump. He replaced the nozzle in its hanger, the motion awkward with his off hand. As he was screwing the gas cap back into place, a high and piping voice said, "Hey, mister. Nice bike!"

A gap-toothed kid stuck his head around the pump, grinning from ear to ear. Johnny turned, shielding the blood-soaked hand from view. He offered a smile. The expression sat poorly on his face. Sometimes he wondered if he'd forgotten how to do it right.

"Thanks," he said. "You like motorcycles?"

"I'm gonna have one when I grow up. Does she have a name?"

Johnny closed his eyes, shutting out the kid's bright eagerness. He hadn't named his bikes until his daughter Emma had insisted on it. For a while, he'd ridden an Indian Roadmaster named Twilight Sparkle without a word of complaint. Emma and Craig were gone now, but he still named his bikes as if she might show up one day, put her hands on her hips in that bossy way she had, and say, "Daddy, you know she needs a name. How else will she come when you call her?"

The irony of *that*, of course, was that Johnny's bikes did come when he called them, whether they were named or not.

He pushed the memory away and pasted a smile on his face. "Not yet. She's new. You got any ideas?"

The kid edged closer, his eyes glued to the graceful lines of chrome.

"Felicia?" he suggested. "That's my mom's name, and she's the prettiest lady I know, just like your bike is the prettiest one I ever saw."

"Leo, stop bugging that nice man," called the mom, tossing some trash into the can.

"I'm naming his motorcycle, Mom!" he called back with injured pride. "I'm being useful!"

Johnny snickered. "You better get back into the car. Angry moms are no joke."

"That's the T. Thanks for letting me look at your bike, mister."

The kid offered his hand. Johnny didn't get many handshakes these days. His aimless drifter vibe didn't endear him to new friends, and he didn't stick around anywhere long enough to have old ones. Despite himself, he'd started a new relationship with a trucker named Dixie, but he hadn't seen her much lately.

He'd been crisscrossing the country for weeks, full of death and fear. Touched and surprised at the gesture, he shook.

"Leo, come here right now!"

The mom's voice had gone sharp and demanding. Johnny turned to see her staring at the bloodstains on his hand with wide and frightened eyes. He released the kid and held his hands out, trying to telegraph his harmlessness.

"Go on to your mom," he said. "She's worried."

But Leo stood his ground, his lower lip thrust out in a stubborn pout. "Mom, you don't get it," he said. "He's a good guy."

"I'm not going to argue with you, Leo. Get into the car this instant!" she snapped.

"Ask him! You're a good guy, aren't you?"

Johnny swallowed. He'd done a lot of questionable things in his life. As much as he wanted to talk to the boy just a while longer and pretend to be normal, he couldn't lie to this woman who reminded him of his dead wife. Roxanne had been a gentle person until their kids were threatened, and then she could have beaten a mama bear in a fist fight.

"I won't hurt you," he said, avoiding the question.

Felicia picked up on the evasion, assuming the worst. Moving with panic-born speed, she yanked her son toward her by the sleeve of his racecar t-shirt. He toppled backwards, protesting all the while, even as she opened the door to the SUV and shoved him in. As soon as the door closed behind him, a fraction of her tension leaked from her shoulders.

When she turned back around, Johnny met her eyes. He didn't dare budge lest she interpret it as a threat and start shrieking.

"I'm sorry," he said.

"We should go."

"That's a well-mannered boy you've got there," he said. "I remember when my son was that age. He went through a phase where he communicated only in dinosaur noises."

Felicia let out a surprised laugh. She still didn't come any closer, but at least now she wasn't looking at him like he might pull out a cleaver and start chopping. Now they were just fellow parents having a friendly chat, except that one of them was covered in road dust and a dead woman's blood.

"I haven't thought of that in a long time," Johnny continued.

"They grow up too fast."

"Some of them do."

"Listen," she said, "I didn't mean to be rude. But he's all I've got, you know?"

"You don't owe me an apology."

"Do you..." she trailed off, but soon continued in a firmer voice, "I have a first aid kit in the trunk. If you're hurt..."

She thought he was injured. He only wished it was the truth.

"I'm already bandaged up good, thanks." Even that lie didn't want to come out. Her obvious concern rattled him. He wasn't used to care, and he wanted to wrap himself up in it. But he couldn't afford that, and he didn't deserve it either. He continued in a gruff tone, "I ought to go wash up, though. Before I scare the pants off somebody else."

"OK. If you're sure."

"I am. You take care of that boy of yours."

She nodded. "You take care, too. Whatever's troubling you, I hope you can fix it. For your kid if not for yourself."

Heartache stabbed Johnny with such force that his hand

went to his chest. There would be no going home to his family after his task was done. He had lost them forever, and no amount of regret would change that.

He nodded, unable to speak even if he'd known what to say.

"We'll pray for you," she said, climbing into the SUV.

Johnny Blaze stood at the edge of the gas station awning, watching until they disappeared down the road. Until this moment, he hadn't realized he was lonely, but there was nothing to be done about it. Instead, he trudged into the dingy station to ask for the bathroom key.

The next morning, Johnny woke beneath the scratchy bedspread in a by-the-hour motel. After the near crisis with Leo and his mom, he'd decided on a shower and sleep. Every hour that passed gave Lucifer more time to sow mayhem and death, but Johnny had been hunting his vessels for weeks now, and he'd been running on fumes. He couldn't afford to make mistakes born of exhaustion. No more stray bloodstains.

Now that he was refreshed and kitted up in a new dollar store undershirt and blood-free leathers, he could finish this. Lucifer would return to Hell where he belonged, and Johnny would no longer carry around the guilt that came with unleashing the Prince of Darkness and causing the apocalypse.

After returning his room key to the motel office, he climbed back onto his bike and took the highway going south. The stench of Lucifer's puppets tugged at him, a psychic stink that turned his stomach with dread and excitement. There was nothing to be excited about, not for him. But to Zarathos, the trail promised vengeance. That was all the spirit ever wanted, and it didn't care much about collateral damage. It had gotten worse lately, too, but Johnny hoped that defeating Lucifer would settle things back down.

The trail burned into his nostrils as he pulled onto a two-lane highway. It smelled like his kids' hair right after a bath mixed with the stench of a burned-out crack house. It was the perfume of Hell, a place that took your most treasured memories and corrupted them. In the movies, Hell always reeked of burning flesh and brimstone, but Johnny knew better. Hell smelled like regrets, if-onlys, and might-have-beens.

The trail took him down the back roads of Georgia, and he took advantage of the long stretches of road, opening up the bike and reveling in the wind that ruffled his hair. When he rode, he could sometimes forget his grief and anger. But the peace it offered was only momentary. When he pulled to a stop at a crossroads, the real world came flooding back, bringing the pain of loss along with it. A police car stopped opposite him, its driver staring at his cycle with unabashed admiration.

Nothing to see here, officer. Honest.

Zarathos strained at its leash, and it took every ounce of Johnny's control to keep the spirit under wraps. Steam rose from his shoulders, wisps curling out of the sleeves of his new shirt. His heart went into overdrive as he struggled to keep the spirit contained.

The cop's eyes remained glued to the bike. He didn't notice the smoking man atop it as he drove past. In his wake, Zarathos subsided, leaving nothing but a vague feeling of regret.

"What the hell is up with you?" asked Johnny aloud.

The spirit didn't answer in words. They didn't really need them after all this time. Instead, Johnny received a wave of emotions: duty, fulfillment. *Need.*

Great. Not only did he have to carry an inhuman spirit around inside him, but it was turning into a revenge junkie. He'd have to do something about that, once this Lucifer thing was taken care of.

He rode on, but he couldn't recapture the feeling he'd had only moments before. In everyone else's eyes, he was a murderer. No one saw the grieving father of two dead children, or the lonely widower, or the rider struggling under the weight of an unbearable curse.

He shook himself out of the unaccustomed fit of self-pity as he nudged the bike onto an exit ramp. Normally he avoided dwelling on his family because it made him maudlin, but the kid at the gas station had torn down his defenses. He had to rebuild them before he faced Lucifer yet again. The battles had gotten hard enough on their own; he had no need to make them worse.

His heart sank as he passed sign after sign for Fort Kenning. As his hunt had progressed, Lucifer began to make things harder. Picking an army base took the hunt to the next level. After all the times he'd been thrown in the slammer, he wouldn't make it onto base, and he refused to flame up and tear through the gates. That would bring the military down on him, and Zarathos would leap at the opportunity to burn them all and sort the rest out in the afterlife. He couldn't allow that to happen.

Maybe the trail led somewhere near the base, but not onto it. He tried to convince himself of the possibility, but every passing mile led him closer to the front gate. He stopped just before he got there, frowning at the line of cars waiting to be admitted. Then he nosed the bike around to head back into town. He needed a plan, and maybe a cold drink to go with it.

It didn't take him long to find a bar. A line of bikes sat outside, and he took a moment to look them over, but none of them called to him like Felicia did. The 1977 Low Rider could have left them all in the dust.

He bellied up to the bar, ordering a brew and a sandwich to go with it. A young Black guy in a putty colored uniform entered the bar just as his beer arrived, all glistening with condensation.

"Who's got that classic Harley outside?" the guy asked, his gaze sweeping the room. "She's gorgeous."

Johnny took a thirsty gulp and then raised a hand. "That would be me."

The guy walked over. "My pa had a bike just like it when I was a kid. Any chance you're looking to sell?"

"Sorry, friend. No can do."

"Well, can't blame a man for trying. I'm Harrison."

"That your first name or your last?"

The guy blushed. "Last name. Spend too much time in the Army, and you'll be calling your mama by her last name."

Johnny gestured to the seat next to him, the vague outlines of a plan forming in his mind. "Well, Harrison, have a seat. I'm always happy to pass the time with a fellow road hog."

"Don't mind if I do."

The soldier slid into the stool next to him, gesturing for a drink. When it arrived, he held it up to toast, grinning widely.

"Here's to new friends, new roads, and new adventures," he said.

"I'll drink to that," answered the Ghost Rider.

# CHAPTER TWO

Over the next hour or so, Johnny and Harrison swapped road stories. Most of Johnny's were heavily edited to remove the parts where he turned into a flaming skeleton and brought justice to evildoers, but he still enjoyed himself. He'd always been a loner, but he must have been getting soft in his old age.

Whenever possible, he steered the conversation toward the base, looking for an excuse to ask his new acquaintance to escort him through the gates. Harrison's reluctance to talk about his "boring" life on base didn't make that easy. Johnny ordered up another round because he didn't know what else to do. As he mulled it over, Harrison stood up, straightening his uniform with fastidious care. Once he was satisfied, he clapped Johnny on the shoulder.

"Be right back," he said. "Got to drain the snake."

"Don't let me stop you."

He watched as the soldier wound his way through the room, stopping for a quick word with a group of officers at the pool table. The wasted time nagged at him. Lucifer would sense his approach soon enough, if he hadn't already, and every passing second increased the likelihood that someone would die. On a military base, Lucifer would have a lot of toys to play with, and it was only a matter of time before he got access to them. As much as Johnny disliked the idea, he ought to go into the bathroom, knock Harrison unconscious, and escort him back to base to put him to bed. The kid would be in a load of trouble later, but it would save lives in the end.

He stood up, sighing. He already felt like a jerk, and he hadn't even thrown a punch yet. But before he could make his move, a loud klaxon split the air. The officers dashed for their drinks, draining them in swift gulps. From behind the bar, the cute young bartender called, "I'll hold your tabs, boys. You stay safe now." Harrison hurried out of the john, still fastening his pants, and made a beeline for the door.

"Sorry, man," he called to Johnny. "Emergency siren. Got to report for duty immediately. Will I catch you later?"

"Uh…"

Johnny searched for words, but "take me with you!" wasn't going to work. He leaped to his feet, throwing a few crumpled bills down next to his glass. In a few hurried steps, he caught up with Harrison.

"No way you're enlisted," the soldier said. His pace didn't falter as he hurried toward the door with Johnny at his shoulder. "Not with that scraggly-as-heck hair."

"No, but bikes are good in an emergency," Johnny replied, thinking fast. "The roads'll be a mess. I'll follow you just in case somebody important needs a ride."

"Suit yourself," Harrison replied.

The two of them mounted up on their bikes, Harrison pausing for one precious second to admire the Low Rider's sleek form. In tandem, they pulled out into the street. Johnny had been right about one thing: cars and pickups clogged the road, sending traffic to a standstill. The two motorcycles weaved their way toward the gates as the high wail of police sirens joined the insistent honk of the emergency klaxon.

As they joined the line at the gate, Johnny steeled himself for what they would find on base. Nothing would have surprised him. Lucifer could have been riding down the street on the back of a nuke, and he wouldn't even blink. At this point, he'd seen everything.

Although that was true, he still shouted in surprise when the tank smashed through the gates.

# CHAPTER THREE

The chain link rattled, and concertina wire tore free with a tortured screech as a tank barreled through the fence. The heavy sand-colored vehicle moved unexpectedly fast, mowing down everything in its path at what had to be at least thirty miles per hour. The guards scattered moments before it pulverized their little hut. Then the war machine began to trundle down the road as desperate soldiers leaped from their cars to avoid being crushed under its massive weight.

"You take left, I'll go right!" Harrison shouted, his face wild with fear and elation. "We'll get around it!"

He gunned his motor and took off, driving too fast for the crowded conditions and panicked crowds. Johnny had no idea what the plan was beyond splitting up, but it didn't much matter. He knew who was inside that tank, and Harrison's plan wouldn't work.

With a practiced flip of the hand, he pulled his shotgun free of the holster mounted on the side of the bike. The shells wouldn't put a dent in an armored tank, but he didn't expect them to. Instead, he called upon the Hellfire that simmered within him constantly, a burning lake of pain and regret. Everything he had lost, every pain he'd endured, increased his capacity to draw upon it, and he would need to go deep to take out such a heavily armored vehicle. The shotgun burst into flames as he poured the power of Hellfire into it.

Zarathos surged inside him, desperate to get free. The spirit wanted a chance at Lucifer, but Johnny couldn't risk changing yet. Once, they'd controlled the Rider in perfect balance, Johnny's mortal values offsetting Zarathos's inhuman single-mindedness. But as he'd worked his way through Lucifer's puppets, Zarathos had gotten squirrelly. Sometimes Johnny worried that he'd give up control and never get it back.

A woman screamed. People tended to shriek when he lit things on fire, so he didn't think much of it until he looked up to see the tank's massive turret shifting as it lined up on its target.

Him.

The Hellfire had gotten Lucifer's attention. Johnny gunned his Harley. The tires squealed as he veered off to the right, trying to buy himself the precious moments he needed to line up his shot. A plume of fire split the air as the tank fired on him. The shell whistled past, a gout of hot air blasting his cheeks. Then a bright red sports car, empty of passengers, burst into flames.

*Whoom!*

The resulting fireball blasted Johnny with heat, peppering his flesh with bits of burning metal. The pain scourged him.

It was time. He would have to risk transforming. The only alternative was death.

He called upon the power of the Ghost Rider. It came with a sickening ease, shunting his thoughts and feelings off into a corner of his mind and replacing them with a single-minded need to enact justice on the wicked. Vengeance boiled the marrow of his bones, surging out of him with implacable fury. Flames burst from his collar and sleeves. His flesh faded away, exposing the smooth white surface of his grinning skull. Beneath him, flames ran along the sides of the classic Harley, twisting its shape into the familiar lines of his Hell Cycle. The wheels burst into fire as chrome twisted like liquid, rebuilding the powerful machine into something deadly: fire and vengeance on wheels.

"Oh my God, what is that?" someone screamed.

The bike responded to the Rider's unspoken command, scorching a line into the pavement as it evaded the path of the swiveling gun. The bike screeched to a stop, leaving an arc of burnt rubber on the pavement in its wake, buying precious seconds to set up his shot. He took unwavering aim at the armored vehicle and fired with superhuman precision. The shell screamed towards the tank, a red streak of fire like an arrow piercing the air. It went down the barrel of the mounted gun, straight into the belly of the assault vehicle.

The tank exploded with a deafening bang, releasing a fireball that lit the nearby trees.

The Ghost Rider watched with implacable calm as fragments of superheated metal went flying with such speed that they buried themselves in tree trunks and car hoods. Somewhere behind him, a man yelped in pain. A large piece of armor flew at the Rider, sizzling as it struck his jacket, knocking him from the bike. He stood up. About fifty feet away, a young Black soldier lay next to a still-running motorcycle, his face slack with unconsciousness.

Inside the Rider, Johnny and Zarathos warred for dominance.

Zarathos had work to do, and the spirit was eager to hunt. But Johnny refused to leave Harrison out in the open like this. In a time of crisis, the young man had rushed toward the danger. That kind of bravery was worthy of respect, and Johnny refused to leave him in the middle of the road.

The tank opened with a screech of burning metal, and a blazing figure emerged from the raging fire. People screamed in horror as Lucifer made his way from the wreckage. He wore the body of a middle-aged man in a scorched military uniform, but there was no mistaking him for just a normal person. The intense flames melted the flesh from his bones as he pulled himself from the wreckage, grinning in anticipation. A young woman leaned out of her car window and vomited on the pavement at the sickening sight.

There was no time to lose, but Johnny refused to relent. If he let Harrison die to serve his own purposes, he wouldn't be any better than the King of Hell. He certainly wouldn't deserve the power of the Rider.

This logic convinced Zarathos when all other arguments had failed.

"*Innocent,*" he said aloud in a voice like rusty metal.

He picked Harrison up and moved him to safety as burning debris continued to patter down around them. Then he turned to face Lucifer, the Prince of Lies, ready to do battle and send yet another fragment of his soul back to Hell where it belonged.

But Lucifer wouldn't be fighting. He emerged from the flames and stood wavering on the street. Bits of flesh fell from his melting body and sizzled on the pavement. He staggered toward the Rider, lips burned away to expose an eerie grin. Zarathos returned it with a toothy smile of his own.

"*Too easy,*" he said, reaching out to grab onto the shambling figure. "*But it's time to go home now.*"

Lucifer's jaunty tones emerged from the man's mouth, the mellifluous voice at odds with the burned body that produced it.

"Too easy? Would you rather I begged for mercy?" he asked, his face oozing sickeningly with every movement. "Oh, please, Mr Rider! Let me go! I can't possibly get up to any trouble in this state, could I?"

"*No mercy. Not for you.*"

"Well, never fear. My next shard will give you plenty of amusement. It'll be like coming home." The burned almost-corpse let out a wheezing cackle. "And we know how much you long for home, Johnny."

The eerie laughter of the corpse was cut off as the Ghost Rider's crushing grip squeezed any semblance of life from its bones. He met the body's eyes, searching for the demonic spark hiding in their depths. With a howl of agony and scorn, the six hundred and fifty-seventh fragment of Lucifer's soul came free, and the Ghost Rider returned it to Hell where it belonged.

Its job completed, the spirit retreated, its flame fading to blue and then flickering out entirely as the flesh returned to cover his bones once more. The bike twisted, becoming a classic Harley again. Johnny looked down at the burnt corpse at his feet. This had been way too easy.

He should have been relieved, but Lucifer didn't do easy. He was playing another one of his games, and Johnny didn't like that one bit.

# CHAPTER FOUR

An abnormally gentle Florida spring shower began to fall as Topaz locked the shop door behind her. She paused, tilting her head back and letting the drops patter onto her face. She'd always loved the rain. After a long day's work, there was nothing like curling up with a book, a light blanket, and a steaming cup of ramen while the A/C blasted in her face. She had a few historical romances stashed under her bed that she couldn't wait to bust out. Sometimes she felt silly for hiding her reading material like a child, but the last time she'd left one of her books out, her roommate Satana had highlighted all the risqué parts and left critical comments in the margins.

The rain soaked her clear through as she crossed the small town square. At first she'd been skeptical about settling here despite Satana's insistence that a town named Salem was the perfect place for three modern day witches to hide. But she loved it here. She loved the rows of palm trees that ran down Main Street, and the stately brick of the college buildings. She loved the rowdy crowds of undergraduates that crowded the aisles of Mystic Energies at the beginning of every year, eager to buy tarot cards and Ouija boards. Then, later in the year, the curious dabblers would trickle off, leaving them with a dedicated core of customers who were actually interested in learning something. On occasion, they'd run across a student with some true magical talent, which never failed to excite.

As she passed Mac's Bar, she raised a hand to the group of guys clustered outside, eager to get a head start on the evening's revelries. A pasty, red-haired boy with the patchy beginnings of a beard looked her up and down with frank admiration, elbowing his buddy, a stocky Latino.

"Hey, Topaz!" said the buddy, grinning. "Where's your sister?"

She had no family that she could remember, but their coven had decided early on to keep their story simple. When they moved to Salem and opened the shop, they'd changed their names. Jennifer's surname, Kale, would attract too much magical attention, and Satana's would attract the demonic. Topaz had never had a last name or any paperwork to prove her identity, not until now. Now they were the LeFay sisters. Everyone in town knew the name was fake, but they never would have suspected the truth in a million years. They thought the witches were frauds when in reality they were three of the most talented mystics in the world, with a combined power that would rival the great Doctor Strange himself.

Topaz pushed away the thought of Stephen Strange and smiled at the boy. She didn't need to ask which sister he wanted. The boys always wanted Satana, to her eternal delight. Topaz always tried to talk some sense into them, but it never worked.

"You should stay away from her," she said, not unkindly. "She'll chew you up and spit you out."

"Sounds like fun," said the Latino kid, puffing up his chest and winning a back slap from his friend.

Topaz rolled her eyes and continued on toward home. It had taken some time for the coven to find a house they all liked. Even though there were only three of them, they had such wildly disparate tastes. Jennifer was practical to a fault, except when it came to libraries, which could never be big enough. Satana wanted the kind of dramatic ambience usually seen in vampire movies. Topaz had wanted a comfortable home full of squishy sofas and treasured heirlooms. She'd lived many places, but she'd never had a home before. They'd finally settled on a rambling Victorian house on the outskirts of town, and after almost five years, Topaz still loved it as much as the day they'd moved in. Sometimes she wondered what she'd done to deserve such happiness.

She turned up the walk toward the front door. The fitful rain had washed away the ever-present yellow film of pollen that coated their front step, leaving only a few stubborn deposits at the corners. The sight reminded her that she needed to ask Satana for more stinging nettle to mix up a fresh batch of Aller-G Tea for the shop. The succubus was very territorial about her garden, and Topaz couldn't blame her. She'd always been good with plants, but Satana could have grown orchids on the moon.

To her surprise, she entered the house to find Jennifer waiting at the dining room table. On her average day off, Jennifer didn't even leave the library to pee. Topaz had always wondered how she managed that, but some things were better left unasked.

Today, the sorceress sat at the ornately carved table, bent over another one of her dusty old books, with twin mugs full to the brim with steaming noodles.

Topaz paused on the front mat, carefully removing her wet things and hanging them to dry. "I hope one of those is for me," she said. "I'm starving."

Jennifer smiled, tucking a velvet ribbon into the crease of the pages to hold her place before closing the book. Topaz had always felt comfortable with Jennifer, and they had a lot in common. Although Jenny was fair and blond while she had dusky skin and dark, curly hair, they shared the same build and a heart-shaped face. They both preferred a no-nonsense style, dressing for comfort, while Satana looked like a dominatrix on her off day more often than not.

Jennifer pushed one of the mugs across the table. "Was the shop busy today?"

"Oh yeah. Lots of panicked undergrads asking for teas that will keep them up to study for exams and magic amulets that will change all their grades to As." Topaz grinned, pulling the mug closer and curling her hands around its heat. "They're so cute."

Jennifer frowned.

"Is something wrong?" asked Topaz, her gaze sharpening.

The blond sorceress took a deep and steeling breath before pulling something from her pocket and sliding it across the table. It was an ornate golden key, its stem strung with beads of rose quartz. A familiar lock of curly black hair had been laced through the hole. It had been tied off with a neat bow of red ribbon, secured with a dot of red candle wax.

Topaz picked up the token, ignoring the way it made her skin crawl. Even the most inexperienced practitioner could have identified it from a mile away. Rose quartz, keys, and the color red tended to figure prominently in beginner love charms. She didn't need to touch the hair to know it was hers. After all, she spent hours wrestling with those curls every day.

"Where did you find this?" she asked.

"I went into your bag to get the herbal guide I'd loaned you." Jennifer flushed, holding up the book in question. "I should have asked before rummaging around in your stuff, but I just needed to look something up real quick. I sensed it as I was pulling the book out. I'm sorry for going through your things, but…"

Topaz nodded, eager to reassure her friend that trust hadn't been breached. "I meant to give the book back to you yesterday anyway." She paused, frowning. "This is probably just a joke. Not a good one, but still."

"A joke?" Jennifer arched a brow. "I don't find it funny."

"Well, no. They'll have to be stopped, but…"

Topaz trailed off. She didn't want to explain it, but she knew that whoever had placed this charm didn't really intend to brainwash her into love. After all, she was so desperate and lonely that she would have dated just about anyone if they'd only asked. The truth wasn't pleasant, but that didn't make it any less true.

Jennifer frowned, her expression grim. "I don't like the idea of idiots throwing love spells around in our town. Can you identify the worker? I tried, but the traces are so faint. Empathic magic has never been my strong suit."

That was an understatement. Empaths needed a certain amount of vulnerability to walk the web of connections that bind all living beings, and Jennifer kept herself locked up tighter than the Sanctum Sanctorum. Her sense of self was too strong to merge with the resonance of the One. But now wasn't the time for lectures on magical theory.

Of the three witches, Topaz was the strongest empath, but the whisper of magic from the charm was so faint that it would take her utmost concentration to identify it. She rolled her shoulders back, taking a deep breath and emptying her mind. Before she could make any headway, the front door opened, letting in a blast of humid air. She shuddered, her concentration broken.

Satana Hellstrom carried a pair of brown paper grocery bags into the house, setting them down on the tile as fat drops blew in through the open door.

"Honey, I'm home!" she called.

"I'm not your honey," said Jennifer.

"More's the pity," replied Satana. "I'm bored. A steady diet of undergraduates has jaded me. Do you see how jaded I am?"

The succubus didn't look jaded. She wore a black suit with an uncomfortably narrow pencil skirt and high heels that could have doubled as tent spikes in a jam. Satana changed hairstyles like some people changed clothes. Currently, she sported a platinum bob. But Satana could become anything she wanted down to the bone, while Topaz had always been just herself.

"Don't eat too many noodles," Satana continued. "I'm grilling steaks tonight."

"In this weather?" asked Jennifer.

"I like to live on the wild side." Satana's impish grin faded as she saw the charm on the table. She dropped the bags on the table and leaned over to take a closer look. "What in the blazing fires of Hell is that?"

"Someone tried putting a love spell on Topaz," said Jennifer.

Her quiet voice cut through the room. Satana straightened, her pupils glowing red with anger. A faint scent of brimstone saturated the air. By this time, the other two witches had gotten used to her fragrant flare-ups. Once they'd taken all the batteries out of the smoke detectors, they'd become quite bearable.

"Please don't tease me," Topaz begged. "Not this time."

As the resident wild child in a house full of homebodies, Satana could sometimes get to be a little much. Sometimes, she bragged that she'd made Topaz blush every day for an entire year. If anything, that was an understatement.

"I only joke about things that are funny," Satana snarled. "This is not."

"Agreed," said Jennifer. "Topaz is going to figure out who made it so we can have a little talk with them."

"Delightful."

Satana began cracking her knuckles. They sounded like fireworks. Topaz tried to concentrate, but the incessant crackle grated on her nerves.

"Could you please stop?" she asked. "I can't focus."

The succubus stared at her for a moment, her eyes completely red in an expressionless face. Wisps of steam poured off her shoulders and hair. Then she relaxed, regaining control with visible effort, her eyes fading to their usual dark brown.

"I'll put the steaks in the fridge," she said. "We can celebrate with them later after we nail this guy's—"

"Satana," Jennifer cautioned. "Language."

"Oh, fine."

With that, Satana swooped up her groceries and carried them into the kitchen. In her wake, Jennifer cracked one of the windows to let some fresh air in. Topaz smiled in appreciation as the odor of burning things faded away.

"Thanks," she said.

"She's just being protective," said Jennifer, staring toward the kitchen.

"Oh, I know. It's kind of nice, actually."

"You enjoy having to keep your pretend sister from eviscerating people who displease her on a regular basis?" Jennifer arched a brow. "You really have changed."

"You know she just says those outlandish things to get a rise out of us. She doesn't really mean them." Jennifer snorted, and Topaz felt compelled to add, "Most of the time."

"Well, I won't argue with you, since you're the empath." Jennifer nudged at the charm on the table. "Speaking of empathy…"

Topaz cleared her mind, focusing on the soothing patter of rain on the windows and the distant slam of cabinet doors as Satana put the groceries away. She felt the deep ties that linked her to Jennifer and Satana, her sisters in spirit if not in name. She sensed the flicker of magic in the love charm, and the tenuous string that tied it to its maker.

"I'm going now," she said, her voice sounding impossibly far away to her own ears. "Watch my back."

"I'll pull you out if it goes sideways," Jennifer promised.

What a wonder it was to hear that and know that it was true. The three of them hadn't always been this close – in fact, they'd hated each other when they first met. But now, she trusted them both with her life.

She furled up her consciousness and followed the thread of magic toward the person who had tried to ensorcell her. She had a few things she wanted to ask them, like why they would choose Topaz when Jennifer and Satana were better at... well, just about everything.

# CHAPTER FIVE

The deep blue of twilight covered the sky by the time the coven returned home. The rain had trailed off, leaving behind a deep, damp smell that reminded Jennifer Kale of rebirth and new beginnings. A peaceful silence blanketed the neighborhood, or it would have if Topaz and Satana would take a breather. They'd been chattering nonstop since they had left Steven Leach's house. He'd tried to deny ownership of the love charm at first, but Satana had scared the truth out of him. People tended to spill their secrets when confronted by someone literally smoking with fury. He'd 'fessed up eventually, and then Jennifer had talked some sense into him while Satana loudly debated the use of a variety of household objects to rearrange his face.

If left to her own devices, Jennifer would have chosen a subtler approach, but she had to admit that Satana got things done. Over the years, she'd gotten used to it, and most of the time it didn't bother her. But she worried. One day, this perfect house of cards would come crashing down, and she hoped she'd be strong enough to save it. After all, nothing lasted forever, no matter how much you wanted it to.

"We should have brought the car," Satana complained, pulling her five-inch heels off and padding down the sidewalk in her bare feet.

"If you'd bought something less conspicuous than that hot rod, maybe. He would have taken one look at it and ran," replied Jennifer.

"Or he would have assumed that his spell worked, and Topaz was coming by to seduce him with her hot wheels," Satana grinned, her eyes alight with impish delight. "Honestly, 'Paz? What is it with you and men named Steve? Are you trying to collect the whole set?"

"That's enough of that, please," said Jennifer.

"Yes, Mom. But can you imagine, our little schoolgirl and that yob?"

"I'm almost afraid to ask, but what's a yob?" asked Topaz.

"A yob is a geeky little boy with delusions of grandeur. I got it from TV, since *someone* gets all prissy when I swear," said Satana.

"I don't care if a man isn't muscular..." said Topaz thoughtfully.

"No, but trying to take away your free will is a dealbreaker."

"You can say that again."

For one rare moment, Topaz and Satana exchanged looks of complete agreement, as Jennifer looked on in approval. She often found herself playing referee between Satana's gleeful troublemaking and Topaz's carefully maintained innocence. Not that she minded. It was almost like having siblings again.

"You should have let me teach him a lesson, Jenny," said Satana, obliterating the mood. "I'm disappointed."

"You know the drill," Jennifer replied with the infinite patience of someone who has had this conversation a million times before and expects to have it again very soon. "You take the lead in combat situations. Topaz is primary for interpersonal problems. But when it comes to magical issues, I've got trump. You can like it or lump it."

"You know, you're really hot when you're forceful like that." Satana fanned herself.

"You sound like one of those creepers who come into the shop," Topaz declared. "Please take it back?"

But Satana changed the subject instead, stepping out onto the cracked concrete of Main Street with a blatant disregard for the crosswalk just a few yards away.

"You know, we could solve a lot of problems, if you just let me lead on everything. Little Leach would toe the line after I shook my fist in his face," she said.

"It's less the fist and more the red eyes and brimstone," murmured Topaz, following her across the street.

"Good idea. I can shake them in his face, too."

"Actually," Jennifer said from the crosswalk, raising her voice to speak over them. "I've been thinking we need to offer some classes."

"Classes?" asked Satana, her voice blank. "What kind of classes?"

"Arcane ethics. We're seeing a distinct uptick in local dabblers getting in too deep. It would be better if we could head those problems off before they started."

"That sounds boring. I prefer the fist-shaking."

"If my brother had gotten that kind of guidance, he might still be alive," said Jennifer.

The comment threw a bucket of cold water on the banter, but she couldn't bring herself to regret it. She understood the need to wind down after an altercation. Steven Leach had known that – if it worked – his love charm would override Topaz's free will, but he'd rationalized it. He thought himself so desperately in love that it justified any action necessary to win her affections. When Jennifer had pointed out that he would be making the woman he claimed to love into a slave, he'd protested that he wouldn't have made her do anything she didn't want to, ignoring the fact that he'd tried to manipulate her into wanting it in the first place. The whole thing left a sour taste in Jennifer's mouth, and the rest of the coven needed to take it seriously.

The silence stretched between them, until Satana murmured, "Well. That was a thing you said."

"It's true," Jennifer retorted.

"I'm sorry," Topaz interjected. "I started it. But the whole situation makes me so uncomfortable, and I was trying to bury it in humor."

"I do that," said Satana. "I won't deny it."

"Right? I keep wondering what would have happened if I'd had no magic at all? Would I be in his arms right now, thinking I wanted to be there when I didn't?" Topaz shuddered. "Honestly, things like this are why I think I should swear off love for good."

That comment brought Jennifer up short right at the mouth of their walkway. This was the first she'd heard about such a thing, and if a diehard romantic like Topaz was making vows like that, her trauma was deeper than Jennifer had realized.

She exchanged a look with Satana, who wore an expression of angry concern that was equal parts reassuring and concerning. If Satana took this seriously, Jennifer wasn't overreacting.

"What do you mean?" she asked.

Topaz sighed, looking down at the ground. "Do we really have to get into this now?" she asked, but before she could continue, Jennifer held up a hand for quiet.

Now that they'd drawn close to the house, something nagged at her. She'd warded the place with obsessive thoroughness, layering protections atop the rooms and grounds over the course of six full months. No way would she leave the *Tome of Zhered-Na* unattended without sufficient protection. When it came to the magical book that had resulted in her brother's death, she couldn't be too careful. She didn't even take it outside her heavily warded bedroom if she could avoid it. No sense in tempting fate.

Nothing had tripped her magical shields, but something tickled at the edge of her senses. She focused, expanding her awareness to test her shields, holding up a hand at the ready and drawing in a bluish globe of raw magical power just in case. Satana took in these preparations and snarled, her eyes flaring with red. Her nails sharpened to claws, and a wickedly graceful set of horns sprouted from her head as she developed her demon form, taking a step forward to ensure that any physical threats would hit her first. Topaz exhaled with the long, slow concentration of a Buddhist at prayer, a soft golden glow spilling from her to touch her coven, lending them calmness in the face of the unknown threat, the eye in the center of the storm.

The empathic boost sharpened Jennifer's senses, helping

*Marvel Untold*

her to drop internal walls she tended to forget about without the magical assistance. Her awareness unfurled, taking in layer upon layer of protective spells. All were intact, and she could sense the lurking darkness of the Tome, safely hidden away within the walls of the old Victorian. Reassured, she swept the grounds, trying to pin down the source of her discomfort.

A familiar presence approached them from around the side of the house. She sensed him only a moment before she saw him, and a mingled sensation of caution and relief ran through her. She let go of the growing power she held in her hands but did not lower them. They might be family, but they weren't always friends.

"Johnny Blaze," she called. "What brings you to my home?"

"It's good to see you, too, cousin," he said, stepping out into the glow of the streetlight and offering what he probably thought was a charming smile.

"So, we're not trying to kill each other this time?"

"I hope not. I'm out of clean shirts," he replied. "Hellstrom. Topaz. Good to see you."

"Here in Salem, our last name is LeFay."

Jennifer put stern emphasis on the name. She held no illusion that they couldn't be tracked. They hadn't even bothered to change their first names, because their magic spoke for itself. Any mystic with a decent amount of skill would sense their power from miles away. Cloaks could only do so much. But still, there was no need to invite trouble, and the Ghost Rider tended to do just that.

"All right," he said. "Can I come in?"

"That all depends on what you want."

"Advice for starters. Help if you'll give it."

This was her call, but for something this big, they all needed to be in agreement. They'd each run up against Johnny before, and not all the encounters had been pleasant. She wouldn't make them vulnerable to him again without their express approval. She looked at Topaz, the question written in her eyes.

"I'll follow your lead on this one," the psychic murmured. "I don't know him as well as either of you do. He thinks he's telling the truth, though."

Jennifer turned to Satana, telegraphing the same question.

"When the Rider comes 'round, the doo-doo is about to hit the fan," said Satana. "I'd rather have advance warning if it's all the same to you. Let's hear him out."

"Thanks for the vote of confidence," said Johnny. "Doo-doo?"

Satana sighed. "I catch a lot of grief for my language, remember? Well, Jenny? What's the play?"

Jennifer nodded, the decision made. The cousins didn't always see eye to eye, but Johnny fought the good fight in his own way. If he was willing to face her ire, he must be dealing with something of critical importance.

"Come on in, Bonehead," she said, pulling out her keys. "We'll hear you out."

# CHAPTER SIX

A short while later, the four of them sat around the circular wooden dining table, mugs of tea wafting steam into their wary faces. No sooner did Topaz sit down than she bounced up again.

"Almost forgot the sugar!" she exclaimed, grabbing it from the cluttered kitchen counter and returning to the table. "Sorry about that. Would you like some, Johnny?"

He eyed his cup with the skepticism of a longtime coffee drinker and nodded, dumping five heaping spoonfuls into his mug. Satana grinned. Over the years, she'd gotten used to Topaz's teas. From the smell of it, this was either the one that promoted peace or the one that encouraged honesty. Of course, such simple spells didn't work on Satana Hellstrom, but if they made the Rider spill more than he'd intended, she'd drink them by the gallon.

She watched him drink in silence. Although she'd never been friendly with the Rider, she had to admit that he was attractive enough, with his tousled blond hair, lanky frame, and grizzled features. In a different world, she might have been interested.

But Johnny had shown himself entirely too eager to kill off members of the Hellstrom clan, starting with her brother. Sometimes Satana had wanted to kill Daimon herself, but that didn't mean she could condone such behavior. She would hear the Ghost Rider out, but she harbored a healthy level of distrust regarding every word that came out of his mouth. After all, she hadn't survived this long by being naïve.

At least Jennifer wore an expression of suspicion that mirrored her own. Sometimes the sorceress could be squirrelly when it came to family. She'd nearly gotten them all killed when the Hellphyr had taken over her brother, but at the end she'd done her duty at Andy's request. She'd put him out of his misery. Over the intervening years, they'd managed to avoid contact with the magically talented Kale clan, and Johnny's appearance threatened to upend the fragile balance they'd managed to achieve. Satana would have to watch Jennifer to be certain she was handling her cousin's appearance as well as she seemed.

"So, what's going on?" Satana asked. "I'd love to sit around all night and have a slumber party, but I have steaks to cook. If I don't get something to eat soon, I'll have to pick one of you. Probably Johnny, since I hate him by default."

The Rider met her eyes, his cheeks flushing but his gaze steady and calm. "I don't have any beef with you, Satana. Not right now. Maybe we'll come to blows someday, but it'll have to wait. What I've got to do is too important," he said.

"I'm listening," Satana replied. "And I haven't tried to kill you yet."

"I appreciate that." Johnny took a sip of his tea, winced, and set the cup down. Some of Topaz's concoctions took a little getting used to, but at least they worked. She made a sedative tea that Satana sometimes drank. The succubus rarely slept, but it took the edge off enough for her to get a little rest. The first time she realized how well it worked, she picked Topaz up and spun her around in a wild hug. The empath's squeal of shock still made her smile whenever she thought about it.

"What's so funny?" asked Jennifer, suspiciously.

"You don't want to know," replied Satana with perfect honesty. "So, Ghost Rider, are you going to tell us what brings you to our humble abode or not? Would you like some crayons to draw us a picture?"

"We don't have crayons," said Jennifer.

"I do," added Topaz. "I also have a unicorn coloring book if he wants it. Satana gave them to me for my birthday." She folded her hands and fixed him with a stern look. "But I'm with her. I'd like to know why you're here, please."

"Like I said, I need advice. And some help, if you're willing to offer any. It's a long story with a ton of background that you probably don't need, and there's really no sugarcoating it anyway. What it boils down to is that I got myself stuck in Hell. When I managed to break out, I accidentally let Lucifer out with me. I didn't realize it at the time, but that's neither here nor there," he said.

Satana stiffened. As the lone half-demon at the table, she had the most experience with the denizens of Hell. They used to be her neighbors, back in the awful old days when she'd called the place her home unsweet home. Back then, her father Marduk had pretended he was Satan for kicks and giggles. Then she'd met Lucifer. It hadn't been a pleasant experience.

Over the past few years, she'd tried to cultivate control over her demonic impulses, but she slipped sometimes. Like now. Her nails thickened into claws, which scraped into the surface of the wooden table as she clenched her hands into involuntary fists.

Both Johnny and Jennifer drew back from the table, but Topaz reached out and took Satana's hand in hers. Her gentle fingers stroked the hard chitin of Satana's claws, and her green eyes met the half-demon's red ones.

"Let me help," she said. "It's OK."

The obvious concern in her voice brought Satana back under control without any magical interference needed. With effort, she banished the claws, replacing them with her usual red manicured nails. She patted her hair into place. No horns, but her hair had reverted to the luscious black waves of her natural form. That more than anything shook her. Her father had pulled her strings for years, and her independence from him had been hard won. She wasn't about to go back to the days when the mere mention of his name threw her off her game.

"I've got it under control," she growled. "But he's lucky I don't leap across the table and pull his guts out. If he brings Lucifer down on us, I still might."

To his credit, Johnny didn't try to make excuses. Instead, he watched her with sad blue eyes.

"You know what he's capable of," he said. "It'll be Hell on Earth if he isn't stopped, and it's my fault he's here in the first place. I let him out. It's my job to put him back."

"Damn straight it is. Where do we come in?" she asked.

"When he came through the portal with me, he couldn't quite fit. He broke into fragments – six hundred and sixty-six of them, as irony would have it. Each one took over a body. You can guess what he did with his newfound freedom. More blood and death than even I can handle. It hasn't been pretty," he said, shuddering. "I've been tracking them down and sending them back to Hell."

"And he's running," said Jennifer. "Do you need help tracking him, or what?"

"No, he wants to be found. Every puppet I destroy makes the remaining ones that much stronger. Eventually, there will be only one left. All Lucifer's power, concentrated in one body. That's been his goal all along."

"Jesus," said Satana. "I'd cross myself, but I'd probably burst into flames."

"It's not funny," Jennifer said, scowling.

"Would you rather I dig a few more furrows into our table? You either get sarcastic Satana, or murderous Satana. I assume you'd prefer the former."

Topaz put hands on both their shoulders, and this time she didn't ask for permission. A soothing calm washed over Satana, and the angry tension in Jennifer's shoulders eased. The demoness shook off the touch with a rough mutter of thanks. She didn't want to be soothed. If there was ever a time to be pissed off, this was it.

"It's bad," said Johnny, drawing their attention back to him with more tact than Satana would have given him credit for. "But I've been making good progress. I've got nine more fragments to go, and then, if I'm still alive, I'm gonna sleep for about two years."

"I don't get it," said Topaz. "If you've got it handled, why are you here?"

"That's where things get sticky." Johnny took another sip

from his mug and winced. "I can sense the fragments. I'm not sure how to explain it except to say that they stink."

"Hellfire has a certain aroma," said Satana. "Any demon can smell it if you get close enough. I imagine the Rider has a highly developed sense for it, given your job."

"Exactly. But the latest one has me worried."

"Why?" asked Jennifer, her expression wooden.

"Because it smells like a Kale, and it's here in town," said Johnny.

# CHAPTER SEVEN

In the wake of Johnny's announcement, the silence was deafening. One by one, they all turned to Jennifer, who had frozen with a mixture of incredulity and fear. If he was right, the implications couldn't have been worse. But she couldn't believe it. No Kale could enter the city limits without triggering every single one of her alarms. Heck, she'd known last year when a distant cousin with barely any magical power at all went to Key West for spring break, and he hadn't come within a hundred miles of Salem.

Johnny had to be mistaken. She shook her head, taking a sip of her tea.

"There's no way," she said. "If there was a Kale here, I'd know."

"I'm sure you would, but..."

She interrupted him before he could get going again.

"It's my job to know, Johnny," she said. "If that's all you've got, I'd like to eat. I'm getting hungry enough that I might resort to cannibalism, too. Satana, can you grill up those steaks, or would you rather get takeout? Is there enough for Johnny as well?"

"I got enough. And I'll cook them so long as you promise not to continue the conversation without me," the succubus replied.

"The conversation is over," said Jennifer.

"No, it isn't," said Satana, her expression mulish.

Jennifer nearly spat out a retort, but Topaz kept a hand on her shoulder, encouraging calm. The sorceress felt anything but calm. A flash of insight hit her like a freight train: this way lay death. She'd never had premonitions before, but the certainty was undeniable. She knew it down to her marrow even if she couldn't have articulated how she knew; confronting Lucifer would mean the end of their coven.

She took a deep breath, trying to uncover the source of the feeling. It wasn't just nerves. After Andy had died, she'd spent months on edge, waiting for another tragedy to strike. This felt completely different. Before, her anxiety had fueled her caution, but now the bone-deep knowledge that this was a dangerous road fed her anxiety. After all, who in their right mind would take on the Prince of Darkness when they had another option? It didn't matter where the feeling had come from, because exercising extreme caution just made sense in this situation. Johnny might not like that, but he'd have to understand. More than anyone, he knew what Lucifer was capable of.

Satana forestalled any further argument by heading into the kitchen, unruffled by the sorceress's obvious displeasure. In her absence, Jennifer, Johnny, and Topaz all stared at each other in awkward silence. Over the next few minutes, Topaz shifted in increasing discomfort before finally blurting, "So it's been a long time since you've seen each other?"

Johnny arched a brow. "Yeah. I see you've finally gotten some pants that button, Jen."

"They were my favorite pants. They were comfortable, and they had decent pockets. You have no idea how rare that is in women's clothing."

"I'd wear a paper bag if it had good pockets," Topaz agreed. "I remember those pants. You wore them all the time when we started the coven. What happened to them?"

"Oh, they were falling apart. I could deal with it when the button fell off, but not so much when they got holes in indecent places. I had to get rid of them."

"Too bad," said Topaz.

Johnny pushed back from the table, looking around. The dining room had been painted in a rich shade of purple, and sconces on the walls emitted a gentle glow. Topaz's houseplants crowded every inch of the sizable window seat, stretching long tendrils of ivy up along the walls to the ceiling. Random knickknacks cluttered the mantel as well as the floor beneath it, golden statues of Ganesh bumping elbows with delicate porcelain fairies and lion dogs.

"Nice place you've got here," he said.

"We're happy," said Jennifer. "It's home. You think you'll ever settle down again?"

A spasm of pain crossed his face. He rubbed at his chin as if to hide it, his fingers rasping over the stubble. Jennifer hadn't welcomed his arrival, and she didn't trust him any more now than she had when he'd shown up, but her heart still went out to him. After all, he was family, and she didn't have much of that left despite his ridiculous claims to the contrary.

"That didn't go so well for me the first time," he said. "I got a girlfriend, though. I think you'd like her. She doesn't take crap from anybody."

"Then what in the heck is she doing with someone like you?" Jennifer asked, teasing.

"Beats me." He grinned. "She's a trucker, so she doesn't have to see me much. Maybe that explains it."

"What's her name?" asked Topaz.

"Dixie. If I knew you all wouldn't turn me into a newt, maybe I'll bring her to visit someday."

"We'll see," said Jennifer.

Satana's entrance with steaks, salad, and home-brewed beer put an end to the stilted conversation. They all tucked in with relish, limiting their talk to observations about how good the food was.

The fragile peace couldn't last. Satana finished her food first, pushing her plate away and scowling until Jennifer couldn't take it any longer.

"Why are you acting like a toddler?" she asked.

"I figured you shouldn't be the only one," replied the succubus.

"Uh…" Johnny looked from one to the other, his eyes wide with alarm. "Maybe we should talk this out."

Topaz waved him away. "Don't worry. They bicker to siphon off steam when they're stressed. It'll pass in a minute."

"No, it won't," said Satana. "Not until Miss Perfect here is willing to admit that she could be wrong for once."

"You'd like that, wouldn't you?" shot back Jennifer.

"No, I wouldn't. But if there's a Kale here and we don't know about it, you and your precious book aren't the only ones in danger. Especially if Lucifer's involved. I've kind of got a personal stake in that one, don't you agree?"

The words hit Jennifer like a blow to the stomach. Satana rarely talked about her upbringing, but once every few months, nightmares would make her scream in abject terror. The first time, Jennifer had been convinced the Hellphyr had escaped from the book to murder them all in their beds. But it had just been Satana, stuck in the grips of some remembered horror. Jennifer would never forget the succubus's uncharacteristic vulnerability or her panicked embrace in the short moments before Topaz banished the dreams away. Every time she had those dreams, she clung to Jennifer like she'd been drowning.

They never spoke about it, but Satana's unconscious mutterings had given Jennifer a pretty good idea of what those nightmares entailed. Whatever had happened to her in Hell had scarred her beyond even Topaz's ability to heal it entirely. At some point, Satana would have to exorcise her own demons, quite literally. Until then, of course she'd be concerned where Lucifer was involved. Jennifer had been so distracted by the Kale connection that she hadn't even stopped to consider the rest of the story. Johnny knew the powers of Hell as well as Satana did, and he wouldn't have risked her ire for nothing.

Jennifer clenched her fists, letting the silence draw out as she thought this over. Then she nodded.

"You're right," she said.

"Damn straight I am," growled Satana. "We need to hear the man out."

"Sorry. I shouldn't have been so self-centered."

Satana waved off the apology. "Yeah, well, you know I wouldn't actually bite your head off, right?"

"You might try."

Jennifer forced a smile, and after a moment, Satana grinned

back. Topaz watched with quiet approval, meeting Johnny's eyes from across the table. He didn't move a muscle, like he was afraid he might accidentally rekindle the animosity between them if he made the slightest mistake.

"See?" Topaz smiled. "All better now."

"You sure?" Johnny's eyes flicked from one woman to the other.

"We're allowed to disagree, Bonehead," said Jennifer. "So long as we do it like adults."

"If you say so."

"I'd like to hear more about Lucifer," said Satana. "In detail."

"And I'd like to know what makes you so sure that one of my relatives is involved," added Jennifer.

Johnny grabbed his mug and gulped down the cold tea. "I'll tell you, Topaz. It was less unnerving when they were fighting," he said.

"Tell me about it," she replied. "I live with them."

"What do you all want to know?" he asked.

"Let me sum up, and you tell me if I have any of it wrong," said Jennifer, all business now that she'd decided on a course of action. "You've been hunting these Lucifer shards for a while now. I have no doubts that you'd be able to sniff out the infernal. We've all seen the Ghost Rider at work, right?"

Her gaze swept the table. Satana nodded. Topaz held her hand up, shaking it in a so-so motion.

"Not exactly, but I know enough to agree with you," she said.

"OK, so have you noticed any patterns, Johnny? Is Lucifer picking his puppets based on some criteria?" Jennifer asked.

He answered without any contemplation necessary. "None," he said. "They're all over the map when it comes to location and characteristics. The last one I took out was a soldier in a tank. Before that, it was a middle-aged soccer mom."

"At least that one would have been easy," said Topaz. "But the tank? I'm surprised you're in one piece."

"The Rider's pretty impervious to damage," Johnny replied. "And you'd be surprised. That soccer mom nearly took my head off. I'd take a million tanks over her, any time."

"Never underestimate an angry middle-aged woman," said Jennifer, smiling. "It doesn't go well."

Johnny shifted with an amusing level of discomfort. "Well, there's no pattern that I can see, but maybe you could magic one up."

"So, the King of Hell just happened to possess a member of one of the most powerful magical families in the world?" Jennifer asked. "Statistically speaking, you have to admit that it's an awfully big coincidence."

"It is," Johnny allowed. "That's why I'm here. Either he lucked out, in which case I'm potentially screwed. Or he's messing with my senses, in which case I'm also potentially screwed. I'd kinda like to know which one it is before I march up to him and hand him my head on a plate."

"Oh," said Jennifer. "Now I get it. You need us to figure out what kind of tricks he's playing."

Relief weakened her knees, and if she hadn't been sitting, she might have toppled over. Scrying, she could do. There wasn't much danger in that, right? She quieted her mind, alert for the heavy feeling of dread in the pit of her stomach, but she sensed nothing. Either this was a safe road, or her momentary grasp on precognition had passed. That was the problem with premonitions. They didn't come with a manual.

"It's probably a long and distinguished list, the tricky yob," added Satana, nodding in approval.

"Enough playing," said Jennifer, back to her usual briskness now that it seemed the crisis had been averted. "I'll clear the dishes. Satana, you check the perimeter while Topaz prepares the space."

"And what do I do?" asked Johnny.

"You can help with the dishes. Otherwise, stay out of the way until Topaz is ready for you. She'll need your memories to fuel the scrying," said Jennifer, stacking the plates.

"That's not terrifying at all," he replied.

"I'll be respectful of your privacy," said Topaz. "We just need to see what you've got on this fragment. It's the easiest way to track it."

"I appreciate that," he said. "My memories aren't exactly fit for human consumption."

"Cousin," Jennifer said in gentle tones, "you *are* human."

He pursed his lips. "After everything I've seen and done, I'm not sure that's true anymore."

Before she could answer, he picked up a couple of mugs and carried them to the kitchen. More worried about Johnny than ever, Jennifer followed him with a stack of plates, and they all got to work.

# CHAPTER EIGHT

Squinting in the dim stairway, Johnny followed the witches down a set of rickety wooden steps into the basement, gazing around in curiosity. At the bottom stood a long, empty space, with a plain concrete floor and cinderblock walls cluttered with shelves. Perfect walls had been chiseled from the earth with the same magic that held the groundwater at bay. But still, a moist chill seeped through the soles of his boots. The room had been freshly swept, leaving the floor empty of debris. As he wandered around, he scanned the shelves, expecting some freaky witch stuff, but there wasn't a single bat's wing or skull to be seen. It was mostly candles and iodized salt. Disappointing.

"Do you have stock in a salt company or something?" he asked, indicating the shelf full of canisters.

"Shut up, or I'll turn you into a newt," said Satana.

"Can you really do that?" he asked.

"I'm not sure. We'll have to experiment and find out."

"Children," said Jennifer, her patience obviously fraying at the edges. "That's enough. Johnny, I want you to stand right here. We'll be drawing circles around you. Whatever happens, do not breach the circle until you're instructed to. I don't care if something goes wrong and you think we need your help; let us handle it. If you leave the circle, it will only hit us with magical backlash atop whatever problems we're dealing with."

"In short, you'll make it worse," said Satana. "And that would tick me off."

"I understand," said Johnny. "But if Lucifer retaliates, I've got the juice to stop him. I don't doubt your abilities, but I don't think you've got the Hellfire for it."

"I do," said Satana, uncharacteristically quiet. "But nothing like what the Rider can summon up. I'd be able to delay him, but not much more."

Johnny nodded. "If the doo-doo hits the fan, one of you has to let me out while Satana holds him off. Deal?"

"That works." Jennifer paused. "I should have asked this before. If Lucifer has managed to get his hands on a Kale, could he access their magic?"

The question made Johnny's jaw clench. How dumb did she think he was? He had a reputation for burning first and asking questions later, but that didn't make him stupid. The fiery rage he barely held in check leaped up within him, eager to make her pay. The eagerness for violence disturbed him. It had been a simple question; why was his fuse so short all of a sudden? Zarathos didn't feel anger, so he couldn't blame it on the spirit. He didn't like it, didn't understand it, and so he tamped it down and hoped that stifling it would make it go away.

He took a deep and calming breath.

"Do you honestly think I would have come here, risking the possibility that you might try to string me up by my feet, if he couldn't? We haven't exactly had the closest relationship," he said.

"Yeah, well, whose fault is that?" she demanded.

Regret settled in the pit of his stomach like lead. You'd think he would have gotten used to it by now, because what-ifs and if-onlys had haunted him every day for the past few years, but this one hit him hard. He'd spent so much time mourning the family he'd lost that he'd pushed away what little he had left. Maybe it was for her own protection, but she didn't know that.

"Both of ours." His quiet admission stopped her in her tracks. "Like Satana said, I might be a bonehead, but I can be taught. I've made a few mistakes, and this is something I can't afford to screw up, so I'll eat crow if I have to. Is that what you want?"

"No, you're right," she said, taking him by surprise. "I guess I'm just as much to blame for our shaky relationship as you are."

"Guess we can be messed up together, then," he said, the ghost of a smile flitting across his lips.

"This is all very touching," Satana interjected, "but if you two are done with your moment, I'd like to go fight the devil now." She paused. "I can't believe I just said that. What am I, nuts?"

Jennifer nodded, her demeanor brisk and businesslike, like some internal switch had been flipped. "As much as I hate to admit it, Satana's right. We can continue this later if you want. Shall we go on?"

"Yeah," said Johnny. The last thing he wanted was a heart to heart, but he owed her. "Sounds like a good idea to me."

"If Lucifer can access this hypothetical Kale's magic, I'll have to shield from that," she continued. "Topaz, you'll take lead on the scrying. Satana, you're on perimeter."

"Who lets me out of the circle if Lucifer throws us a curveball?" asked Johnny.

"Me," Topaz volunteered. "Satana's better equipped to hold him off, and Jennifer will be busy. Besides, establishing an empathic bond with the Lord of Hell would be suicidal." She broke off, shuddering.

"Johnny, you stand here."

Jennifer placed him in a spot at the center of the room while Satana handed out containers of salt. The three witches began pouring the mineral out onto the ground in a complicated pattern. Although none of them spoke or lifted their eyes from the ground, they managed not to run into each other despite the space constraints. The air grew thick with power as they worked. Johnny began to sweat even though he just stood there. It was like breathing in a sauna, the air close and heavy with the threat of lightning.

When they finished, he stood in a smaller circle, like the center of a wheel. Three spokes emerged from this central hub at even intervals, terminating in circles enclosing each of the witches. A larger, thicker circle surrounded the entire structure.

Jennifer looked at Satana and nodded. "Seal it."

Satana bared her teeth at Johnny, her mouth overflowing with significantly sharper fangs than usual. She bit down on the meat of her palm, slicing the skin open on the razor-sharp surface. Red blood welled, filling the air with its coppery aroma. She held it over the circle, allowing a single carmine drop to fall into the salt.

Magical power flared with an intensity that even Johnny could feel. All the hair on the back of his neck stood on end, and Zarathos swelled inside him, sensing a potential threat.

*Down, boy*, he counseled. *They're friendly.*

The spirit waited. If it had breathed, it would have held its breath just as Johnny did. But nothing happened. The suspense was awful, and his foot had begun to itch, but he didn't dare move to scratch it. As the silence stretched on, he couldn't bear it any longer.

"What's going on?" he asked.

"Verbal updates please," said Jennifer. "So Johnny can follow along."

"OK," replied Satana. "It's safe. The perimeter's secure."

"Establishing the link with Jennifer," Topaz said in a dreamy voice.

"Johnny," said Jennifer, "I want you to think of the fragment and the moment you thought it might be attached to a member of my family. Think of where you were. What you heard. Were you hot? Was it windy? How did it smell? Construct a complete picture of it in your mind."

Johnny closed his eyes and tried his best. He wasn't into this woo-woo imagery stuff. Roxanne had gone through a yoga phase once, and she'd talked him into trying it, but he couldn't take the stuff seriously. She'd been frustrated, but he'd made it up to her later.

But this was different. He pushed away the lingering feeling that this whole process was a load of garbage and thought back to the moment when he'd climbed onto his bike, ready to chase down the next fragment. He'd just left a diner, gravel crunching beneath his boots. Birds chirped in the trees, and the thick Georgia air stuck his shirt to his back. He remembered the scent of Hell on the breeze, pulling him toward his next quarry. But this time, it had a new layer: a familiar scent of cinnamon that reminded him of his cousin Jennifer. He hadn't thought of Jen in a long time. Frankly, he tried to avoid anything to do with family as a matter of principle. But the resemblance was undeniable.

He'd stiffened on his bike then, overcome with the worry that Lucifer might have taken possession of *her*. He concentrated, trying to find some bit of proof that his infuriating cousin wasn't one of Lucifer's puppets. To his immense relief, the undertones were all wrong. He wouldn't have to kill Jen, but he had another problem. The scent was too close to be anything but another Kale, and he knew mystical power when he smelled it.

That couldn't be good.

He remembered how the realization had made his stomach sink. How his hands had trembled as he fired up the bike. How he'd resolved to come here, no matter what the price, because Lucifer could not be allowed to consume that much power. Not if he had anything to say about it.

"OK," he said. "I've got it."

"Here we come," said Topaz.

Other than a slight tickle at the back of his mind, he sensed nothing. That disturbed him. If Topaz could enter his brain with such subtlety, what would stop her from rummaging around in there any time she wanted?

"It's called integrity, Johnny," she said. "Also, you're opening your mind to me. It's much more difficult if you haven't. Trust me, you'd notice."

"That's reassuring," he muttered.

"Now focus," she ordered.

He did. After a moment, Jennifer said, "You track Lucifer by *smell*?"

"I'm not sure it's really a smell. It's more like a memory, maybe? But that's not quite the right word for it. I can't make sense out of it myself."

"No, I get it," said Topaz. "Your brain finds a way to interpret the amorphous. You don't have a frame of reference, so you translate it into terms we can understand. Magic works the same way."

"Back on task," ordered Jennifer. "Topaz, let's follow the scent."

The two witches closed their eyes while Satana scanned the room for threats. This time, the silence was much shorter. Topaz broke it with a moan, the sound so soft that at first Johnny wondered if he'd imagined it. Then she did it again. He leaned forward, watching her worriedly. As his hand neared the plane of the salt circle, magical power nipped at his fingers. He shook them out, hissing.

Topaz whimpered.

"What's going on?" he asked.

Satana shook her head. The worried furrow between her blazing red eyes failed to reassure him.

"I don't know. I should be able to feel their minds, but it's like they're not there," she said, following that up with an inventive string of curse words.

"What do we do?"

Jennifer's head snapped back, as if she'd taken a right hook to the face from some invisible boxer. Blood gushed from her nose. Her eyelids flickered with frantic movement, but they did not open.

Satana snarled, brimstone steam beginning to curl out from the collar and sleeves of her expensive business suit. Her entire form quivered as she fought for control.

Johnny had no room to criticize. Zarathos surged within him again, and it took all his considerable willpower to keep the spirit leashed. He couldn't afford to fly off the handle now, although he wanted to. The need to protect his people was overpowering in its intensity. But he had to identify the threat first, or risk Zarathos haring off on his own and leaving the witches to fend for themselves. He gritted his teeth, suppressing the urge – no, the *need* – to transform.

"Satana? Hey!"

Johnny's shout got her attention. She focused on his face, her eyes clearing, although they still burned crimson with fury.

"I'll try to pull them out," she said. "If it goes badly, or if we're not speaking to you by a count of one hundred..." She hesitated. "Break the salt. The inner circles only. Do not touch the outer circle, or I'll burn all the hair off your body, one strand at a time. I hear the eyelashes hurt the most."

He hesitated. "Break the circle? Won't that hurt?"

"Oh, it will. It'll hurt you, too. Use your foot. The boots might shield you some."

"But–"

Topaz whimpered with pain. It was all the motivation Satana needed. She closed her eyes, snarling something in a guttural language that made his skin crawl. Johnny recognized the rhythms even though he didn't understand the words. It was the language of Hell, and every syllable burgeoned with infernal power.

The salt caught fire.

Hellfire surged up from the protective sigil, wreathing them all in flames. Zarathos didn't like that at all. The spirit made another desperate leap inside him, trying to wrest control of their body. His flesh boiled as the Rider struggled to emerge. Pain flared in his jaw as he clenched his teeth so hard they ground together, concentrating with all his might to hold the spirit at bay.

"They're friends!" he told Zarathos. "This isn't a threat!"

But the spirit was beyond logic or conversation. All Johnny could do was hold onto himself with everything he had. Johnny wouldn't have trusted Satana under many circumstances, but he refused to stab her in the back. Besides, she was trying to rescue Jen. But Zarathos couldn't understand that. The spirit had never been good at big picture reasoning. It was like a Hulk with a nose for the demonic; it sensed evil, and it wanted to smash.

As the seconds ticked away without attack or injury, the urge to transform subsided. Johnny relaxed, massaging his sore jaw. He'd forgotten to count. He started at thirty to make up for the lost time.

Nothing had happened by the time he got to ninety.

"Satana?" he called. "Ten seconds."

No answer. The suspense was killing him, and no one would know if he shaved off a few seconds. He had to do *something*. Transformation came with a risk, but if he didn't take it, they might all die here.

Johnny and Zarathos merged into the Ghost Rider with sickening ease. The spirit of vengeance slid one motorcycle boot through the salt without a second thought for the flames. The circle broke.

Hellfire rushed in, encasing him in a burning cyclone. Something fell off the wall with a clatter, the sound almost swallowed by the hungry hiss of the flames. The wavering figures of the witches stood on the other side of the flames. The Rider lacked the magical knowledge to determine what had happened to them, but the whiff of demonic influence was enough to drive him to action. He marched forward, breaking the circle that surrounded Satana. Flames rushed in on her, buffeting her slim figure. But she didn't burn, and that was enough to stay the Rider's hand. She was human enough to resist the unnatural fire, and so she would escape his vengeance. For now.

He broke the circle around Jennifer. She screamed as the fire rushed in on her, but it didn't touch her. Moving faster now, he scraped his foot through the salt that ringed Topaz, scattering the burning fragments. The circle filled with leaping flames, cycling from red to purple to yellow in rapid succession. Then it flared in a bright burst of white light that caused even the Rider to shield his eyes.

The fire went out. The three witches slumped to the ground in unison.

Flesh crept back over his skin as Johnny exerted control of his body once more. Zarathos retreated with less of a fight than he'd anticipated, but he wasn't about to look that gift horse in the mouth. Not now. He knelt next to Jennifer, searching for a pulse, but there was no need. She coughed in his face.

"Nice," he said.

Her eyelids flickered and opened. As she roused, he turned on his haunches to check on the others. Satana shook her head, groggy. Topaz held a hand to her temple as she sat up. It looked like they would be all right.

He let out a relieved breath, but the feeling didn't last long.

"What the heck happened?" he asked. "Care to share with the rest of the class?"

"You broke the salt," muttered Jennifer. "Didn't you listen to a thing we said?"

"He saved us," said Topaz.

"He was following my instructions," added Satana. "You want to take your frustration out on somebody? It should be me."

Jennifer whirled on her, wiping at her bloody nose. "Are you nuts?"

"It worked, didn't it? If we hadn't merged our magic, we wouldn't have gotten out of there."

"And if we'd gotten stuck, Johnny would have been imprisoned, too. Did you think of that?"

"I decided to trust his skills. Is he or is he not the Ghost Rider?"

They were nearly yelling at each other. Johnny stepped between them before it came to blows. He'd never been much of a peacemaker, but he knew how it felt to lose your temper and regret it later.

"Hey," he said. "Everyone cool it. It all turned out OK. You're gonna need new shelves, and the candles shattered, but that's not so bad. Even the salt survived so you can set it on fire later."

The three witches turned to him with varying expressions of incredulity and amusement.

"Johnny Blaze, are you trying to be reassuring?" asked Jennifer.

"I'm trying to keep you all from killing each other. If you all croak on me, who's gonna tell me what happened?"

Satana barked out a laugh.

"You were right," Jennifer said, ignoring her. "It's a Kale, and they grabbed onto us as soon as they realized we were looking. We couldn't get out."

"They're powerful," said Topaz. "I couldn't pick up a thing."

"So they've got mortal magic," Johnny said. "*Lucifer* has mortal magic."

Jennifer nodded, her expression bleak. In perfect tandem, both Johnny and Satana began to curse at length. After a moment, even Topaz joined in.

# CHAPTER NINE

"We're leaving," Jennifer declared.

The declaration took Topaz aback. She'd already been knocked off-kilter by the aborted attempt at scrying. She thought she'd shielded herself as well as possible to protect her delicate human psyche from a direct link with the King of Hell. But they hadn't seen a thing. The moment they'd made contact, they'd been clapped into a mental prison, and not even their combined strength had been able to budge it until Satana joined them. Their quarry was too strong for them to overcome.

The experience had shaken her, but she hadn't even considered running. Her first instinct was to call for her former master. She might be wary of Stephen Strange, and she definitely couldn't trust her conflicted feelings toward him, but he alone had the magical prowess to stand against such a powerful opponent.

She was tempted to suggest it, but Jennifer and Satana had their own reasons for mistrusting him. Although he'd put their coven together, he hadn't been honest with them. If he'd only told them the truth, Jennifer's brother might still be alive. So, she held her tongue.

Johnny didn't.

"Leave?" he demanded. "What do you mean, leave?"

"We are taking the *Tome of Zhered-Na* and leaving Salem," said Jennifer. "We won't be returning."

"Wait. What?" asked Topaz.

"Don't you think we should have a say in this, O great and powerful sorceress?" added Satana, an angry edge to her voice.

Jennifer whirled to face her, hands clenched in bloodless fists. "This is my call," she said. "I'm the guardian of the *Tome of Zhered-Na*. You know what will happen if Lucifer gets his hands on it? Have you put some thought into that? I have. I've seen it, and it's not pretty."

"Care to fill me in before you walk out on me?" asked Johnny, an edge to his voice.

"I'm not hiding out with the Tome for kicks and giggles, Johnny," replied Jennifer. "There's a nasty demon imprisoned in it, one with the power to take out all the mystics in the world, including the Sorcerer Supreme. Do you know how long the Earth will last without magical protection?"

Johnny shook his head. Jennifer's flashing eyes swept across the room. Topaz could sense the fear beneath the fury, and that more than anything else convinced her this was real.

"A week?" she said softly.

Jennifer sighed. "Not even. I've seen it."

"What do you mean, you've seen it?"

"Premonitions. I started having them after Johnny arrived. Lucifer wants the book; I am sure of it without a doubt. I don't think it's a coincidence that he's come to Salem. If he wasn't making a move for the Tome, he'd steer clear of us to avoid catching our attention, to avoid facing all four of us instead of just Johnny."

"Exactly. We can take him," Satana persisted. "If I'd been there from the start, things might have gone differently. That's how we got out. Breaking the salt allowed us to work together."

"We're more balanced when it's all three of us," Topaz agreed. "Stronger."

"And I can handle Lucifer. We're better off together," added Johnny.

But the sorceress shuddered, her eyes focused on something they couldn't see. Fear came out of her, an intense wave that nearly knocked Topaz off her feet. Whatever images danced before Jennifer's eyes, they frightened her to the core.

"It won't work," she said, her voice bleak. "I believe in you. In us. But this time, we're outgunned. We have to run."

"We can't do that," said Topaz.

Jennifer stared her down, incredulous. "Why not?" she asked.

"I understand how important the book is. Lives depend on keeping it safe. But Lucifer's strolling around with the powers of one of the strongest mystics I've ever seen. A Kale, no less. Let's say we leave Johnny to face them alone, and he manages to drive Lucifer out. If the mystic survives, how are they going to live with what he made them do?" Topaz shuddered. "I'm not going to leave someone to deal with that alone when I can help. When someone messes with your head – with your reality – like that, it can break you."

Tears prickled at her eyes. She didn't like to talk about her past, because she'd lost so much. She had no sense of family, no home, no people. She'd traveled through India for a while, trying to find some connection to her roots, but the sense of belonging she'd longed for never came. The place held so much beauty, but none of it belonged to her. For a long time, she'd had no real identity. She'd become whatever people wanted in her desperate need for acceptance.

She knew how much it hurt to be abandoned, and that wouldn't happen again. Not on her watch.

"They probably won't survive it," added Satana, brutally matter-of-fact. "You think you know what the Lord of Hell is capable of? It's worse."

"Tell her, Johnny," urged Topaz.

The three witches turned to face him, and Topaz's burgeoning hope faded at his expression. He shook his head with obvious regret.

"I should have been clearer," he said. "Lucifer possesses bodies at the moment of their death. There's no bringing them back. The first one had a heart attack in his sleep and woke up with Lucifer at the wheel. Last week, there was a soccer mom – Muriel Lefevre – who died of cancer and then got up and started shooting her family with a shotgun. She got all but one before I brought her down. Whoever this person is, they're already gone. I'm sorry."

The revelation hit Topaz like a sucker punch to the stomach.

"I guess there's nothing to fight for, then," she said, deflated.

It all seemed so futile. Regardless of what they did, Jennifer's relative wouldn't survive. What good was making a stand if there was nothing left to stand for?

"Wait," said Johnny. "That's not what I meant."

"We've got to get the book to safety," said Jennifer. "But we won't leave you high and dry. I'll spend the evening making an amulet to shield you from the worst of the magic. We'll leave early tomorrow."

Topaz sighed, looking around the basement. "I'm going to miss this place," she said.

"Maybe we can come back someday, if Johnny lets us know that it's safe," said Jennifer. "But it's selfish to ask for that, given the circumstances."

"You've got to reconsider," he begged. "How am I supposed to find them?"

"How do you think we can help?" Jennifer shot back. "If we fail, they take the book. Then you're facing Lucifer's puppet plus the Hellphyr. We're doing you a favor, even if it doesn't seem like it." She paused, taking in his frustrated expression. "You'll see someday. Or maybe you won't, but I'm not going to live my life to please Johnny Blaze. Now, if you'll excuse me, I have some packing to do."

She hurried up the stairs, Topaz on her heels.

# CHAPTER TEN

To her surprise, Satana found herself pitying the Ghost Rider. Jennifer's rejection had left him standing in the middle of the salt-strewn floor with a gobsmacked expression on his face, like he'd called in a Hail Mary and ended up with a dud. He sighed, running his hands through his hair. She picked up the broom and began sweeping up the salt, more for something to do than for a need to clean.

"Aren't you supposed to be packing?" he asked.

She shrugged. "It's a waste of time. I'll just throw everything through a portal once I know where we're going. The packing's really just an excuse so they don't have to stare at your tragic expression and feel guilty over it."

"But you don't feel guilt."

"Not often, and not for your sorry butt." She paused to survey the messy room and dropped the broom. "To heck with this. There's no sense in cleaning up if we're leaving anyway. I'm going out to the garden. You can come along, unless you feel like sitting down here and enjoying the pervasive aroma of burnt salt."

He hurried up the stairs after her, his eager acceptance at odds with his carefully cultivated gruff expression. If he thought he was fooling her, he was an idiot.

She led him through the house and out the back. The kitchen door screeched when she opened it, a nails-on-the-chalkboard sound that made her want to clap her hands over her ears. She'd been meaning to fix it for weeks. Now she never would. Jennifer might say that they'd return once the danger had passed, but Satana knew her too well. One security breach was one too many. Jennifer wouldn't dare risk the book by returning here.

The garden sat in a fenced-in area off the side of the house. The succubus had never tried to grow things before they came to Salem, but to her surprise, she'd found that she had a knack for it. Under her care, the bare space had transformed into a riotous jungle. Dark, glossy leaves dangled over the winding path to her favorite bench swing, which was enclosed in a nest of deep blue bougainvillea. She sat down on the rocking seat and patted the spot next to her.

"Have a seat," she said. "I won't bite unless you beg."

Johnny grunted but did as she'd asked. He took a moment to appreciate the space, looking around with interest. Satana liked that. Pleasures were meant to be savored, and so many people drank them down without pausing to enjoy them, leaving them always hungry. She'd learned not to do that the hard way.

"It's nice out here," he said.

"I'll miss it."

"Then why leave?" She opened her mouth to reply, but he held up a hand to forestall her. "Don't lie to me, Satana. I know you agree with me."

"Who said I was going to lie?" she asked, soaking her voice with every ounce of innocence she could muster up.

"I've met you before, remember?"

She laughed. "How could I forget? You're attractive when you're angry, you know that?"

"You got a thing for flaming skeletons?" he grumbled.

"That's not what I meant, and you know it."

He shook his head. "No games, Satana. Not now. There's too much at stake, and *you* know *that*."

"Touché." She leaned back against the bench, trailing her hand through the cool leaves as they rocked back and forth. The motion soothed her. "But it doesn't matter if I agree with you or not."

"I wouldn't have pegged you for a blind follower."

"You're lucky we're in my happy place, or I'd pop your head off for saying that," she replied.

"Look," he said, begrudgingly, "I'm sorry. But you've got to understand my frustration here. You're hanging me out to dry when you could help. Even if I manage to find the next shard, how am I supposed to win? You know what he's like, Satana. Even if his magic won't affect me, he can turn innocent people against me. I can't kill innocents. I won't. But I don't have the magical juice to protect them without you." He slumped. "This is a recipe for disaster, and you know it."

"You're the Rider. Figure it out."

"I've done the calculations already. I don't like them."

She frowned. Although she didn't know Johnny Blaze as well as his cousin did, she'd always been good at reading people. On a typical day, he was the kind of guy who would muscle through any obstacle, bleeding from a thousand wounds and insisting that he was just peachy. The emotional wall that usually separated him from everyone else had been cracked, its edges blunted. Something must have shaken him hard to make him this vulnerable, especially to the likes of her.

"You're awfully maudlin," she observed.

"Yeah, well, the impending destruction of life as we know it will do that to a guy. Especially when he knows it's his fault."

"Don't be a moron. I've fought you, remember? I know what you're capable of, and I also know you were holding back. If you let loose, you'll go through Lucifer like a knife through silk, magic or no magic."

"That's the problem," he said, standing up from the bench to pace on the stones before her. "I can't let loose."

"Explain," she said, frowning.

"Zarathos has his own priorities, and they don't always match mine. We used to balance each other out OK, but lately, not so much. Sometimes when I transform, stuff happens that I wouldn't do when I'm completely myself. But I'm responsible for that, even if I'm not steering at the time. It's my body." He stopped and stared at the ground. "It's been hard to hold on lately. I'm angry all the time. Maybe that's his fault, or maybe it's me, but it doesn't matter in the end, does it? One of these days, I'm worried he'll take over, and I won't be able to get back out again. That probably sounds stupid."

"It doesn't."

Satana's mind boiled over with painful memories. Years of servitude to her father's cruel whims. Being pulled through time and space to a summoner's circle, bound to do their bidding regardless of her feelings on the matter. The frustration of being nothing more than a magic-bound slave, unable to control her own actions. Sometimes, she wondered how long she had before it happened again.

"Then why won't you help me?" he asked. "You know I wouldn't beg if it wasn't important. Talk Jennifer into it. There's got to be a way around those premonitions. She'll listen to you."

A bitter smile stretched her lips. "On any other topic, yeah. We're usually pretty good about deciding on things as a group, but the *Tome of Zhered-Na* is an exception to the rule. If the demon gets out, or if Lucifer uses some of the ancient spells on those pages to kill people, it's her fault. She's the one with the blood oath to protect it. It'll break her if she fails."

He winced. "Join the club. If I bring about Hell on Earth, it'll break me, too. I'll do anything to stop it."

"Yeah," Satana sighed. "What a mess."

"If you refused to go, she wouldn't force you."

"But it wouldn't do any good. Against a threat this strong, you need all three of us. You saw that during the scrying. There isn't much that can beat demonic, human, and heavenly magic working in balance. Separately, we're barely in the big leagues, but together, we can really throw down if we have to."

"So it's no use if we don't convince Jennifer."

"Precisely. And if we can't, my best option is to keep the coven together." She paused, deep in thought. "If you came with us, do you think Lucifer would follow?"

"No," Johnny answered without hesitation. "He'd stay here and burn the town to the ground. Eventually, he knows I'd come back for him. And if this Kale is really powerful, I can't afford to leave this fragment until the end. It gets more powerful with every kill, and that magic could tip the scales. Heck, it already has. The longer I wait, the worse it'll get."

"Damn," she muttered. She liked none of this. The presence of another Kale, the threat to her coven, Jennifer's sudden wave of precognition – none of it boded well. She would have loved nothing more than to join Johnny, if only for the opportunity to blow off a little steam with some well-placed violence. But she couldn't turn on her coven mates like that. They needed her, whether they realized it or not. "Well, if I come up with a brilliant idea overnight, I'll let you know."

"I'm being dismissed, huh?"

She nodded, waving him toward the house. "I need some time to think. Go on in. You can bunk down on the sofa. Topaz can point you toward blankets if she hasn't gotten them out already. Knowing her, you've probably got them already, along with fluffy slippers and your own little shampoo."

"Too bad you're not staying here. You could open your own B&B."

Satana chuffed. "Yeah, something like that."

# CHAPTER ELEVEN

For once, the garden failed to soothe Satana. After the witches had first moved to Salem, she'd been restless and dissatisfied. She'd never been the type to settle down, and she wasn't even sure that she liked these people. Jennifer was too serious and Topaz too uptight. They'd been at each other's throats from day one. At first, she'd only stayed to prove Doctor Strange wrong. He'd been certain they couldn't survive without him, dogging their steps with constant offers of help despite their emphatic denials. She'd wanted to make him choke on his skepticism.

In those early days, they'd moved from place to place. Jennifer and Topaz had wanted a house, and Satana had gone along with it even though she didn't expect to stay. Then they moved to Salem and started the shop, which had provided some entertainment. Satana loved teasing the undergrads who came into the shop, and they loved it even more than she did. The constant low-grade thrill kept her succubus hungers at bay. They'd never disappeared, but they didn't control her like they sometimes had.

She kept putting off her departure, by a day, and then a

week, and then a month. In the meantime, she'd fallen in love with the garden, coaxing exotic flora from the soil. Topaz grew useful things in her indoor herb garden, but Satana specialized in plants that were beautifully exotic and sometimes deadly. Except for the bougainvillea, which was there just because she liked its scent.

She'd never really had a home, and now she did. Not the house. It was fine, but the garden brought her comfort like nothing else had, and now she had to give it up. It made her angry enough to spit fire.

Restless, she left the swing and began walking without any particular destination in mind. Her half-demon constitution allowed her to go without sleep much longer than the average human. She hated sleep anyway. Too many memories awaited her there. During the long nights when everyone else rested, she'd crisscrossed these streets more times than she could have counted. She knew them like the back of her hand. Maybe the familiar walk would bring her some peace. At the least, she could make her goodbyes.

She found herself standing in front of the neon sign for Mac's Bar. Normally, she did her drinking at the Pit, a dive bar outside town that was more likely to feed her need for conflict and forgive her for breaking things. Mac's was either too civilized or too juvenile for her taste, depending on the night. But she didn't think that under the circumstances Jennifer would be happy to have to bail her out again. They'd always been able to wipe the slate clean with some well-applied magic, so any trouble with the authorities never lasted, but that wouldn't matter. Even Satana knew that introducing complications wasn't the best idea tonight.

She pushed the door open. The stocky, bearded bouncer took in her appearance with a dazed expression. He held out his hand and opened his mouth, but no sound came out.

"Are you asking me to dance, or did you need something?" she asked.

He went scarlet.

"I'm... You're..." he stammered.

"Come on now," she chided gently. "Spit it out."

"Can I have your ID? Or your number? Or both?" His eyes went wide with admiration and horror. "I'm sorry! Forget I said that, miss. You're safe with me."

"I'll forgive you this time," she said, grinning.

She tried to push past him, but he stopped her with the briefest of touches, like he was afraid he might melt into a puddle of goo after too much contact with a woman like her. He was probably right. The guy had mass and muscle for days, but she knew the type. Down deep, he was a teddy bear.

"Sorry!" he repeated. "But I still need to see that ID."

She had cash and cards in her suit pocket, but she didn't feel like digging them out. She'd had enough of being bossed around for one night, and at least this was one demand she could refuse.

"What's your name?" she asked.

"Colin."

"Well, Colin, I'm glad you're here. Sometimes the boys can get a little aggressive, you know. It's ever so reassuring to know you're here to keep me safe," she purred.

He swallowed hard, nodding with such vehemence that she could hear his beard brush against his shirt. It was almost too easy. A little flash of skin, a little nudge of magic, and voila! A devoted slave.

"S-sure," he said. A trickle of sweat ran down his temple. "If anybody gives you guff, you ask for me. We don't tolerate that kind of thing here. I'll even walk you home if you need it."

"Thank you, Colin," she said.

She reached out and tugged on his beard before trailing her fingertips down his shirtfront. He wavered on his feet. Then she entered the bar, the request for ID all but forgotten. She grinned as she crossed the room, feeling all eyes on her. Maybe things had gone sideways, but at least she still had this high.

She slid into a spot at the bar and ordered a drink from the bartender, a pert blond with a heart-shaped face who probably made a killing on tips. They exchanged bemused looks as a frat boy sauntered past, his eyes glued to them both, and went face-first into a wall.

Satana nursed her drink, debating her options. Maybe she would pick one of those lucky frat boys and give him a night to remember. She needed something to do, or she'd spend the entire night dwelling on the problems that Johnny had brought to their doorstep. That would only upset her, and she needed to be on the ball for whatever came tomorrow.

That decided her. The lucky boy who had enough guts to sit down next to her would get a chance. If they played nice, she'd make their night. And if they didn't…? Either way, she wouldn't be bored.

She didn't have to wait long. Someone slid into the seat next to her. She didn't look up, allowing her long black hair to shield her face from view. Whatever they said first would give her an idea of what kind of fun she'd be having tonight. She wasn't sure whether she wanted them to sweep her off her feet or bomb spectacularly. Either way, she needed the release, so they'd better get on with it.

"You're looking good, daughter," said a familiar voice.

Satana jerked to attention, spilling the remains of her drink all over the bar. Ice cubes skittered into her lap. The bartender was there in a flash, handing over a rag and cleaning up the mess with swift efficiency. Satana murmured a thank you, but her attention was on the man on the stool next to her.

Her father.

For years, Marduk had called himself Satan, even to his daughter. It had taken her years to learn his name, and to this day, she still suspected it might be a nickname. After all, true names had power. Daddy Dearest wasn't the trusting sort. Plus, he lied like some people breathed.

He was wearing his academic face, choosing to appear as a thin old man with a receding hairline and a penchant for sweater vests. He thought this made him more approachable. His tendency to smile all the time was intimidating in his horned demonic form, but with this face on, it made him look like an unhinged creeper.

"Whatever you want, the answer is no," she declared.

"But you haven't even heard me out yet," he said, smiling.

"That wasn't an accident."

"Come on, now. Is that any way to greet your dear old dad?" He held out his arms. "Give us a kiss."

"I'd rather stick my head in that blender over there."

"I wish you wouldn't. I just got this sweater vest, and I'd hate for it to get stained."

Satana wanted nothing to do with this nonsense. She threw a few bills onto the counter and made for the door. Marduk grabbed her by the arm before she could get very far. His hand was much too hot by human standards. If she wasn't half-demon, it would have left a mark.

"Leave me alone," she began, but before she could really let loose, someone tapped her on the shoulder.

"This guy giving you a hard time?" Colin the bouncer asked, folding his beefy arms and frowning at Marduk.

"The brave knight comes to the rescue? How delightful!"

Marduk grinned wider. The combination of overdone glee and his flyaway hair gave him a manic clown vibe. Unnerved, Colin took a step back, but a glance at Satana steeled his resolve. He pointed to the door.

"I think you'd better leave now, old man," he said.

"Or what? Will you make me?" asked Marduk.

"Yeah. Yeah, I will."

"I would like to see you do that, young man. I would like that very much. Such displays of strength do impress the ladies, don't they?"

"That's enough."

The bouncer reached toward Marduk, but Satana grabbed his hand before he burned himself. She didn't know why. What did she care if some stranger made a misguided display of masculine aggression and got a few blisters for his trouble? He'd made the choice of his own free will, and she had no obligation to keep him safe. For years, she'd kept the peace in Salem city limits because she lived here. As of tomorrow, she wouldn't.

But she'd stepped in anyway. With dawning alarm, she

realized this wasn't just about defying her father. She'd grown to love this place despite herself. Damn it.

"He's not worth it," she said to the bouncer. "If you toss him out, he'll just make more trouble."

His brow furrowed with uncertainty. "You sure? You don't have to put up with his garbage, you know. We have a nice place here. We look after our women."

Marduk giggled. "Son, this pretty little girl could rip your head off. I think your chivalry is a bit misplaced."

"I don't like your tone, mister," said the bouncer.

"*Dad*," Satana interrupted. "Knock it off."

Colin froze. "That's your father?"

"Unfortunately."

"Is he drunk or something?"

"I wish. He's always like this."

"I've always had a bit of the devil in me," admitted Marduk.

Satana groaned. Colin glanced between the two of them. His excitement had faded now that his prime opportunity to impress the pretty lady had evaporated. Satana almost pitied him, but she had bigger fish to fry. Like finding out what brought her father to her doorstep after five blissful years of no contact.

"OK," Colin said. "I guess you can stay then? But if you try any funny business, I'll toss you out the door myself."

"I'm looking forward to it," said Marduk gravely.

"Shut up," said Satana.

Confused and defeated, the bouncer returned to his station by the door. Satana sat back down, gesturing for the bartender to bring her another drink. When it arrived, she sucked the whole thing down in seconds. Including the ice.

"Impressive," said Marduk. "Now can we get down to business?"

"What will it take to make you go away for another five years?" she demanded. "Or ten. Can we go for ten this time?"

He clapped a hand to his chest. "You wound me, daughter. Honestly, our family is so dysfunctional. I think we ought to try therapy. Call your brother and ask him to join us. I'll make an appointment for tomorrow."

"I won't be here."

"So you *are* leaving. I'd hoped I was wrong." Marduk's smile faded. His mouth flattened into a thin-lipped grimace. It was not an improvement, and Satana's stomach sank. Marduk's meddling meant one thing: news of Lucifer's latest target had traveled fast. The buzzards were already circling in anticipation of a meal. "Honestly, Satana, that's the worst plan I have ever heard. You girls will get yourselves captured, and then Lucifer will open up the Tome and throw a nice little splatter party with the Hellphyr as the guest of honor. What are you thinking?"

"It's not my call."

"Oh, right. It's your sister's. Wait a minute. If you're my daughter, and all of you LeFay girls are claiming to be sisters now, does that mean that I'm Jenny and Topie's dear old dad, too? I ought to hunt them down and give them a lecture."

"They don't like you any better than I do."

"No, but they might listen to sense. The smartest thing to do is give the book to me. I'll keep it out of Lucy's hands while you put him down like the dog he is."

Satana smirked. "That's your game? You're losing your touch, old man. You can't honestly expect me to agree."

To his credit, he shrugged. "Not really, but you can't blame me for trying. And you do have to admit that it would be better for it to be in my hands than in Lucifer's. I'd protect you and your so-called sisters. He'd hunt you down first just as a matter of principle."

"The answer's still no."

He nodded. "Fine. But running is going to get you killed. I advise against it. I do wish you'd let me help."

"And you're going to do that out of the goodness of your heart? I don't buy that for a second."

"I wouldn't insult you by pretending that my concern is anything but self-serving. If you have the Tome, I have some chance of getting my hands on it eventually. If Lucifer snaps it up, that opportunity is lost forever."

"Well, at least I can believe that one," she muttered. "But we both know you'd hop at the chance to take it yourself."

"Of course I would." He held his palms up, unable to deny her point. "At this point, you're a beggar. You can't afford to be a chooser, too," he said.

"You've got nothing to offer that I want."

He gestured for a drink, secure in the conviction that he'd roped her in. She stood up instead, determined to prove him wrong.

"What about some information on Magda Kale?" he asked. "The one Lucifer took over."

With a thump, she sat back down. She didn't trust him, and she never would, but she could trust in one thing: he would always act in his best interests. Sometimes, they'd align with hers. Long ago, she'd stopped wishing for his approval or affection. This was the best she was going to get, and now she would take advantage of it.

"I'm listening, old man," she said.

He smiled like a cat that had just eaten an entire flock of canaries.

"I knew you would," he said.

# CHAPTER TWELVE

The next morning, Topaz rose before dawn. She liked watching the sunrise from the front porch, enjoying the birdsong and fresh air before the heat and humidity drove everyone inside. It had been a particularly wet spring this year, and she hadn't been looking forward to what summer would bring. Some days, a nice walk outside in the Florida summer made her imagine she was taking a stroll through a bowl of hot soup. But she'd miss it.

She clutched her teacup and curled up on the porch swing, trying to suck in every bit of enjoyment out of this last morning spent in the house. Everything had extra poignancy today. When she put the kettle on, she thought about the fact that it was the last time she'd use this particular kettle. The last time she'd curse under her breath at the temperamental stove. The last time she'd sit in this exact spot and watch the sun peek over the rooftops and outline the palm trees.

When she was young, she'd dreamed of traveling the world, performing feats of magic that would make everyone love her.

She'd wanted to be special. But when she stood shoulder to shoulder with Jennifer and Satana, she'd realized that she had no idea who she was. She'd spent years trying to please everyone but herself. So, she'd turned her back on everything she knew – on the only man she'd ever loved – and set off on her own.

The past few years had brought her a surprising contentment. At the end of the day, it came less from the house and more from the people in it, but she still grieved. She couldn't stand between Jennifer and her duty to keep the book safe, but she didn't want to leave the memories they'd built up over the years. The first day they'd moved in, Satana had thrown herself onto this exact swing, which tore free and crashed onto the ground, carrying the succubus along with it. The rest of the day, the only thing Satana wanted to talk about was her booty's destructive power. While they were lugging the dining table through the front door, she'd declared that her booty could destroy cities better than Godzilla, and they'd all cracked up. For the first time, the place felt like home, and the witches like family.

Topaz didn't want to lose that, but she understood where Jennifer was coming from. She'd lost her brother to the Hellphyr. Maybe the witches had begun as roommates, but now their bonds went deeper than that. Jennifer would want to protect them. Running made sense, but Topaz didn't have to like it.

Sighing, she went inside to refill her cup. To her immense surprise, Satana was slumped at the dining room table. The succubus had never been a morning person. Although she only rested a couple of hours each night, she slept hard. Sometimes things got broken in the process.

"You OK?" she asked. "Want some tea?"

Satana pinched the bridge of her nose. "You got some of your headache blend? I could use it."

Topaz pulled it off the shelf. She'd considered packing up the teas last night, but now she was glad she'd held off. Satana must have really thrown down the night before if she was asking for tea. She never got hangovers, while Topaz could get drunk by looking at the bottle from across the room.

A few minutes later, she slid the steaming cup across the table.

"Here you go," she said. "Sounds like last night was wild, even for you."

Satana gulped down the entire thing in one go, heedless of the fact that the water had been boiling just moments before. She let out a sigh of contentment before slamming the empty cup down on the table.

"I saw my father," she said.

Topaz stiffened. The tromp of quick footsteps on the stairs announced Jennifer's arrival before she actually came into view. She stuck her head out from around the banister, her blond hair still wet from her morning shower.

"Did I hear that right?" she demanded.

Satana nodded. "We should talk. All of us," she added with a significant look toward the living room, where light snores suggested that Johnny still slept despite the early morning ruckus.

"I'll wake him up," said Jennifer. "Topaz, you want to put some more water on? Something tells me we're gonna need it."

Fifteen minutes later, Johnny's eyelids remained at half-mast, but he joined them at the table anyway. Topaz gave him a cup of her caffeinated tea, and after a couple of sips he looked nearly human. Next to him, Satana drummed her nails on the table with increasing agitation. Topaz didn't like that one bit. The succubus tended toward unflappability. Whatever she had to say must be bad.

"Can we get on with it?" she asked.

Jennifer nodded, obviously impatient. "Please. I'd like to hit the road before the traffic gets bad."

"Well," Satana replied, "what I have to say might change those plans. I'd say I was sorry about that, but we all know I'd be lying."

Johnny perked up. "What happened?" he asked, his voice like gravel.

"My dad came for a nice, friendly visit last night. I haven't seen him in five years, which suited me just fine. At first, I thought it was a social call."

"Demons do social calls?" asked Topaz, surprised.

"Most of them involve decapitation," Satana explained. "And usually, there's no tea."

"And this is why I don't associate with demons."

"Anyway," Satana continued. "It turns out that he's kept tabs on us this whole time, and he knew we were planning to run for the hills. At first, he tried to convince me to give him the Tome instead. To keep it safe from Lucifer."

"Over my dead body," Jennifer said, with all seriousness.

"Yeah, that's a lie if ever I've heard one," observed Johnny.

"You think?" Satana snapped. "Jeez, Bonehead, I never would have thought of that, even though I'm half-demon myself. I'm so glad you're here to explain these things to me."

To his credit, he hung his head. "Sorry. Still waking up here."

"Well, I don't think he really expected it to work. But he did give me some information about Magda Kale."

Jennifer's hand spasmed, slopping tea over the rim of her mug. "Who?" she asked.

"Magda Kale. Lucifer is walking around in her body as we speak," replied Satana.

Jennifer considered a moment, then shook her head. "I don't recognize the name," she said.

"I think you're second cousins, but honestly, all those terms get confusing. Does anyone really know the difference between a second cousin and a third cousin?"

"I do," Topaz interjected. Her heart went out to this unknown woman. Did she know somehow that her body was the vessel for the Prince of Darkness? How horrible that would be. "But I'm pretty sure that question was rhetorical."

"It was. Shut up," said Satana.

Topaz smiled. She didn't take the brusque attitude as an insult. On the contrary, it comforted her in this uncertain time. Some things might change despite her wishes, but Satana would always be a jerk. She was *their* jerk. If anyone tried to hurt their coven, she'd do anything to protect them.

"There's probably a good reason you don't know her, Jen," said Satana. "According to my dear old dad, she's a powerful psychic and illusionist. She could have been hiding in plain sight this whole time, and you wouldn't have noticed her. Not unless you knew to look, which you didn't."

"Hm." Jennifer's brow furrowed in thought. "Continue."

"Magda's magic is a bonus for Lucifer. She can ensorcell people, so he could raise up an army. The minute he realized what he had going, he started plotting to make this fragment the last one. Imagine that. All Lucifer's power, plus all Magda's. No one would be able to stand against him."

"We would," Jennifer said, her jaw tight. "Especially with the Rider on our side."

"But that's the point, isn't it?" Satana continued. "If we leave, it doesn't matter whether Johnny is on our side or not."

"Which is what I've been saying all along–" Johnny started.

Before he could get going, Topaz shook her head. Satana and Jennifer needed to work this out on their own. If he made himself a target, they'd just turn on him, and nothing would get resolved. For the first time, she'd begun to see a way out of this mess, and she didn't want him to ruin it.

Thankfully, he fell silent, taking her unspoken cue.

"I'd stay if not for the Tome," Jennifer said into the silence. "You know I would."

"The Tome is safest here, behind your shields," said Satana. "Once we're separated from Johnny, Lucifer's going to take it. We don't have enough Hellfire to stand against him. He'll burn through us, and then he'll use Magda's power to open the book. He'll release the Hellphyr to go hunting. You remember what happened the last time it got out."

The three witches exchanged bleak looks. None of them would ever forget, not if they lived for a million years.

"What happened?" asked Johnny, his expression bleak. "It's bad, isn't it?"

Jennifer folded her arms and shrank away from the table, making a point of withdrawing from the conversation. Topaz stepped into the breach, eager to save her from having to tell the tale. Johnny needed to know, but at least she could spare the sorceress this pain.

"Doctor Strange formed our coven to chase down the *Tome of Zhered-Na*, in which the demon Hellphyr is imprisoned," Topaz explained. "Only a member of the Kale family can open the book and release the demon."

"So I've heard," replied Johnny.

"Well, Marduk found the Tome first. He set up a library and hired Jennifer's younger brother to catalog the collection, knowing that the magic of the Tome would call to him. It worked. Andy opened the book, and the Hellphyr possessed him. It began hunting down all the local mystics, using Andy's body to do it."

Jennifer flinched. Topaz reached out toward her, but the sorceress pulled away before they made contact. Although the empath could dampen grief, she hadn't made the attempt. It might have made things easier, but some things needed to be felt, no matter how much they hurt.

"I was Stephen – Doctor Strange's – student at the time. He recruited us to recapture the Hellphyr. Without the book, it's practically impossible. The ritual requires three different types of magic working in concert: heavenly, mortal, and demonic. He threw us together and put us on the trail."

Topaz tried to keep her voice light, but it cracked at the end despite her efforts. She'd wanted so badly to please her teacher. Her feelings toward him had verged on the unhealthy; she could see that now. He'd been everything to her. Teacher. Friend. Lover. She'd done his every bidding without question, certain of his goodness and wisdom.

Now that she'd learned to stand on her own two feet, she still believed in him. Stephen always tried his best to do what was right, but he could also be egotistical. He manipulated people without even realizing it. Part of her still loved him and always would, but she could no longer trust him implicitly. She had learned the error of her ways and would never be so naïve again.

"Marduk is trying to play us just like he did last time," said Satana, her voice dripping with bitterness. "He wants the Tome and the Hellphyr for himself. With every kill, the Hellphyr grows stronger, absorbing the magic from its victims. He nearly fed it enough to defeat us last time."

"He needn't have bothered." Jennifer sagged with defeat, elaborating for Johnny's sake. "The three of us didn't get along at first. We'd been thrown together with only the flimsiest of explanations. We moved into the Sanctum Sanctorum to train, but it didn't go well."

Satana blushed. "Sorry about that."

The apology surprised a smile out of Jennifer. Not a big one, but a smile, nonetheless.

"I'm the one who put my big butt in the way," Jennifer said.

"Never trust a big butt and a smile," said Satana. She took in the blank looks from around the table. "Come on. I can't be the only person here who knows that song."

"*Anyway*," said Jennifer, "Satana nearly took my head off by accident. I stormed off on my own, and naturally, I went to see my brother."

She fell silent again, staring down at the table. Just like that, the swell of good humor disappeared, and once again, Topaz stepped in to fill the silence.

"We fought the Hellphyr," she explained. "But we couldn't save her brother. He begged her to end it. He'd finally realized what he'd done, and he couldn't live with it."

"It was all my father's fault." Satana bared her teeth. "I'd like to rip his throat out."

"I'd hold him down," said Jennifer. "But that's neither here nor there. The point is, Johnny, we can't let the Tome fall into the wrong hands. The Hellphyr will feed on mystics until it's too strong to be stopped. That's why we have to run."

"But Magda's counting on that," said Satana.

"*Lucifer* is," corrected Johnny. "Important distinction. Magda's power might be left behind, but it's dangerous to think of the puppets as the people they used to be. It's much harder to pull the trigger that way."

"Fine. Whatever. The point is that I wouldn't trust Marduk to babysit a pet rock, but he can be counted on to do what's best for him. He'll do anything he can to avoid living under Lucifer's rule," said Satana.

"But we only have his word on that," Jennifer pointed out. "And I'm the keeper of the Tome. I still say we go."

"This is a mistake," Satana protested.

"I can't help if you leave me behind," added Johnny.

Jennifer shook her head, her expression mulish. She'd made up her mind, and nothing was going to budge her. Within moments, the conversation had degenerated into a shouting match. Satana stood up first, but they all followed suit, yelling so loud that they couldn't hear anything but their own desperate arguments.

Topaz couldn't take it any longer. She could understand their fear and worry, because she shared it, too. The odds were undeniably stacked against them. But she couldn't sit by while her family turned on each other. She drew on every ounce of her power, pouring it into her voice. When she spoke, it rattled the tchotchkes on the shelves, knocking one of the porcelain fairies onto its side.

"Enough!" she boomed.

Everyone froze, staring at her in shock.

"This is beneath us," she said in her normal voice. "This is the kind of behavior that got us into trouble when we formed this coven, and as I recall, when we walked away from Stephen, we vowed never to act like this again. So, are we going to be toddlers today, or would we like to put our big kid pants on?"

A slow grin began to stretch Satana's lips, and Topaz whirled on her.

"This isn't funny," she said. "Out of all of us, you know that best. Cracking jokes and keeping secrets isn't going to get the job done."

"How stupid do you think I am?" asked Satana, her good humor fading away. "I have tried. I've made my arguments, but she won't listen. She's blinded by fear."

"And you aren't? The only difference I see between the two of you is that she admits her fear but refuses to face it down. You're the opposite. You want to charge in blindly without admitting that you're afraid in the first place."

"How is that going to help?" Satana threw up her hands. "Fine. I'm terrified. I'm not afraid of the Hellphyr. If I die, I die. I've done it before. It's not exactly spring break in paradise, but I can handle it. But if Lucifer takes over this plane of existence, there's nowhere for me to run. I'll get picked up by my father or the Prince of Lies. Either way, I'm a slave, and I can't go back to that. I won't."

Topaz turned to Jennifer. Bright spots of color flushed the sorceress's cheeks, and tears glistened in her eyes.

"It's my job to protect you from things like this. I can't be responsible for more death. Can't you see that?" Jennifer begged.

"Do you believe in us or not?" asked Topaz. "That's what it comes down to. Because I do. I spent years as a student, terrified to do the wrong thing. To do anything at all on my own. I couldn't make a decision to save my life. Don't you remember?"

"It took you three weeks to choose a paint color for your bedroom," said Satana.

"And you had to resort to eeny-meeny-miny-moe," added Jennifer.

"Well, you two taught me to believe in myself. In us. No one else made this coven work. We did. My magic has developed in completely unforeseen ways. I can't think of the last time I worked one of the spells that the Sorcerer Supreme taught me. Now I shape the power to my whim, and not to the words in a dusty old book."

"There's something to be said for dusty old books," muttered Jennifer.

"There's something to be said for faith," countered Topaz. "Now, do you believe in us or not?"

"Of course I do." Jennifer laced her hands together, fidgeting. "But I have this awful feeling. I can't explain it, but I just know that if we try to make a stand, we're going to fall. I've seen it. If I ignore that, and something happens to one of you, I'll never forgive myself."

"Premonitions are warnings," said Topaz thoughtfully. "But they're not set in stone. The future never is. I believe in what you're saying, Jen. It's just that I believe in our coven more."

A deep silence fell over the table. Johnny, who had been

watching the confrontation with grim thoughtfulness, stood up. As the three witches turned to face him, he cleared his throat, drawing their attention.

"I'm not sure this matters," he said, "but I came here to consult with you, Jen. I figured I'd get the information I came for and then leave. In the middle of the night, if I had to. Not because I don't trust you, but because I've got to protect you. I don't stand up with many people, because they can't keep up with the Rider. They die, and then I come back to pick up the pieces and face the music. It hurts, every time." He paused, allowing his gaze to skim over them each in turn. Topaz nodded in encouragement. Satana smirked in bitter acknowledgment of his point. Jennifer just waited, listening without any indication of her thoughts. "But I'm willing to admit when I'm wrong. I need you here. The three of you have got a good thing going. If anyone can stand against Lucifer and his new wizard skills, it's you."

Jennifer took a deep breath, steeling herself.

"He's not a wizard," she said. The three of them all piled on, talking at once and rendering each other unintelligible. She held up a hand for silence and continued, "I'm just saying, if we're going to work together, we need to speak the same language."

"So we're not running?" asked Topaz, hope growing in her belly.

"If all three of you are going to call me out like that, yeah. I'll stay with you. I won't stand against Lucifer directly, but I'll help as much as I can. I do believe in what we've built here." Jennifer swallowed hard. "But I'm scared to lose it."

"Oh, it's terrifying," Topaz agreed.

"We'll probably die," added Satana in bright and cheery tones. She paused to take in the scowls around the table. "What? Too much?"

"Definitely too much," said Topaz. "Let's get to work."

# CHAPTER THIRTEEN

When Jennifer exited the house with the *Tome of Zhered-Na* in her arms, the others already waited for her. They'd cleared out a sizable spot at the center of the garden, moving the swing and a cluster of pots to create a large open space. The sun stood high overhead, blazing down on them with a bright intensity that made her squint. Most witches avoided working spells at high noon, since the power of the sun came with a price. During this hour, the veil between worlds was extra thin, and malicious spirits would seize on any opportunity to cross over. But between the four of them, they would deal with the backlash. She needed the boost in order to pull this off.

She hadn't attempted the *Spear of Varnae* before. For all the time she spent studying the Tome, she hadn't used many of its spells. The more magical power she threw around, the greater the likelihood that someone like Stephen Strange might show up on their doorstep, eager to get a glimpse at incantations that had been lost to history. If the Sorcerer Supreme did darken their doorstep, things would get ugly. Satana would want to punch him, and Jennifer would have to stop her, if only because she had dibs.

The perspective of years had allowed her to realize that Strange wasn't responsible for her loss. Marduk had set the plan in motion leading to Andy's death, and Strange had only reacted to it. By the time he'd realized what had happened, it had been too late to save anyone. But she still rankled at his treatment of them. She respected Strange's magical chops, but he needed to work on his people skills. Maybe listen to a podcast or two. But she wasn't going to tell him that, and she'd avoided doing anything that would catch his attention. She'd had no need for earth-shattering spells anyway. Not until now.

For now, her newfound premonitions were silent. She hoped that meant they'd avoided the awful fate she'd seen so vividly: Topaz screaming under Lucifer's psychic assault, Satana kneeling at his feet. The *Tome of Zhered-Na*, unleashed upon the world, the demon free of its pages to feed on blood and magic. The vision still haunted her, though. She didn't know how to balance what she'd seen with what she knew of her coven mates – their bravery and skill and caring. But when it came to the book, she was their leader. Her family had sworn a blood oath, and that made her responsible.

The Tome brought complicated feelings to the table, too, and she couldn't deny that. The sight of its unassuming brown leather cover made conflicting emotions swell within her: regret, responsibility, and anger at their forefront. During their first year in Salem, she hadn't even read it, but worry about the Hellphyr eventually drove her to crack it open. Now, she understood the bindings that imprisoned the demon, leaving her free to study the spells within. Some of them were original incantations from Zhered-Na herself, unseen by anyone but her Kale ancestors. Strange would have had a fit if he realized it.

Her coven treated the book with the respect it deserved. Topaz stared at it, her mouth slack with awe and nervousness. Satana flashed Jennifer a thumbs up, always eager to approve of a display of power by her fellow witches. Johnny stood a few steps back, his arms folded and fingers tapping with impatience. He tilted his head in the subtlest of let's-get-a-move-on gestures.

"So, what's the plan?" asked Satana.

"I'm going to use an incantation from the Tome," said Jennifer.

"Wow," murmured Topaz. "That's a first."

Jennifer smiled despite herself. "I can't decide if I'm excited or terrified, to be honest," she said.

"If anyone's meant to use the book, it's you," said Satana. "You'll do fine."

"What does the incantation do? Please tell me there's no salt this time," said Johnny.

"What do you have against salt?" asked Jennifer.

"Nothing. I just keep finding it everywhere. Like in my…" He trailed off, flushing. "You know what? Never mind. Forget I said anything."

Satana threw her head back, laughing. The louder she cawed, the more red he got. Jennifer held up a hand, signaling silence. To her surprise, Satana acquiesced. It looked like today was going to be a day of firsts: Jennifer's first use of the book. Satana's first time listening without complaint. Hopefully it ended with their first win against Lucifer himself.

"No salt," Jennifer said. "I'll be using the *Spear of Varnae*."

"What's that?" asked Johnny.

"Varnae was a powerful sorcerer and the first vampire. After he was made undead, he made more use of his vampiric abilities than of his magic, but a few of his incantations still exist, including this one."

"Thanks for the history lesson," said Johnny. "What does it do? Is there an actual spear? Remember, I'm an idiot."

"How could we forget?" asked Satana.

Topaz elbowed her, and she subsided.

"The Spear isn't a physical weapon. It's a blunt force magical lance that you can use to break all kinds of magic. Illusions, charms, time effects, the Spear pops them like a bubble. Supposedly," said Jennifer. "I've never used it, but the book suggests that it packs a punch."

"You think it can get through Magda's shield?" asked Topaz.

Jennifer nodded, trying to maintain her flimsy optimism. "I think it's our best bet," she said.

"What do you want us to do?" asked Johnny.

"Be ready," said Jennifer. "This spell creates a magical bridge. If we can reach across it, so can Lucifer."

He nodded, patting his chest, where a heavy chain sat coiled around the black leather of his jacket. The handle of his shotgun jutted up from behind his head. Johnny Blaze had come ready to fight. Even when he wasn't a flaming skeleton, he didn't look like the kind of man you'd want to tangle with in a dark alley.

"I haven't killed any Lucifers in about three days," he said, "and I'm going through withdrawal. Let's get on with this."

"If something comes through, Johnny kills it. Topaz and Satana, you stick together. This time, we won't be taken by surprise by Magda's magic. She should be incapacitated by the Spear, but I don't expect it to last long. We need to know where she is. Figure that out and get out before she can retaliate," Jennifer instructed.

Satana slammed a fist into her open hand. "Why stop there? If you can make a bridge, let's go for a nice social visit. I have a few things I'd like to say to my old pal Lucy."

"Johnny's the one who can send Lucifer back to Hell, and he won't be able to use the bridge. We've got to track her so we can hunt her down and end this for good," said Topaz.

"Oh. Yeah," Satana said, nonplussed. "My bad."

As Topaz made reassuring murmurs, Jennifer opened the *Tome of Zhered-Na*. It didn't look like much. Just your average leather-bound book with a demonic skull on the cover. The pages looked cracked and brittle with age, but to Jennifer's surprise they'd proven to be quite sturdy. The black, spidery text inside skipped from one ancient language to another without any attempt at instruction or explanation. A record of a failed magical experiment might be followed by an earth-shattering spell with sketches of ancient Atlantean creatures scribbled in the margins next to it. The jumble of material had made for some interesting reading.

Every page thrummed with power, and magical ties bound the Hellphyr into each word. The book served as a conduit to the pocket dimension that imprisoned the demon, and it contained incantations that would allow for travel between the worlds. Jennifer hadn't breathed a word of their existence to anyone, and she never would. When she tried to read those pages, the ink seemed to dance before her eyes. She could read enough to understand the contents, but not to fully grasp the spell. That must have been intentional. Such power wasn't meant to be wielded except in the direst of circumstances. She would have destroyed the book if she could have done so without releasing the demon.

But now she was glad she hadn't. She held it up before her, imagining her ancient ancestress, the powerful Zhered-Na, doing exactly the same. With painstaking care, she drew a sigil in the air with her free hand, power flowing from her fingers to outline the shape in purple light as she traced lines of magic into the very fabric of reality. The magical sign hovered before her as she began to recite the words of the spell, the ancient Atlantean tongue flowing from her lips like she'd been born speaking it.

The words sat heavy in her mouth. The faint rustle of the leaves stopped as a deathly hush fell over the garden. As the incantation poured out of her with increasing speed, emotion welled deep in Jennifer's chest. All her anger, all her fear, every ounce of determination and will that she possessed was sucked out of her with the words, pouring into the sigil. She would not let the dire fate she'd foreseen come to pass. She would die first. The soft lines twisted, straightened, hardening to a razor point. She pictured Lucifer, wearing the body of a woman she'd never met, but one who was family, nonetheless. A memory of panic washed over her as she thought of the impotent fear that had consumed her during the attempted scrying, and that emotion also poured into the incantation.

The glistening magic formed into a glowing lance of purple light, crackling with power. It jerked at Jennifer's mental restraint, eager to seek its target. She was the spear, and the spear was her. As she released the weapon to seek its target, she screamed aloud in rage and destruction, purple light spilling from her eyes to wreathe her head in magical flame.

A boom shook the neighborhood as the spear rent a hole in time and space, setting off car alarms up and down the street. Jennifer sagged as the weapon vanished, taking all her furious energy along with it. Weakness dragged her toward the floor. The purple glow of power flickered and died.

Before she could hit the ground, Topaz took her by the left arm, supporting her weight. Satana appeared on her right, sliding a hand around her waist. Johnny stepped in front of them all. He had transformed while she cast the spell. Hellfire flames wreathed the smooth bone of his skull as he stood ready to protect them from whatever happened next.

The air shimmered. Smoke poured out of the hole in the sky. It flickered with mystic energies, obscuring their view of what lay on the other side. But Jennifer didn't need to see with her eyes. She could feel the spear surge through the air toward its mark. She jerked as it struck true. She tried to tell them what had happened, but her mouth wouldn't work. Her lips had gone as numb and lifeless as her legs.

The rent in the sky widened, and Hell itself came pouring out.

# CHAPTER FOURTEEN

Satana could smell the demons before she saw them. Johnny Blaze had been right about one thing: Hell had a particular stench to it. To her, it smelled like burning motor oil. She'd recognize it anywhere. When the demons began to drop out of the sky like a particularly awful rain, it didn't surprise her one bit.

She had to give Lucifer credit for one thing – the guy was creative. Every time she thought she'd seen the worst that Hell had to offer, she'd see a new and twisted demon that put all the rest of them to shame. Each creature was unique, but they had all been designed to elicit fear, an advertisement for the horror they brought in their wake. They hadn't been made to kill. That would be too easy. No, they'd been built for torture of the mind as well as the body. And now they streamed into Satana's space. Her garden. Her *home*.

Jennifer sagged in her arms. The sorceress couldn't even stand, let alone fight, and Satana wouldn't leave her helpless against demons. She'd been in that situation before, desperately wishing for help that would never come. She refused to allow that to happen to anyone else. Not on her watch. If anyone was going to be doling out terror on her turf, it was her.

The Ghost Rider unleashed his chain, pulling it taut and sending Hellfire coursing along its links. As he whipped it around his head, Satana shouted a warning. The garden patio wasn't that big, and the thought of taking a flaming chain to the face didn't appeal.

"Watch it!" she said.

"Back up!" shouted Topaz, echoing her thoughts.

Together, they dragged Jennifer backwards. Although the sorceress still couldn't support her weight, she held onto the Tome with a death grip. Satana thought she should take charge of it. The last thing they needed was one of the demons to snatch it up. But the moment her fingers grazed the cover, Jennifer's eyes snapped open.

"No!" the sorceress slurred. "Danger… ous."

"I know it's dangerous, you idiot. That's why I want to keep it safe," Satana replied without heat.

"Incoming!" Topaz warned.

The Ghost Rider had managed to attract most of the demonic attention. Flaming skulls will do that, and the chain didn't hurt either. A dark splotch on the ground already testified to the demise of one of their hellish attackers. Satana hadn't even felt it die, but then again, she'd been distracted.

But even he couldn't take on the lot of them by himself. A pair of demons had circled around him, slinking toward the witches. The one on the left looked like a cross between a rotting corpse and a spider, with six segmented legs sheathed in putrid flesh. On the right scurried a demon with enormous fangs over an intense overbite. It stalked them in furtive darts almost too quick for the eye to trace.

"Have a seat," said Satana, dropping Jennifer onto the garden swing tucked into the corner of the garden against the fence. The seat clunked against the wood. Jennifer sagged, remaining upright with effort.

By the time Satana straightened, Topaz had already summoned her power, which ringed her in a yellow-tinted glow. The empath gestured toward the fanged demon with a smile that ought to have taken it aback if it had had the intelligence to understand.

"Come into my parlor, said the spider to the fly," murmured Topaz.

"It would make more sense for me to say that," Satana complained. "Since I've got the spider-demon."

Despite her bickering, a satisfied smile stretched her lips. Her entire body relaxed as she dropped the glamour fully, allowing her true form to shine through. Black, glossy horns rose from the crown of her head to come to graceful points above. Her eyes burned with the fires of Hell as she shook her cloven hooves free of those annoying high heels. Relief overtook her, the intense sensation of a muscle clenched for weeks and only now being allowed to relax. It was playtime, and she was ready for it. She beckoned the spider-demon closer with wickedly pointed claws.

"Come play, my pretty," she said. "Mama's hungry."

She rolled her shoulders, loosening the tight muscles. Maintaining a glamour had become second nature, but dropping it always felt like coming home. As much as she might like to deny it, this form – beautiful and deadly and hellish – suited her.

The demon charged. Although its piggish eyes held only the barest animal intelligence, it recognized a challenge easily enough. A smile stretched her lips as she crouched, bracing for impact. It hit her with the force of a freight train, its mass bolstered by superhuman strength. She rolled with the impact, grabbing the creature's torso and taking it along with her.

The move would have worked on a humanoid. She would have thrown it over her shoulder and rolled to stand nearby. But she'd forgotten to account for the extra legs, each of which ended in a prehensile hand. They wound around her waist, leaving the topmost set free. She ended up flat on her back, pinned underneath its weight. The demon's topmost hands began to rain down on her face, landing a flurry of blows. For a moment, the onslaught stunned her, and white blooms of light flared from behind her closed eyelids. She was out of practice, her aggressive instincts tempered by years of suppression and focus. It ticked her off. A primal survival instinct rose within her, and she grabbed onto the demon's wrists, her hands buzzing with red, angry magic. It nipped at the demon's skin just enough to make it release her and retreat. She let it go, wiping blood from her nose and licking it from her skin with a pointed tongue as she climbed to her feet. She wasn't ready to end this fight. Not yet. She had some aggression to work out.

"Come on, big boy," she said.

It charged again, a skittering motion that reminded her of some large, segmented bug. This time, she was ready for it, and she exchanged blow for blow. A stinging haymaker ricocheted off her temple. Stars burst behind her eyes, but she shook them off, driven by her eagerness for destruction. She raked its belly with her claws, which sank deep into the vulnerable flesh. A wild shriek escaped from her lips as her demonic nature reveled in the opportunity to inflict pain.

It howled, driving both its lower fists into her belly, pushing out all her air in a painful whoosh. She allowed the momentum to take her backwards, lashing out with her feet and connecting with its jaw. It whipped around, but before she could catch her breath, it was on her again. It pinned her to the ground a second time, its teeth clacking shut millimeters from her nose.

"Nuh uh," she chided. "I draw the line at scars."

Of course it didn't understand. Hunger consumed the mindless beast, and it had decided that the best remedy to its problem would be to eat her face. She zapped it again, putting a little Hellfire behind it. It jerked in her hands, tearing free once more.

She let it go, wiping at her face with the back of her hand. Her nose still bled. She licked it clean once again as the demon watched with ravenous fascination.

"You want this, don't you?" she asked, holding out her hand. "Come and get it then."

This time, she didn't hold back. She didn't bother blocking, and the demon took full advantage of that fact, lashing out with all four of its forward limbs in a flurry of blows that would have knocked the average cage fighter out cold. Pain tore at Satana's consciousness, rendering the entire world in sharp relief. She gave as good as she got, tearing chunks of flesh from the thing's body.

A particularly heavy blow snapped her head back, and she laughed in its uncomprehending face.

"In the Olympics of pain, I'm a gold medalist," she said. "Is that the best you've got?"

Of course, it didn't reply. A vague disappointment stirred in her belly, and that more than anything told her that it was time to end this. She had squeezed every bit of juice she could out of the encounter. Not that she enjoyed pain. But she'd needed to remember that she could endure it. Whatever her father or Lucifer dished out, she would survive it, and she would laugh in their faces just like she did now.

She grabbed it by the head and poured her power into it. As only a half-demon, she didn't have the reserves of Hellfire that the Ghost Rider commanded, and this move would drain her, but she didn't care. She needed the satisfaction.

The demon caught fire from within. She let it burn for a moment, warming her hands over its screeching body. It flailed too much for her to really enjoy the experience, though. Too bad. She plunged her clawed hand into its burning torso, pulling out its desiccated heart. It gave one weak thump before dissolving into a rancid goo that coated her fingers. She released the corpse with a convulsive jerk, and it fell, burning, at her feet.

"Ick," she said, trying to clean her hand off.

Her head swam, and her balance wavered. With effort, she remained upright, wiping her hand off on her pant leg. When she finally got the presence of mind to look around, she found the others staring at her. A few black smears on the ground were all that was left of the other demons. As they stood there in silence, the spider-demon dissolved into sludge, adding one final burn mark to the tally. No one even blinked. They just kept staring.

"What?" asked Satana.

"You OK?" asked Johnny.

"Why wouldn't I be?"

His incredulous gaze took in the other two witches, who shrugged. He turned back to her with the corners of his mouth twitching.

"No reason," he said. "But now I really don't want to tick you off."

"No," she replied primly. "You don't. Now if you don't mind, I'm going to go take a shower and wash this demon goop off me."

# CHAPTER FIFTEEN

Jennifer let herself out the back door, easing it closed so the creak of the hinges wouldn't give her away. Maybe she should leave a note. It still wasn't too late to go back and put one on her bed, just to explain her logic. She wasn't sneaking off because she didn't trust her fellow witches, or even her somewhat-reliable cousin Johnny. In fact, it was quite the opposite. She knew they'd follow her all the way to their graves, and she couldn't stand to lose them. She'd already lost too much.

After the fight, she'd felt surprisingly optimistic. They'd worked well together. Johnny's presence, which could have destabilized the comfortable camaraderie of their group, had only made it better. She'd gone to the basement with a lightness in her step. For the first time, she'd begun to think that they could really stand against Lucifer and survive, so long as they stuck together. But the ritual hadn't worked. They still didn't know where Lucifer was. Sure, they'd defeated some of his demons, but he had hordes. They'd barely made a dent, and now she didn't know what to do. She'd pulled out the biggest gun she had, and she'd missed the target anyway.

The vision had hit her in the shower. When she finally regained her senses, she was slumped at the bottom of the claw-footed tub, the water pounding down on her. It washed away the blood that trickled from her nose and the cut in her lip, where she'd bitten down on it.

This one had been worse than all the others put together. She would never be able to articulate the torturous horrors she'd seen, and it was probably better that way. For the first time, she understood Satana's nightmares all too well. The King of Hell could be creative when it came to torment, and she hadn't truly understood that until this very moment. If she didn't do something, nothing but pain awaited them. She used to joke about how handy it would be to know the future, but she wasn't joking now.

Her abandonment would hurt the others after everything they'd been through. They'd think she'd lied to them. It hurt her, too. But she couldn't bear to let them suffer like that, and they'd made it clear: they intended to stand up to Lucifer, no matter the cost. If she had to sacrifice her own happiness to save them, so be it. They'd be safe.

She paused at the garden gate, looking back toward the house one last time. Satana's plants rustled in the dark, their heavy leaves restless in the gentle breeze. Somewhere in the ornamental pond, a frog croaked, deep and resonant like a creature from the ocean depths. The bathroom light flicked on, bathing the window casing in a gentle glow. Jennifer could see shadowy movement beyond the dappled glass. She could swear she could make out the rattle of the bathroom pipes, but that was impossible. She couldn't have heard that all the way out here, and she never would again.

After one final look back, she let herself out the garden gate, trying to ignore the lump in her throat. Driving would have been quicker, but the garage door would have announced her plans to everyone not in the shower.

Luckily, Salem was a college town with a thriving bus station. Since this was a spur-of-the-moment plan, she hadn't taken the time to look up the bus schedule, but she hoped to catch something that went north. She could set off some magical flares outside town to get Lucifer's attention and then sneak off. With so many potential exits to cover, Lucifer would be forced to track her rather than setting a trap and waiting for her to fall into it.

To her immense dismay, she arrived to a nearly empty station. A late-night bus left for Atlanta in the morning, but there was nothing until then. She'd been hoping for a red-eye, but maybe they didn't offer those any more. She hadn't taken the bus in years.

She sat down on one of the hard plastic seats and pulled out her phone, searching for other options. The car rental was still open, but she didn't like the idea of driving. She'd engaged in a magical battle from behind the wheel once in her life, and she was surprised she'd survived it. She'd taken out a mailbox and nearly driven off a bridge, and she'd been lucky to escape with minor injuries in the end. She didn't relish the possibility of repeating the experience while fighting a magically endowed Lucifer fragment.

A rideshare service might work. She was frantically googling it when a shadow fell over her. She jerked to attention, her heart thumping in her chest. Lucifer couldn't have found her this quickly, could he?

But it wasn't a Luciferian puppet wearing the vaguely familiar face of one of her distant relatives. Satana scowled down at her, arms folded and foot tapping. She'd pulled on her frightening businesswoman clothes, and steam rose from her shoulders. Someone was mad.

"Just what do you think you're doing?" she demanded. "You can't abandon us like this."

A wave of anger drowned out the apology that had risen unbidden to Jennifer's lips. Her eyes flashed as she leaped to her feet, staring Satana down.

"This isn't what it looks like!" she declared.

"Hm, let's see. You took the magical book that the King of Hell is lusting after, and then you snuck off to a bus terminal without a word to anyone. Why on earth would I think you're sneaking off? Silly me," replied Satana, her voice dripping with sarcasm.

"I'm protecting you!" Jennifer said. "You don't understand what I've seen, Satana. What I know."

Her voice grew in volume despite her efforts to keep her temper under control. Behind the Plexiglas barrier that surrounded the ticket counter, the dozing attendant jerked to attention. Satana either hadn't noticed their audience or didn't care. She shouted right back.

"You're underestimating us!" she yelled. "Jeez, Jen, do you really believe half the stuff you've said about our coven, or was it all blowing smoke up our skirts?"

"Of course I believe it. I'm trying to protect you. I can't stand to lose you like I did my brother, and I knew you'd be too stubborn to listen, so I snuck off. I don't expect you to understand."

"You don't?"

Satana's voice went deathly quiet, and under any other circumstances, that would have given Jennifer pause, but she was too far gone to recognize the impending explosion. She was drowning in a pool of shame, grief, and terror, and nothing else seemed to matter at that moment. Nothing other than getting away so that her coven sisters didn't meet the same gory end as her brother.

"No, I don't," said Jennifer. "Your father was a manipulative demon of a man who pitted you against your own brother like you were on a reality show based in Hell. I've known that from the beginning, but I don't hold it against you. It is what it is."

"How kind of you," Satana purred.

"So let me go. It's the only way to save you."

For the first time, the sorceress felt a pang of misgiving deep within her. She'd liked it much better when Satana was yelling. Shouting back had made her feel justified in sneaking off. The demoness hadn't understood, just like Jennifer had anticipated. But Satana's quiet fury was harder to stomach.

"Excuse me, ladies? You can't fight in here."

A querulous voice cut through their argument, drawing their attention. They both turned to see the squirrelly guy from the ticket counter, clutching a cordless phone in one sweaty hand. He gulped as they stared him down, taking one involuntary step back and clutching the phone like it was a security blanket.

"You can't fight in here," he repeated. "I've called the cops."

Satana whirled on him, her eyes blazing.

"Do you mind?" she said. "We're having a conversation here."

He took another step back, spluttering. The succubus

turned back to Jennifer and rolled her eyes. Jennifer couldn't help it; she laughed. The guy's forehead wrinkled with comical amounts of confusion, which only made her laugh harder. Satana turned around, put her hands on her hips, and stared him down.

"You see what you did?" she demanded. "You ruined our argument. I was having fun."

"You... what?" asked the ticket man.

"Oh, leave him alone," Jennifer urged. "He's just doing his job."

The mere mention of his job reminded him that he had a backbone. He straightened, brandishing the phone at them.

"I am!" he said. "This is a nice station. We don't tolerate any..." He trailed off, searching for the words.

"Funny business?" suggested Jennifer.

"Exotic animal trafficking? Trapeze artists? Alternative lifestyles?" prompted Satana.

Jennifer snickered, the last vestiges of her anger ebbing away. Satana maintained an admirable poker face, but she'd obviously chilled out, too.

He looked back and forth between them, his mouth hanging open, as he tried to decide if they were making fun of him, and if so, whether he wanted to do something about it. Satana arched a brow. He backed away as if she'd threatened him – and honestly, if anyone could make an eyebrow threatening, she could – and took refuge behind his Plexiglas. From there, he watched them with stern resolve, secure in his authority now that he thought himself safe.

"I like him," said Satana. "I'm gonna send him a nice fruit basket."

"He'd throw it out and call the cops."

"That's a waste of good fruit if you ask me," Satana sighed. "Do you really think you're leaving?"

A host of excuses and rationalizations leaped to Jennifer's lips. But she had no time for any of them.

"Yes," she said, and kept it at that.

Satana nodded, taking a seat on one of the uncomfortable plastic chairs, her elbows on her knees. After a moment's hesitation, Jennifer plopped down next to her.

"You should get out of here," she said.

"You know," said Satana, ignoring her, "you're wrong. I do understand your logic."

Jennifer perked up. "Then let me leave before he finds me. I've warded the Tome, but it's a delaying tactic at best."

Satana held up a finger, and Jennifer sighed.

"I'm not done. You were right about my family. You were a jerk about it, but you were right. I was Marduk's lapdog for years. Daimon and I are siblings, and I'd have his back in a pinch, but we don't see eye to eye on a lot of things. I'm a talk show producer's dream guest. But it doesn't mean I don't know what family is. Over the past few years, I've figured it out."

This wasn't a huge revelation. After all, Jennifer felt the same way about their coven. But hearing it from Satana – angry, impulsive, demonic Satana – was a different story. Of course Satana cared, but this was bigger than that. Even if she couldn't bring herself to say the word, she was talking about love.

The succubus kept her eyes locked on the floor between her feet and continued, her voice sinking until it was almost inaudible.

"I don't want to lose that," she said.

"I feel the same way," Jennifer offered. "I'm not leaving because I don't care. Quite the opposite, in fact."

Satana lifted her head. Her gritted teeth and tense jawline suggested intense emotion being held back by sheer effort of will. She shook her head, hard.

"I don't think that. But that's not what I'm concerned about. We're balanced when it's all three of us. We smooth out each other's rough edges. I'm not sure if the empath has any sharp edges, but if she did, she doesn't anymore," she said.

"If anything, we give her a little edge. She needs it."

"Point conceded. But once you're gone, that all falls apart. I won't leave Topaz on purpose, but I'm not sure I'll have a choice."

Jennifer frowned.

"What do you mean?" she asked.

"One of my favorite things about being in this coven is that I can think," Satana explained. "The demon half of me just wants things, and it wants them now. I spent years being ruled by those impulses, and let me tell you, it's awful to look back on. I don't even know if I wanted to do half of the horrible things I've done. I don't think I ever realized I had a choice until we defied Strange and struck out on our own."

"You don't give yourself enough credit."

"You say that *now*," said Satana, chuckling. "But I distinctly remember you trying to kill me at one point early on."

"I am not apologizing for that again. Honestly, are you going to bring it up every time we argue?" Jennifer asked without any heat.

"Yes."

They both cracked up. Behind his partition, the ticket man

stiffened like they'd started shouting threats. Jennifer glanced at him.

"So, what's the point? Quit stalling, or we'll end up getting arrested."

Satana sighed. She didn't even crack a joke about being arrested, which was very out of character.

"If you leave, I won't be able to hold it together," she said. "Topaz and I are polar opposites. You help bridge the gap. We'll both try, of course, but it won't be long before I decide that corrupting just one of those cute young undergrads won't be too bad. And then, before you know it, I'll have a harem, and Topaz will try to intervene, and we'll end up fighting each other. Even if we both survive, even if you manage to best Lucifer, it'll never be the same. The coven will be broken. I'm not sure what future you've foreseen, but I'd rather face that with the two of you than stare down the barrel of damnation alone."

Jennifer hung her head, absorbing this. She couldn't deny the truth of what Satana was telling her. They were stronger together, not just when it came to fighting Lucifer, but for everything. But she couldn't risk them. She couldn't take any more guilt.

Satana watched as the sorceress struggled with her emotions. When she didn't get the answer she so obviously wanted, she pushed her advantage.

"I understand there's a risk," she said. "But Topaz is right. Whatever you've seen isn't definite. I'd rather make my last stand if the alternative is losing myself again. I'll die someday anyway. I'd rather do it when I actually like myself. I'd rather do it while I'm still me. You can't save my life just to throw away my soul, Jen. I won't let you."

The words stabbed Jennifer like daggers. She took a shaky breath and let it out.

"You don't ever do half measures, do you? You just go for the throat," she said.

"It's a big part of my charm," replied Satana, a faint smile curling her lips.

"Damn."

Jennifer sank down onto the chair next to Satana, resting her elbows on her thighs. She needed the extra support. The truth made her knees weak. She couldn't deny it, though.

"I'm scared," she said in a small voice. "I don't want to believe what I'm seeing, but what if it's right?"

"Then we'll handle it together," replied Satana. "What else are we going to do?"

"I have no idea. But I'll come home. That's a start, at least."

"Yeah." After a tense and worried moment, Satana brightened. "Hey, at least I have something else to hang over your head when we argue now." Jennifer snickered, and Satana put on a wounded expression. "I'm being serious here. Variety is a good thing."

"Right." Jennifer stood and offered her hand. "Let's go home before we give the ticket guy a heart attack."

"You're no fun at all," replied Satana.

Then, to Jennifer's surprise, the succubus hugged her. To her greater surprise, she hugged back.

# CHAPTER SIXTEEN

Topaz couldn't stop pacing. Back and forth across her bedroom, eight steps from the elaborate hand-woven wall hanging near the door to the bed with its filmy curtains, and then back again. She'd already downed two full cups of her calming brew, but the only thing that had done was make her need to pee. She'd tried meditating but couldn't manage to sit still. In desperation, she'd gone back to the infantile exercises she'd done as a child, constructing a mental wall brick by painstaking brick, but it did no good. A million emotions buffeted her, so muddled that she didn't even know which ones were hers any longer.

Being an empath wasn't usually this hard. Ever since she'd left the Sanctum Sanctorum, she'd been developing her psychic abilities. Before that, she'd been more of a dabbler than a specialist. She'd learned anything she could get her hands on in her desperation to impress the doctor. But each of the other witches had a specialty. Satana liked beating things up, and she had a knack for it. Jennifer was so good at ritual sorcery that Topaz thought she could be the Sorcerer Supreme someday, if Stephen decided to step down. But neither of them had terrific social skills, and Topaz liked people. Developing her empathic skills seemed like a smart call, and it had turned out that she was a natural. It was the one thing she'd ever been truly good at.

On the average day, she could shut out the emotions and stray thoughts of everyone around her, but today had not been average at all. Twice now, they'd been rebuffed in their efforts to find Lucifer, and Topaz knew what they had all been afraid to tell Johnny. They were out of options. Magda must have been a terrifically strong sorceress, or maybe Lucifer had found a way to augment her abilities. Either way, the coven could do nothing but sit behind the house wards and wait for their enemy to come to them, and what cost would that carry? People would die, and the reality of it had hit them all hard.

She had to get herself under control, and that meant retreating behind mental walls, if only for a moment. She tended to keep mental lines open between herself and her fellow witches. When Satana was struggling with her instincts and urges, Topaz could help her maintain control. If Jennifer's grief over her brother overcame her again, Topaz could offer distraction or comfort. She never remade or stole emotions, because that felt like the hugest of crimes, but once she picked up on them, she could offer support. From the beginning, she'd made it clear that she would use her abilities whenever she saw a need for them, but she would always make sure they knew what she was doing and respect any requests to butt out.

Since then, the three of them had gotten close. Maybe too close, because right now she had a hard time distinguishing her thoughts from theirs. Did she think that Johnny Blaze was regrettably cute, or was that Satana? Did she want to punch Stephen Strange in the face? Did she regret their past relationship? On the average day, she would have denied it, because if anything, her time at the Sanctum Sanctorum had brought her here, where she was happy for the first time in her life. But she'd made a dreadful mistake. She'd let herself get too close.

The moment she realized what was happening, it got a hundred times worse. The tumult in her head increased as she began to panic. She couldn't calm down while she was being buffeted by Jennifer's fear, Johnny's determination, and Satana's stubbornness all at once. She stumbled out of her room and down the stairs, all her attention focused on putting one foot in front of the other. She had to leave until she could get herself under control.

She took off without any real idea where she was going. The torrent of emotions began to ease as she walked, but it hadn't receded enough for her to think. It took effort to remain upright; the sunlight hurt her eyes. A car horn blared, and she jerked back just in time to avoid being run over. Somehow, she'd ended up in the middle of the street.

"Topaz? Are you OK?"

The voice was familiar, concerned. But she couldn't place it at first. Whoever it was took her by the elbow, and she lacked the strength to resist. They led her up some stairs and sat her down. A short time later, a glass of ice water was placed in her hand. The cold sting of physical contact gave her something to focus on, shutting out the flood of psychic emotions that had temporarily overcome her. She sipped, letting the chill liquid trickle down her throat. As she relaxed, her natural defenses reasserted themselves, leaving her in control once more.

She looked up to see Steven Leach hovering nervously over

her. Steven had been a frequent customer at the shop over the past couple of years. He could have been twenty or maybe forty; it was impossible to tell. His short stature and scrawny build suggested someone not yet full grown, but his receding hairline indicated an older man. Topaz had never found a way to ask without being rude.

She might have gotten around to it, if he hadn't tried to work a love charm on her.

With a spasmodic movement, she set the glass on the table next to her. A quick scan of it didn't set off her magical alarms, but she didn't want to chance it. She could forgive if asked, but she wouldn't forget. She wasn't that gullible.

She was on his front porch. Had she walked here on purpose, or had her feet just retraced the steps of their earlier trip on autopilot? She didn't know. Maybe the residual effects of his pitiful love charm had brought her here. Under normal circumstances, they wouldn't have had the juice to affect her, but once her defenses had gone down, it might have actually worked. That was a scary thought.

"Topaz?" he repeated.

"I should go," she said.

She wasn't afraid of him, not exactly. But the thought of what she could do to him if she gave her emotions free rein chilled her to the bone. As much as she denied it, as much as she hid it, she was angry. About a lot of things, to be honest. She'd never let that fury out to play, because she knew without a doubt how dangerous that would be, but sometimes restraining herself was harder than others. This was definitely one of those times, and she couldn't risk a loss of control, not with everything else going on.

His face twisted with regret as he gestured for her to sit.

"Please, stay a minute. You look like you might keel over," he begged.

"It's not a good idea."

"I learned my lesson about the charm. I knew I shouldn't have done it, but... sometimes it's hard being alone."

"Taking away my free will isn't going to solve your problems, Steven," she said, as gently as she could.

"I know. Of course I know that. But most people look right past me. You were always nice."

"Nice?"

"Yeah. I talked myself into believing that you had feelings for me and just needed a little nudge. I know it doesn't excuse what I did. I promise I won't do it again." He shuddered. "Your sisters are terrifying."

Her heart sank. For all his proclamations of love, he didn't see her at all. Her feelings didn't matter. His interest was rooted in fear. Satana and Jennifer had made a bigger impression than she had once again. She didn't resent them for it, not for a moment. But she wished with all her heart that she could find that spark that made them exceptional inside herself. The only things that made her special were in her service to others, and she was happy to do it, but it still hurt.

"You shouldn't cast love charms because they're wrong, not because you're afraid of my sisters," she said, sighing.

His eyes widened. "Of course! I mean, they are terrifying, and that's a good reason not to do it again. But the thing that bothers me the most is the disappointed way you looked at me."

She tilted her head.

"Really?" she asked. She wanted to believe him, but that didn't make him a liar, and all her senses indicated that he told the truth.

"Absolutely. I was glad to see you, because I thought you might give me a chance to apologize. But then I realized you weren't yourself. Are you sure you're OK? Do you need some more water?"

"No." Topaz took a sip. Now that she was back in control of herself, there wasn't much he could do to her even if he tried. "But thank you for the drink. It helped."

"Good. So, what's going on?" he asked.

She shook her head.

"I don't blame you for not trusting me. I violated that. But I wasn't imagining the part where we were friends, was I?" he said, his eyes fixed on her with wistful hope.

"You didn't imagine it. But you tried to take away my choices. It takes time to recover from something like that. You don't know what it's like to be stuck in a mental prison, not knowing if your thoughts are your own or not. It's awful. Don't ever try to change how people think. Using magic to help make pain more bearable is one thing, but you never take it away. Pain makes us human."

"OK. You're a good person," he replied. "That's what I always liked about you."

Even after everything he'd done, the words bolstered her flagging confidence. She locked eyes with him. Maybe he could make things up to her, if only he could settle the concern that had nagged her for years.

"I'm going to ask you a question, and I need you to tell me the absolute truth. It's important," she said.

He straightened, eager to do anything to make up for his mistakes.

"Whatever you need."

"What do you like about me? Is it just how I look, or…?" She trailed off, unable to finish the sentence.

"How you look?" His forehead creased in confusion. "I mean, you're gorgeous and all, but as they always say, beauty's only skin deep. I might admire a pretty woman, but I wouldn't spend hundreds of dollars at her shop every month just for the opportunity to talk to her if she was a moron."

Despite her best efforts, she flushed. "Jennifer's smarter," she said.

"And Satana is sex in heels. I know. But you're kind, and you're funny in a quiet sort of way. I like that. I like being in on jokes that no one else hears. And you always seem to know when someone needs a word of encouragement or a good old-fashioned lecture. You're just a good person." He hung his head. "Which makes me feel even worse about what I did. But I didn't think you'd notice me any other way."

She took a deep breath, contemplating what he'd said. The words had the ring of truth, as reluctant as she was to believe them. A heavy weight lifted from her shoulders. After all these years, she'd still thought of herself as the consolation prize, assuming that Doctor Strange had only dallied with her because she was convenient, available, and willing. But Steven Leach saw her, and he cared. Both men had tried to take advantage of her good nature in their own ways, and she wasn't going to give them a free pass for that. But maybe she was good enough after all. She'd said it to a million people before, but she couldn't remember ever saying it to herself, let alone believing it.

"I still don't like what you did," she said, "but this helps. I've just decided that I'm officially taking time to work on myself. I'm not ready for a relationship right now. We could still be friends, if you promise not to try to magic me again, and if you can handle my sisters glaring at you all the time."

He made an attempt at a brave smile. Although it was utterly transparent, she applauded the effort.

"It's worth the glares," he said. "You want another drink? I've also got milk and orange juice. I'm afraid I don't keep alcohol in the house."

"I'll take a little more water, but then I've got to get back home. I have important things to do."

"Magic things?" he asked eagerly.

"Important things," she repeated.

"Well, can't blame a guy for trying. I'll refill your water." He gathered up the glasses and then paused. "Thanks, Topaz. You're the best."

# CHAPTER SEVENTEEN

After he cleaned up, Johnny climbed the creaking stairs to the second floor. His tour of the house hadn't included the bedrooms, and most of the doors along the long hallway were shut, so he had no option but to follow his gut. He'd been able to sense Jen's magic once he got to Salem, but in this house, the magic was everywhere, muddling his senses. He picked what he thought was the right door and knocked on it.

He was beginning to think he'd gotten it wrong when his cousin peeked out. She wore a dressing gown embroidered with Chinese dragons, her wet hair hanging lank around her face. When she saw it was him, she pulled the door open and turned her back on him as if to say that she didn't care whether he entered or not. He did so swiftly, latching the door behind him.

She collapsed into an overstuffed armchair, the only available sitting space in the room. Books had been piled on every surface, covering the nightstand, the desk, and even most of the floor. Closed suitcases and packed trunks cluttered the giant four-poster bed. The room should have been stuffy, but a gentle breeze from the open window made it surprisingly cool. The filmy curtains fluttered in a never-ending dance, wafting into his face as he leaned against the wall. He brushed them away absentmindedly.

"What's up?" asked Jennifer, picking up a brush and running it through her tangled hair.

"Just wanted to check on you," said Johnny. "Where did you and Satana run off to?"

Jennifer shook her head, her lips pressed into a tense line. Her obvious anxiety worried him, but he'd never been much for heart to hearts. He never knew what to say, and when he managed to scrape something together, it never came out right. So instead, he took refuge in humor.

"I'm worried about Satana, but I can't check on her. I'm afraid she'll bite my face off," he said.

"She's fine."

"That didn't look fine to me. More like borderline pathological."

"Those are some fancy words coming from you, Johnny Blaze," she said, teasing.

"What can I say? I read a book once."

"Yeah, well," Jennifer waved his concerns away and returned to brushing. "Trust me. I'd have her watch my back any time. That hasn't changed."

"What's going on?"

"With Satana? You tell me. Out of the two of us, you know what it's like to carry a curse around. Except that you can put yours away sometimes. Satana can't. She's got to find a way to balance her two sides, or they'll rip her apart."

Johnny considered this for a moment, the only sound the smooth hiss of the brush through wet hair.

"So she lets her demon out to play a little. Like a release valve," he said.

She nodded. "Something like that."

He ran a hand through his bristly hair. "I guess I can relate to that after all. I've been struggling with it some myself."

She put the brush down and observed him, her keen eyes missing nothing. Johnny squirmed under the appraisal. They had never been close, and in fact they'd barely seen each other after his mom took off. But he knew her well enough to tell that his cousin had changed.

"You've got more powerful since the last time I saw you," he observed.

"I've got confident. The power was always there, but I ran from it."

"I can't throw stones on that one. But it never works out. Running from your responsibilities, I mean."

"Yeah."

The quiet pain in her voice mirrored the heartache that followed him everywhere. Despite himself, he thought of Roxanne's laughing face. His kids, begging for endless rides on his bike until he began to regret ever buying the damned thing. But he closed the door on those memories as soon as they surfaced. Jen needed him.

"You're having more of those premonitions, aren't you?" he said. "You ran, and Satana towed you back. Am I right?"

"I don't need a lecture from the likes of you, Johnathon Blaze."

He held up his hands, urging calm.

"I've got no room to judge. In your shoes, I probably would have done the same thing," he said. "But the premonitions worry me."

"Why?" she blurted.

"You've never had them before, right? They're all new."

She nodded, and his stomach sank.

"It's convenient timing," he pointed out. "Lucifer shows up, and all of a sudden you're having visions of certain doom that make you want to run for the hills. If he wants that book of yours, it would be much easier to get it if you were alone and running."

She opened her mouth to protest but closed it with a snap, her gaze going faraway as she thought it through. He waited in silence, giving her the time to consider his words.

"There's no way to know for sure," she said. "It's a leap of faith either way."

"Yeah, but one way, you're facing the Prince of Lies alone, and the other one, you aren't."

"Yeah." She let out a breath, the tension draining from her shoulders. "You've changed. Last time we met, it wasn't like this."

He knelt down next to her, taking her cold hand in his. "I don't give a crap about what happened before. You tried to knock my block off, and I did the same to you. Maybe sometime we'll do it again, because we're both too stubborn for our own good."

"It runs in the family, I guess."

A surprised smile stretched his cheeks. Sometimes, he forgot what it was like to smile. He'd definitely forgotten what it felt like to have family, and the warm feelings Jen stirred up set off warning bells in his mind. Caring about people was dangerous.

If Lucifer didn't use those emotions against him, someone else would. But he spoke again despite his better judgment.

"Yeah, well, you're my people. If you ever need me, I'll come. Even if we just fought, and you punched me in the face, I want you to come to me if you need help," he said. "You have my word on it."

Her expression softened.

"Thanks," she said.

"It's not an invitation to punch me, just in case you were wondering."

"I hadn't, but I wish I had." She tilted her head to examine him. "You have changed, Johnny. You're not as angry as you used to be."

He hitched a shoulder. "Oh, I'm still plenty angry. But my time in Hell made me realize that it can be used against me if I'm not more careful. I'm trying to be, but damn, is it hard."

"I guess we all have to fight our own demons. Some of them are just more obvious than others. But at the risk of sounding like one of those hokey made-for-TV movies, we're stronger together."

"You know," said Johnny, with wonder rising within him, "you might actually be right."

# CHAPTER EIGHTEEN

Topaz, Satana, and Johnny all sat around the dining room table, eating chips and salsa, when Jennifer entered the room and dropped the *Tome of Zhered-Na* onto her placemat. The book landed with a thud that rattled the bowls. The three of them stared up at her with almost identical expressions of confusion. She would have laughed if she wasn't so keyed up.

"I'm going to open it," she declared.

The statement didn't create the excitement she'd anticipated. Three blank faces stared at her, waiting for the punchline. Except that she'd already delivered it. Satana and Topaz had been pestering her to be less conservative with her magic for years. Johnny had been begging for their help, and she'd just declared she was going against everything she'd once stood for to get it. You'd think they'd be excited.

Johnny scratched his head. "But you already opened it to cast that spell. The spear thing. Not that I don't appreciate the effort, but..." He trailed off, desperate for help.

Unsurprisingly, Topaz took the bait. "What do you think

opening the book will do to help us? Because we're in over our head."

"Precisely," said Jennifer. "Let's look at our status. I didn't get much of a read on Magda, but we can make some conclusions based on what's happened. We know she's a powerful witch. Probably either a ritualist or mentalist."

"How do we know that?" Johnny broke in.

"If you're right, and Lucifer was sending those premonitions, she's got some serious power," said Jennifer.

"Back up a minute," said Topaz. "I haven't heard about this."

"I took the precognition at face value. We've all discovered new magical skills before, and I figured this was just another one. But Johnny pointed out that the timing's awfully suspect. If Magda is a mentalist, she could have used the blood link between the two of us to try to drive me away from you where I'd be weaker."

"And take the book from you." Satana shook her head. "Sounds like Lucifer all right."

"Exactly," said Jennifer.

"Told you so," said Satana.

Jennifer sighed. "I know. We all know."

"So, what does that mean in terms of next steps?" asked Johnny, changing the subject.

"Her shield was impenetrable," Topaz observed. "Out of the three of us, Jennifer and I make the best shields. I specialize in empathy and psionics, so I've got to be able to throw up a good shield off the cuff in the event that I connect with something that wants to take up residence in my brain pan."

"Now, that's an image," muttered Satana.

Topaz ignored her. "Jennifer is better at using ritual to shield, like the salt rings we used during the scrying. Those shields are stronger than mine, because they've got more intent and preparation driving them. They're powered by more than just the worker's will."

Johnny nodded. "Got it. How do we get past that?"

"I'm getting to that," said Jennifer. She rested her hand on the book. For some reason, that made her less terrified about what she was going to propose. "We know Magda is powerful. She was able to block and then counter our attempts to get through her shields. I think we've got to assume that we won't be able to locate her via magic."

"So, what do we do?" asked Johnny. "We can wait until Lucifer starts killing, but I'm not too thrilled with that plan. If he's holding off, he's planning something big. I can guarantee that we won't like it."

Satana scowled. "No way. We're not going to sit by while he feeds on innocent souls. Even I draw the line there."

"Lucifer's gone to an awful lot of trouble to pry me from the *Tome of Zhered-Na*. Maybe he wants it for himself, or maybe he's afraid I'll use it against him. So I'll do just that. I'm going to open the book," Jennifer repeated. Her voice sounded surprisingly calm despite the rolling pit of nervousness in her belly. "And I'm going to release the Hellphyr."

# CHAPTER NINETEEN

"Let out the Hellphyr. Have you lost your mind?!"

The words ripped out of Topaz despite her efforts at calm. Memories assailed her: the constant fear and confusion that accompanied the founding of their coven; the frustrated arguments of three women thrust into a situation they did not understand and couldn't control; the horror that had washed over Jennifer when her brother's terrified face had emerged from the Hellphyr's body, begging to be set free. Back then, Topaz hadn't been quite as good at shielding herself from emotions, and she'd felt every ounce of pain that her friend had experienced. She didn't understand how the sorceress could even contemplate releasing the creature that had taken her brother from her.

"That's just what my father wants you to do!" Satana exclaimed, leaping to her feet with such force that her chair skittered across the hardwood floor and toppled onto its side. "Do you want to play right into his hands?"

"Does he?" asked Jennifer, calm and implacable. "He wants the book for himself. He wants to play off our fears of the

Hellphyr and what it can do, so that he can take control of it. But remember, that book is only useful to him if every member of the Kale family dies. So long as someone of my bloodline lives, the demon can't be released by anyone else."

"It doesn't matter what Marduk wants," Topaz countered, gripping the edge of the table so hard that her knuckles went white. "We have a responsibility to keep the demon contained. If we let it loose, it'll kill mystics. Eventually, it would probably get to Magda, but how many innocent lives will be lost in the meantime? The price is too high to pay, Jennifer."

"It would be," Jennifer agreed. "If we had to pay it. But I can control it. I know I can."

"I don't get it," said Topaz.

"I guess it all depends on whether or not you mean what you've been saying. Topaz, you called me out just yesterday, saying that you believe in our coven. Did you mean it?"

"Of course I did. You should know that."

Jennifer nodded. "And Satana, you've been telling me for years that I'm one of the most powerful sorcerers in existence, and maybe I should... How did you put it? Quit being such a wuss?"

Satana threw up her hands. "I probably said that, but I didn't mean you should lead us in a mass suicide pact. That's what this is."

"I don't think so." Jennifer stood, her blue eyes sparkling. "I think we can control the demon."

"Jesus." Satana began to pace, smoke curling off her body. "I cannot believe I'm hearing this."

"We'll use it as a hunting dog. It'll lead us to Magda, and then we'll put it back into the Tome. We did it before, remember?

And we didn't even like each other back then. We certainly didn't work well together. It'll be easier this time," said Jennifer.

"I vote no," said Satana. "I don't doubt your skills, Jen. I don't doubt us. But we won't just be dealing with the Hellphyr. We'll have to put him back into the book, counter Magda's magic, and fight off Lucifer, all at the same time. We're good, but no one's that good."

Jennifer frowned, but she nodded. "I don't agree with you, but I can respect that. Topaz?"

The empath held up a finger, asking for a moment's thought. She closed her eyes, trying to shut out the hopeful, worried faces of her coven mates. Her friends. Her family. Their heightened emotions buffeted her, and she walled them off with careful deliberation, shielding herself behind a mental wall. Only then did she consider her own thoughts.

She wanted to believe in them. She *did*, but Satana had a point. Confidence was a virtue, but taking on an unwinnable task had nothing to do with confidence and everything to do with ego. They couldn't afford to make such a mistake here. Too many lives depended on it, and not just their own.

"We should ask for help," she said, opening her eyes. "I agree with Jennifer that we are better now than we used to be. But I also agree with Satana that this situation is a hundred times more complicated than the last time the Hellphyr escaped. I think…" She took a deep breath, steeling herself for what would come next. "I think we should call Doctor Strange."

"I changed my mind," Satana declared. "Jen's not the crazy one. You are."

"No way," added Jennifer.

"Look, I understand where you're coming from. But he's the

Sorcerer Supreme. It's his job to deal with things like this," said Topaz.

"No." Jennifer shook her head. "We've seen firsthand his plans for dealing with the Hellphyr. He deputized us to do so, and that's final."

"But he didn't deputize us to deal with Magda," Topaz countered.

Satana marched over, taking her by the shoulders and looking her right in the eyes.

"You can punch me for asking this, but I've got to do it," she said. "Are you still in love with him?"

A defensive kind of anger hit Topaz like a freight train. It took a lot to make her mad. Given her psychic abilities, she'd had to master her feelings before she could even begin her training. It had been difficult. She'd been willful, afraid, and completely alone, without even memories of her family to sustain her. Sometimes, she tried to imagine them, and the home she'd been born into. She pictured a large family gathered around the table at Diwali, lighting candles that floated in bowls of water. Ladies in sari and men in sherwani and jodhpurs. But try as she might, she remembered nothing. Even when she'd gone to India, it didn't give her the feeling of belonging she'd wanted.

She had come to terms with that. She could accept that she'd been abandoned by – or taken from – a family she would never know. It had taken her time to find the acceptance she'd craved, and she'd made mistakes along the way. Her relationship with Stephen Strange was one of her biggest regrets. Yes, he was intelligent, charming, and handsome. But he'd never viewed her as an equal, not truly, and what kind of relationship can be built on such uneven ground? It had been doomed from the start, and she wished she had had the wisdom to see it clearly. Perhaps they might still be friends if she had. Perhaps they would have had a real chance at happiness.

The possibility had nagged at her for a long time, making her question her every move. But in the face of Satana's unspoken assumption, she finally made her peace with how things had turned out.

She drew herself up to her full height, looking the statuesque succubus right in the eyes. Anger thrummed through her, and her power spilled out, despite her best efforts to keep it in. If she'd looked at her reflection in a mirror, she knew that her eyes would crackle with yellow lightning. She gritted her teeth, desperate to keep the power at bay. Even if Satana's question had hurt her, she wouldn't be able to live with herself if she wounded everyone here.

Satana's expression softened, and she patted Topaz on the shoulder.

"I'm sorry," she said. "I had to be sure."

"I didn't even answer," said Topaz, in a voice that sounded far away to her own ears.

"Honey, you are an open book if ever I saw one." Satana shook her head fondly. "You don't need to say a word. Everything you think is written all over your face."

"A poker player, you're not," added Jennifer. "And you've got a good point, but the fact is that I can't trust the man. We've seen what mistrust does to teamwork, and we can't afford to make the same mistake twice. Whatever magical power he'd bring to the table would be negated by the fact that I want to tear his head off."

"I'll hold him down," Satana promised. "It'll be fun."

Just as quickly as it began, Topaz's wave of rage subsided, leaving her shaking with adrenaline. It took a moment before she was able to speak again.

"I understand why you had to ask," she said. "I don't have to like it, but I understand."

"If we ever needed proof of it, there you go. You're a better person than I am." Satana sighed. "I'm not sure it makes a difference, though. I still want to shank the guy. Jen, what do you think?"

"It would be a bad idea," Johnny broke in. When they all stared him down, he held up his hands. "Look, I know my place here. I have no right to influence your decisions when it comes to magic, and I wouldn't want to. It would be like making decisions by throwing darts at a board when you've got Einstein right there giving you advice. I'm stupid, but not that kind of stupid."

"So what's the problem, then?" asked Topaz.

"Strange and I aren't exactly buddies. I ran into him a couple weeks ago. He wanted me to quit hunting the fragments because he doesn't think I'll be able to take out the last one. He thinks I'll lose, and then Lucifer will be loose on Earth. He wouldn't take no for an answer. We fought, and I nearly killed him. I'm not sure he's going to be too keen on helping me right about now."

"We're your second choice?" asked Satana.

He blinked. "Huh?"

"You went to him first, and when he wouldn't help you, you came to us." The succubus threw up her hands. "So much for your faith in our abilities."

"That's not what I said."

"You should have mentioned it." Topaz shook with the effort of keeping her emotions in check. "You know we have a relationship with Doctor Strange. We would have checked on him."

"Would we?" asked Satana, glowering.

"It's the right thing to do!" exclaimed Topaz.

"I wouldn't bother to help Stephen Strange if he was the last man on Earth, and the survival of the human race depended on our ability to get along," said Satana.

"Carry a grudge much?"

Jennifer stepped between the two witches, holding her hands out for silence. The two scowled at each other over her shoulders, completely ignoring her presence.

"That's enough," she said. "Or do I need to send you to your rooms?" She paused, awaiting an argument that didn't come. Satana muttered to herself, too low to make out any of the words. Topaz flushed in shame, hugging her arms to her chest. "That's what I thought. And regardless of the circumstances, I think it's clear that calling in Doctor Strange would be a bad idea. Even the mention of his name is enough to drive a wedge between us, and Lucifer will pick us off one by one if we're not on the same page."

"But–" Topaz began.

Jennifer broke in before she could get going. "Johnny, are you sure Strange was OK? Positively sure?"

He nodded. "I rode away after we fought, but once I cooled off, I circled back around to check on him. One of his friends healed him, and I admit I was relieved. I didn't want to kill him, but calling him in to help is a bad idea. I don't want to chance another confrontation."

Topaz tried to picture the encounter and failed. She'd known that Johnny was powerful, but she hadn't realized exactly how strong he was until this moment. He'd stood against the Sorcerer Supreme and won. How many people could say that? The list couldn't be long. Maybe the three witches together could beat him, but they wouldn't walk away unscathed. For the first time, she began to believe that they truly could send Lucifer back to Hell where he belonged. With the Ghost Rider on their side, how could they fail?

"Where does this leave us?" she asked.

"For what it's worth," said Johnny, "I didn't go to Strange for his help. He tracked me down to lecture me on the error of my ways. But even if he'd been on my side, if I had a choice between his support and yours, I'd choose you. I'd rather have you all watch my back than anybody else."

"Are you nuts?" asked Satana, her lips quirking. "You're lucky I haven't killed you yet."

He grinned. "See? That's exactly what I mean. You have to keep me alive, so you have the satisfaction of killing me later. You wouldn't want to miss out on that, would you?"

Jennifer chuckled, and Topaz shook her head.

"Honestly, I wonder about all of you sometimes," said the empath. She looked around at the others. They looked elated and frightened and hopeful all at the same time. "We're doing this, aren't we?"

"Oh, what the hell. I'm tired of all this wishy-washy crap. Let's do it," said Satana.

Jennifer nodded. "It was my idea in the first place. Of course it has my vote. Johnny?"

"I trust you to keep it in line." He grinned. "And if you don't,

I can always introduce the Hellphyr to a little Hellfire. Between the four of us, we should be able to keep it leashed. Topaz?"

Despite her misgivings, she nodded. It was one thing to say she believed in their skill – and she did – but another thing to put her money where her mouth was. What they were about to do terrified her, but they'd do it together.

"I can't believe I'm saying this, but I'm in."

# CHAPTER TWENTY

Summoning the Hellphyr would be too easy. Before she'd read the *Tome of Zhered-Na*, Jennifer had assumed it would require a complicated ritual, to keep someone from releasing the demon by accident. But Andy had released the Hellphyr without even understanding what it was. As demonic prisons went, it was an awfully flimsy one. Who on earth had come up with such inadequate protections?

When she'd finally gotten up the nerve to open the book for the first time, she'd taken precautions. She'd spent months warding the property and gave Satana and Topaz strict instructions about what to do if things went wrong. They'd even practiced. But nothing had come of it. She'd opened it, and no demons came spilling out.

After she read it, she finally understood. According to the book, Kale blood was the all-important missing link necessary to release the Hellphyr. One corner had a faint red stain on it. Andy must have sliced a finger open on the pages, not realizing that his genetic material unlocked the doors to the Hellphyr's prison.

As a result, she knew what she needed to do, but her hands still shook. She glanced around the basement, licking her dry lips and resisting the urge to ask for the fourth time if everyone was ready. They were all waiting for her to build up the nerve. Her cheeks flamed with embarrassment. Some sorceress she was. She knew what she needed to do, but she couldn't keep from hesitating. What she was about to do here ran contrary to everything she'd stood for these past few years. But maybe, just maybe, she'd been wrong. All this time, she'd been afraid of the Hellphyr and what it could do if she lost control. But she'd never stopped to consider the possibility that she could leash it to her will. After all, she was a Kale, a descendant of the great Zhered-Na herself. She could do this.

"You don't have to do this," said Satana, echoing her thoughts.

Jennifer met her eyes, smiling slightly. "I do, though."

"Bull. You don't owe anybody anything. At the end of the day, our opinions don't matter. *You* have to make the choice." The demoness grinned. "See how wise I am? I should have my own talk show."

Topaz rolled her eyes, but Satana just snickered.

Somehow, the banter made Jennifer relax when nothing else had worked, not even Topaz's infamous tea. She grinned. Her coven could handle this, especially with Johnny on their side. The Hellphyr fed on mystics, but it would be disoriented and starving. Riding on a swell of confidence, Jennifer ran her finger over the sharp edge of the pages, wincing as the thick vellum caught her skin.

"Here we go," she said.

Her fellow witches stiffened, coming to immediate attention.

A swell of magic washed over Jennifer as they shielded the area to contain the demon. Johnny slung his chain off his shoulder, the heavy links clanging onto the ground. As she watched, flames whooshed up from his collar, engulfing his head and eating away at his skin. He grinned at her, dripping flames. Nodded in encouragement.

A crimson drop of blood collected on her thumb. She pinched the skin, trying to pull more of the precious fluid from inside her. Finally, the drop released, falling onto the grainy parchment.

A roar filled Jennifer's ears, and the book turned to burning ice in her hands. Magic lashed at her skin, Arctic cold and scalding hot at the same time. She wanted to drop it, but she couldn't move. All she could do was gasp as the whirling magic made its way up her arms.

The Hellphyr hadn't manifested the way she'd expected. It was trying to jump directly into her body, like it must have done with Andy. The realization horrified and comforted her at the same time. There had been no moment where Andy had looked at the demon and thought, "That slavering demon looks like a real nice dude. I think I'll invite it to party in my body." He'd probably been taken over before he'd realized what had happened. He wouldn't have known the demon had been running him all over town, killing mystics and devouring their magic for kicks and giggles.

Jennifer wouldn't let the same thing happen to her. She had a score to settle with the Hellphyr, and it wouldn't find her an easy mark. She gritted her teeth and marshalled all her mental defenses, trying to drive the demon out.

It was like trying to hold up a downpour with her bare hands.

The demon's awareness trickled through minute cracks in her mental armor, seeping into her mind. It sat there for a moment, a cold tickle at the back of her skull. Then it spoke to her, mind to mind.

*Sister,* it said.

It used Andy's voice. An image of him rose unbidden in her mind's eye, blocking out her physical surroundings – a slight young man with perpetually mussed blond hair. But Andy was dead, and this mirage didn't fill the void his absence left in her heart. She would have punched it in the face if she could have. The Hellphyr might wear his face, but it couldn't replace her brother.

She snarled aloud.

"You have some nerve," she said.

*Don't be stupid, Jenny Boo.*

The old, hated nickname almost undid her. How could the Hellphyr know that Andy had called her that if her brother was truly dead and gone? Could his soul still linger on, stuck in the creature's prison along with it? She concentrated on the image in her mind, trying to find something that would convince her it was genuine. It looked right, but the Hellphyr had walked around in her brother's skin for weeks. That meant nothing.

"Andy is dead. You're nothing but a pale carbon copy," she said.

But she wasn't sure, and the Hellphyr could sense it. Recollections of her childhood with her brother rose within her, pelting her with pleasant memories. Walking down to Mickey's for soft serve cones. Kicking a soccer ball at the park. Curling up on giant floor pillows to watch horror movies late at night after everyone else had gone to bed. He always picked the movies and spent the entire time peeking out from behind his splayed fingers, too afraid to look at the screen.

*Join us*, said the Hellphyr. Or her brother. Or both. *We will be together, the way it ought to be.*

She shook her head. The mental image solidified further. If she reached out, would her hand pass through his? She couldn't bear the possibility. She clutched the book to her chest, torn with indecision. Logic told her that this was a trick. It had to be. But she wanted it so badly to be true.

"Jen? Are you OK?"

Topaz's voice, tinged with concern, sounded miles away. Jennifer tried to look at her, but her head refused to turn. Andy's figure, frowning in concern, filled her vision. He reached out to her, grabbing her shoulder and squeezing, the way he used to when she cried and he had no idea what to say. His hand was reassuringly solid. How had she doubted that? She had wanted him back for years, and finally, she'd gotten her wish.

"What's going on?" asked Johnny, his voice growing fainter by the word.

"I don't know," answered Topaz.

Then she heard Satana, her voice like a whisper on the wind.

"Whatever the Hellphyr is offering you, it's a lie. It always is," she said. "Come on, Jennifer. You're smarter than that."

Although she didn't want to believe it, Jennifer knew the succubus spoke the truth. Even if some part of Andy had been locked away with the Hellphyr, she couldn't release him. People would die. Andy wouldn't want that.

"Satana's right," she said. "You're not my brother."

*But I can give him to you*, said the Hellphyr, doubling down. *If*

*you merge with me, we would be strong enough to raise him. You'd
be together again, for real.*

Another image joined Andy's figure. Jennifer saw herself,
resplendent in her silver and black battle armor, her blonde
hair streaming out from beneath the spiked band that pulled
it back from her face. A purple aura of magic hung around her
body, filling her eyes. Her dream figure gestured, and the glow
surrounded her brother, making his body jerk. A red stream of
Hellfire joined it, the demon's power merging with hers. Reality
cracked with a sound like thunder, a jagged line that sliced the
air, emitting reddish-purple sparks. An amorphous spirit-thing
slipped through the hole between worlds, darting toward the
body with eager anticipation.

Andy screamed; she swore she could actually hear it. It
couldn't just be in her head this time. It sounded so real.

The portal snapped shut with a sonic boom that Jennifer
could feel down to her teeth. Then Andy turned to her, his eyes
sparking with magic. He held out his hand.

*Join me, and we can make this happen,* he said.

She wanted to. All these years, she'd mourned his loss,
beating herself up over her failure to save him. If only she'd
been there when he met Marduk. If only she'd told Stephen
Strange to stuff it and visited her brother despite the Sorcerer
Supreme's stupid rules. But she hadn't, and she'd carry that
guilt for the rest of her life.

Now, she had an opportunity to set things right. To take care
of her brother the way she should have before. Normally, she
didn't hold with necromancy, but maybe just this once…

She couldn't. Necromancy broached moral lines that she
wasn't prepared to cross, and whatever came back wouldn't truly

be her brother no matter how well it wore his skin. The most she could hope for was a close simulacrum, and at the worst, she'd be dooming Andy's spirit to eternal unlife. She couldn't stomach either possibility. The fact that she'd even considered it sparked fury deep inside her. The demon had tried to use her love for her brother against her again. Apparently, it hadn't learned what a bad idea that was the first time.

"No!" she snarled. "Now get out of my head before I put you out."

The demon-Andy cowered in her mental vision, groveling at her feet. It crouched, twining in a boneless kind of way that made a point of its inhumanity.

*But I have no body, mistress,* it yowled. *There is nowhere for me to go.*

Now she understood. The Hellphyr's physical body must have been destroyed when it was imprisoned in the Tome. Her blood – or that of any member of her bloodline – would form a link that allowed the demon to leap into her body. Otherwise, it couldn't take physical form. It was a handy realization, and one that she would have to scribble in the margins of the book to help the next Kale who held it. Just in case she couldn't tell them herself.

"It needs a body," she said aloud.

"On it," replied Topaz.

This time, her voice didn't seem so far away. Jennifer held onto the demon, ignoring its continued attempts to bargain with her. After a while, it fell into a sullen silence. It didn't fool her. She kept her mental shields intact, knowing that the moment she relaxed, it would try to take her over again.

A yellow haze spilled across the corners of her vision, a

psychic thread that linked her to the members of her coven. Now she could sense that Topaz was working on the body, imbuing it with life. A reddish tinge grew at the edges as Satana added her Hellfire to the mix, creating a form that would be hospitable to the demon.

"It's ready," said Topaz.

"Put my hand on it," replied Jennifer, reaching out blindly, still unable to see anything past the demon and the magical haze surrounding it.

After a moment, Topaz guided her hand to a cold, unyielding surface. Jennifer could feel the magical power beneath her fingertips. She reached out with her power, creating a bridge for the Hellphyr to cross. It surged out of her eagerly, seeking a body that it could control without being beholden to anyone. The tickling pressure in her head eased as it left her body, and her vision cleared, searing her eyes with brightness.

She tented a hand over them, squinting against the glare, and looked at the creature before her. The lion dog from their dining room grinned up at her, exposing its metallic fangs. It was about the size of a large canine, with a stocky body that rippled with muscle. An overly wide mouth showed off a large collection of pointed teeth. Ridges across the top of its head suggested a stylized mane. The creature glistened in the sun that still filtered through the trees, a bright golden metal surging with magical power.

It opened its mouth in a soundless roar, shaking its head. Then it pounced.

# CHAPTER TWENTY-ONE

Satana kept a close eye on the lion dog. When Topaz had requested a vessel for the demon, she'd run upstairs to fetch the statue. It had always been one of her favorites, and she hated to lose it to the Hellphyr, but it was the perfect choice. They needed a form small enough for them to control, but big enough that it couldn't slip away. It would try to run the moment it gained its senses, hoping to take them unawares. That's what she would do. She was ready for it.

Or she would have been, if the thing hadn't swelled.

One moment, the possessed statue was about the size of a large dog. The next, it had grown to the size of a pony. Muscles of liquid gold rippled as it tensed, gathering the strength to pounce on Jennifer. It let out a voiceless roar that made Satana's bones shiver.

She hadn't anticipated this. Sure, she knew the demonic trick behind growing to monstrous proportions. The more power a demon consumed, the bigger they could get. Marduk had used the skill to his advantage, towering over his underlings as well as his daughter. If he couldn't manipulate them into doing his bidding, he would threaten to crush them in his enormous hands. He'd done it to Satana once. Although her years in Hell had been punctuated by constant pain and fear, she still had nightmares about that day in particular.

As a half-demon, she'd never been able to match his size, even if she'd been crazy enough to challenge him directly. Lucifer was even worse. The King of Hell could grow to Godzilla-like proportions. She'd never seen it herself, but the awed terror of the demons who'd seen it convinced her the rumors were true.

But the lion dog shouldn't have been able to grow like that. The extra matter had to come from somewhere, and demons didn't have the ability to create anything. They could only siphon power from someone else, and the demon hadn't had the time to latch on to another power source. They would have sensed it if it had. The rapid growth should have torn the thing into pieces and ejected the demon's spirit out into the ether.

Satana had only dabbled with the trick herself. When she was full in the throes of a succubus binge, she'd grow to maybe six and a half feet and sit atop a throne, looking out at her followers. But ever since she'd been with the coven, she hadn't done it. Sucking power from other people no longer held the appeal it once had. But if the Hellphyr could grow without an external power source, why couldn't she?

The possessed statue launched itself into the air. Instead of dodging, Jennifer stumbled backwards, disoriented by the sudden attack and still off balance from whatever illusions the Hellphyr had tormented her with. Based on her agonized expressions, Satana could have made an educated guess, but it didn't really matter right now.

Everything happened so fast. The Ghost Rider lashed his

burning chain, trying to snare the attacking beast. But the small space made maneuvering difficult, and the Hellphyr moved with a surprising speed. The fiery links whizzed past the metallic dog without making contact. The Rider swung the chain back around, preparing for a second strike, but it wouldn't get there in time. If the statue hadn't grown, it would be no big deal. But at this size, its weight would crush Jennifer to death.

Satana's eyes often went red with fury, but this time she actually *saw* red, impinging on the outskirts of her vision and blanketing everything in a haze of crimson. Some long-buried territorial instinct came rushing out of her. There was only one demon who belonged in this house, and it wasn't this upstart dog-thing. The Hellphyr needed to know who was in charge.

She leaped at the demon dog. Mass wasn't on her side. It would bowl her over, shattering her bones and her spirit along with them. Then it would go through the only people Satana had ever loved, other than herself. She could not let that happen.

Over the past few years, Satana had let her demonic side out to play in small doses, bleeding the edge off her aggressive impulses. But ever since she had joined the coven, she hadn't fully embraced it. She didn't want to lose control and find herself on an island surrounded by mind-enslaved cultists desperate to meet her every whim. She still felt guilty about that, even if it hadn't been a conscious decision at the time. If she allowed them free rein, her demonic impulses would take her over again, robbing her of the ability to make her own decisions and turning her into a creature of instinct, ruled only by her hunger. She'd avoided it for years, but she could do so no longer.

As she flew through the air toward the demon dog, she

reached for the burning, sulfuric power that simmered inside her and let it loose for the first time in ages, pouring every ounce of her power into it. Unbidden, the dam that held her emotions at bay broke under the pressure, buffeting her with feelings she'd denied for way too long. Fear, protectiveness, and resolve washed over her in turns. Running underneath it all was a sensation she'd never felt before, one that she didn't want to recognize.

Love.

She loved Jennifer and Topaz. She would sacrifice herself for them, if necessary.

For the first time in her existence, her eyes pricked with tears. Emotion swept away all rational thought. It combined with the demonic power that she'd kept under wraps for so long, swelling like a pot about to boil over.

With an explosive bang, her body expanded, tripling in size. She hit the possessed statue like a freight train, her giant, red, demonic figure slamming into the Hellphyr's golden form. They flew through the wall of the basement, scattering bricks and powdered mortar everywhere. The momentum carried them into the garden, where they smashed into a brick retaining wall. Shards of masonry went flying as they punched through, rolling onto the ground on the opposite side. Satana didn't even notice. She had her hands locked around the Hellphyr's neck as it clawed at her torso, the two demonic beings struggling for dominance.

Her bodysuit ripped under the onslaught, but she didn't even register the pain. She grabbed the statue by the head, wrapping her arms around its golden mane, and pulled. Her muscles strained as she poured every ounce of strength and fury she had into them. Metal shrieked as the statue's head began to separate from its body.

The Hellphyr let out another of those bone-rattling silent screams. Satana snarled, twisting its head so she could look into its metallic eyes and the faint red fire that flickered in their depths.

"I will rip your head off before I let you hurt them," she said, in a voice that shook the ground. "I will pull you limb from limb and eat the pieces."

It froze, sensing the truth behind her words.

"Choose now," she continued. "But know that if you hurt my people, I will not stop until there's nothing left of you but dust."

The smooth metal beneath her hands shimmered, shrinking back down to its original size. She kept hold of it, staring into the depths of its eyes, overcome by the need to dominate. She couldn't stop. Some small part of her wailed that she shouldn't have let her demonic nature out of the bag, because now she wouldn't be able to put it back in again. If she hurt her friends, she would never forgive herself.

But even though she couldn't manage to look away from the cowering demon dog, she could sense her fellow witches as if they were connected by invisible lines. She could feel Jennifer's worry and Topaz's astonished awe. Running beneath both was a sensation she recognized, although she'd only just now experienced it for herself. They were family now, and they had her back just like she had theirs.

For the first time in her life, Satana didn't feel alone. For the first time, she quit fighting her connection with her sisters and just accepted it. They were annoying and naïve and too damned

*Marvel Untold*

nice, and half the time they didn't even laugh at her jokes. But they were hers, and that realization more than anything else allowed her to regain control of herself. She smothered her violent appetites in a wave of protective determination and tore her eyes away from the statue.

"*Get out of the way,*" ordered the Ghost Rider, its sepulchral voice harsh and demanding.

She could hear the rattle and crackle of the chain behind her. With effort, she released the shrinking statue and stepped back, clenching her fists. Her instincts raged inside her, desperate to rend and tear, to dominate and humiliate. To feed. But she would not let them out. Brick by painstaking brick, she rebuilt her mental shields, walling her demonic urges away until they were needed again.

The Hellphyr didn't move a muscle. It stared up at her in awe and fear, remaining quiescent while the Ghost Rider slipped the chain over its neck. As the Hellfire touched its metallic skin, the demon dog shook all over, bowing its head as its mouth worked in silent fear. But it didn't fight. Instead, it crept behind the Ghost Rider like a frightened puppy on a leash, cowering there.

Satana stared down at the Rider's flaming skull. For the first time, she realized how big she'd grown. She had to be at least twelve feet tall, the top of her head brushing against the palm fronds of the tallest tree in her garden. If she wanted to, she could reach down and squish the Ghost Rider like a grape. That idea amused her, and she let out a chuckle so deep that it belonged in a haunted house.

The burning skull grinned at her. Of course, it always grinned.

"*Change back, Satana,*" it ordered.

"You first," she said. "Age before beauty."

It shook its head, not taking its empty eye sockets off her. Flame whirled in their depths, and not for the first time, Satana wondered what it would feel like to be on the receiving end of his Penance Stare. She had done so much to be ashamed of, but for the first time, she realized she was more than what her blood made her.

The Ghost Rider shuddered, and Satana remembered what Johnny had said about struggling to retain control when he manifested. About how Zarathos had its own agenda. She'd empathized at the time, but now she realized how dangerous that might be for someone like her.

He said, "*Your soul is corrupt. I should send you back to Hell where you belong.*"

The threat should have left her quaking in her boots, because he wasn't wrong. But instead, she remained calm, buoyed by the tangible support that flowed to her from Topaz and Jennifer. It reminded her of soothing ocean waters, lapping at her legs.

"I belong here with my family," she said.

"She does," added Topaz, stepping up next to the demoness. If Satana had been her normal size, they would have been shoulder to shoulder, but at her increased mass, it was more like shoulder to thigh. Topaz looked up at her. "Although I hope you can shrink back down again, because otherwise you won't fit in the house."

"I'll try, if the flamehead here agrees not to try and knock my block off," said Satana.

The Rider considered this for an insultingly long moment before taking one deliberate step back. Its impassive skull stared at them as if eager to reengage.

"We want Johnny back," said Jennifer. "No offense, but you don't play well with others."

The Ghost Rider stared at her another long moment, but it was impossible to tell what it was thinking without the benefits of expression. But finally, the flames faded away, leaving Johnny Blaze to hold onto the reins. Or in this case, a flaming chain leashing a possessed dog statue.

He looked up at Satana, shaking his head.

"Damn, you're big," he said. "I can't decide if that's attractive or terrifying."

"Both," said Jennifer, surprising them all. "Definitely both."

"I am attractive at any size," Satana declared.

The banter made it easier to concentrate. She pulled her power back, allowing her dimensions to return to normal. The process was surprisingly easy, although it made her stomach turn, and her head spun as her body tried to make sense of what was happening. Good thing she didn't need to run, because she'd probably stumble over her own feet.

Back at her normal height, she looked down at the Hellphyr, still cowering behind Johnny's legs, and gnashed her teeth at it. It tried to disappear into the ground, but Satana didn't buy it. She wasn't fooled by its terrified act. It would try to escape again, once it thought it had lulled them into complacency. But it wouldn't get away. Not on her watch.

# CHAPTER TWENTY-TWO

Johnny Blaze had never owned a dog. He'd spent most of his life on the road, dispatching demons and criminals with impunity. There hadn't been much room for pets. Even when he'd retired the Rider and spent those few precious years with his family, he'd resisted his kids' constant requests for a puppy. He could never guarantee that one of his old enemies wouldn't escape Hell and hunt him down, and he had to be ready to take his people and run at any moment. A dog would have only slowed them down.

In the end, he'd been right to worry. Even without the dog, he hadn't been able to save them.

So far, the Hellphyr had been a model pet. The demon didn't have any annoying animal urges to pee on everything or sniff butts or demand constant attention. Johnny wasn't fooled by the show of submissiveness and remained on high alert. However, he did give passing consideration to the idea of getting a dog after the last Luciferian shard was sent back to Hell where it belonged. It probably wouldn't happen, but the thought was nice.

"OK," he said, tightening his grip on the chain, "what's next?"

"I'll put the Hellphyr on the scent," Jennifer replied.

She'd returned to her usual implacable, all-business demeanor, at least on the surface. But Johnny knew that her internal struggle with the demon had rattled her. Overcome with uncharacteristic sympathy, he reached out toward her, but she turned away before he made contact, leaving his hand hovering in the empty air. Feeling foolish, he dropped it before Satana made one of her witty comments and turned his attention back to the possessed statue. Jennifer crouched next to it without any apparent fear, although her shoulders tightened like she anticipated a blow as she put her hand on its head. Johnny tensed, trying to see past her mask to catch any signs of distress.

After only a few seconds, she withdrew, wiping her palm on her pants as if trying to rid herself of the demon germs.

"It doesn't like the idea of following directions, but I promised it a nice mystic snack at the end, so I think it'll lead us to her. It doesn't seem to think that the shield will be a problem," she said.

"Are you really going to let it eat Magda?" asked Topaz, shocked.

Jennifer shrugged. "She's dead, remember? She's not gonna care. The only drawback that I see is that it'll make the Hellphyr stronger. But I'd rather face that than a Lucifer with Kale-level magic."

"That's a mental image I've been really trying to avoid," said Satana, shuddering.

"But he's got a point nonetheless," countered Jennifer. "You think it would work, Johnny?"

"Afraid not," he replied. "The Hellphyr might chow down on Magda's magic easy enough, but there's no way another demon could devour the King of Hell. Doesn't matter how powerful it gets. If it was possible, it would have happened already. Lucifer's a jerk."

"Understatement," murmured Satana.

Topaz relaxed. "Well, I'm relieved. I can't say I'm looking forward to fighting Lucifer, but it doesn't feel right to feed anyone to demons. That's full on evil, no matter how you justify it."

Jennifer cast a worried glance at Satana, who was examining her nails with rapt attention. She didn't seem to take Topaz's comment personally. Heck, she didn't even seem to have registered it.

"Should we go?" asked Johnny.

He was eager to avoid another long discussion. Sure, the witches had created a system that worked for them, and he could see why they talked things out at length. They were all so different that they needed some kind of structure to ensure they were on the same page. But Johnny was used to working alone. When he wanted to do something, he did it. He didn't have to get approval from the committee. As much as he envied the obvious closeness of the coven, he didn't think he could handle the constant need to talk things out. The only person he'd been willing to do that for was Roxanne, and she was gone for good.

To his immense relief, the witches didn't start up again. They were all ready for action. They'd dressed in dark-colored active wear that would allow them to move around in a fight and camouflage any bloodstains. Even Satana wore practical shoes. Their long hair was secured back in buns or braids, reducing potential enemy handholds and increasing visibility. Johnny shouldn't have been surprised. He'd fought with or against Jennifer and Satana before, and both of them had acquitted themselves well in battle. If not for the powers of the Rider, they would have kicked his butt twenty ways to Sunday.

He didn't own any clothes other than jeans, leather, and white t-shirts, because that took too much effort, so he'd dressed the same way he did every day. It had worked out just fine for him so far. But he could still appreciate their effort at preparation.

"We should go, then," he said, shaking the chain. "But this guy is gonna attract attention. Any ideas?"

They had to walk, because the Hellphyr couldn't guide them in a car. They had to follow it, like a dog on the hunt. But he couldn't exactly walk a living statue down the street on a flaming chain. With no idea where the search would take them, they might not be able to stick to the shadows or alleyways. They'd cause a panic.

"We'll need an illusion," said Jennifer. "This shouldn't be tough."

"On it," said Topaz.

The three witches encircled the Hellphyr. The demon cowered like a frightened puppy, belly to the ground, as they closed in. Of course, Johnny couldn't see what they did, but the air grew thicker, as if signaling an impending rain. The space around the possessed statue shimmered like heatwaves off blacktop, and a grating, high-pitched hum grew in Johnny's ears. The growing blur around the Hellphyr made his eyes water. He rubbed them, keeping a strong grip on the chain. This seemed like an opportune time for the demon to make a run for it, but it froze in place as the witches worked their magic.

When the noise and tumult died, a large mastiff stood before them, its eyes glowing red. The dog's powerful body was approximately the same size as before, with a barrel chest and large slavering jowls. Johnny took one look at the creature's powerful jaws and frowned.

"You really think it's a good idea to give the Hellphyr those teeth?" he asked. "Can't you turn him into a chihuahua instead?"

"The teeth aren't real," Topaz assured him. "It's just an illusion."

"Still would be nice if you made him a little yip-yap dog."

Jennifer shook her head. "It was hard enough to get him – *it* – into that statue in the first place. I'm not willing to mess with changing its mass now and risk something going wrong."

"Fair enough," Johnny replied with grudging approval. "I can handle it."

"How kind of you," Jennifer replied, smiling faintly.

Once they put it on the scent, the Hellphyr led them straight to the town square, which was full of late afternoon shoppers. Small groups strolled from window to window while hurried soccer moms desperate for a jolt of caffeine darted into the coffee shop on the southeast corner. A few teenagers did skateboard tricks off the gazebo steps.

The demon jerked at its chain, desperate to follow some scent that tickled its nose. It hadn't expressed any interest in people or other animals so far, so Johnny wondered what had caught its attention.

"The dog's getting agitated," he mumbled.

"That kid with the purple hair has a bit of talent," murmured Topaz.

He followed her pointing finger toward the skateboarders just in time to see a petite elf of a girl with brightly colored hair execute a fancy jump off the steps. The board spun beneath her, and she landed without a wobble to a roar of approval from her friends.

The Hellphyr jerked again, its jaws snapping at the air.

"We'd better move on quick," Johnny suggested. "Keep an eye out for any other folks that'll agitate Rover here."

"On it," said Jennifer.

Johnny shook the chain, and the demon glared at him. For a moment, he thought they were about to have a problem, but then it continued on, leading them steadily toward the northwest end of town.

As they passed by, the neon lights in the window of Mac's Bar flickered to life. Satana tensed, and Topaz slung an arm over her shoulders. She'd been abnormally quiet since her earlier display of demonic powers, and Johnny wondered if he ought to be worried. He'd ask, but something told him she'd shut down that mode of inquiry right quick. He'd have to leave it in Topaz's capable hands. Although he didn't know her as well as the others, the empath had an accepting air about her, like you could tell her anything and she wouldn't be ruffled at all. If he spent enough time with her, Johnny could even see himself confiding in her, which is why he made a vow right then and there to stay away. He'd packed his grief away for a reason, namely the fact that uncontrollable tears didn't go very well with smiting down evil.

A pretty young brunette approached them down the street with her golden retriever leaping at the end of its leash in its eagerness to meet a new doggy friend. The young woman's eyes skittered over the group of them, coming to rest on him with a brilliant smile that confused him. Most of the time, people crossed to the other side of the street when they saw him coming. The grizzled biker look didn't exactly win him friends. Maybe the presence of the witches made him seem safer. That, or the dog.

He'd really have to consider getting one. Not that he wanted to pick up chicks – Dixie would filet him – but maybe he'd get run out of small towns less often if he had one. A small dog that could ride in one of the saddlebags, maybe. He'd have to think on it.

The Hellphyr stopped in its place, watching the capering dog with incomprehension. It didn't seem interested in it the way it had been in the purple haired girl, but Johnny didn't want to chance it. He yanked on the chain, ordering the demon to sit. It turned its head to stare at him balefully.

Topaz stepped forward, smiling. "Sorry," she said, "our dog is kind of a jerk."

The young woman's expression flickered with disappointment, but she recovered quickly.

"No problem," she said. "I can just cross here."

She crossed the street, looking back at Johnny over her shoulder.

"Should I get her number for you?" asked Satana, smirking.

He shook his head in wordless exasperation and turned around just in time to see a little girl run right up to the disguised demon. She was about four years old, with tufty, white-blonde pigtails just like his daughter Emma used to have.

"Doggy!" she exclaimed, holding out her hands.

At the end of the chain, the Hellphyr began to shake with

that silent growl. Johnny didn't know if this girl had some hidden magical talent or if the demon just didn't want to be petted, but he'd be damned if he let some innocent little girl get hurt. He yanked the demon dog back, thrusting his body between them and swiping the girl up in one arm.

"Stop!" he yelled. "That dog's dangerous!"

The little girl burst into frightened tears. Her mother came running up the sidewalk toward them, eyes round with terror, and grabbed the girl from his arms. He couldn't tell which she was more afraid of: him, or the dog. She backed away, cradling the girl's head against her shoulder.

"I'm sorry," he said, his voice husky with emotion. "I just don't want her to get bitten."

He might as well not have spoken. The mom continued to back away, shaking her head.

"Emma, honey, you know you can't run up to doggies without asking," she said.

"Wait!" Johnny said. The woman froze, fear written all over her face and in the lines of her body. "Her name is Emma? My daughter was an Emma, too."

"That's nice," said the mom. "We have to go now."

"But–"

The mom kept backing away as he reached out. He didn't even know what he intended. Patting the kid on the back would accomplish nothing other than freaking the mom out even more than she was already. This wasn't his Emma, no matter how much she reminded him of the daughter he'd lost. He could no longer hold her while she cried. He'd never tear his hair out because of her teenage stubbornness or walk her down the aisle. She was gone, and most days he avoided thinking about that, but here it was, right in his face. His heart seized with a grief that threatened to bend him double. But he gritted his teeth and stubborned his way through it, just like he always did.

The lady hurried away, casting furtive backward glances over her shoulder. Johnny didn't move until she turned the corner and vanished from sight. Then he shook the chain, half-wishing that the demon would try to escape. He could stand to hit something right about now. But the stupid beast just panted at him, the ghost of a doggy grin on its fake canine face.

Johnny debated punching it anyway. After all, the Hellphyr was a soulless killer. It deserved more than a good punching. He took a step forward, cocking his fist. Striking the demon wouldn't bring his family back, but the pain in his hand would distract him from the emptiness in his heart.

Jennifer stepped into his path, staring him down. She didn't seem too concerned about facing down an angry Rider, and for a moment, he was tempted to flame up just to teach her a lesson. But the urge vanished in seconds, overcome in a wave of shame.

"You need to hold it together," said Jennifer. "I'm not sure what's going on with you, but we can't face down Lucifer if you're falling apart."

"I know that," he barked. "I've done this over six hundred times before, remember? I'm the expert on Luciferian extermination."

"Well, then, do we need to give you a minute? Or do you need..." His cousin stumbled, her voice going uncertain. "Do you need to talk?"

To his surprise, he found that he wanted to accept, but now

wasn't the time. He missed having a family, and the sometimes adversarial blood relationship he'd shared with Jennifer to date didn't quite scratch that itch. It would be nice to lean on someone, just this once. But he couldn't bring himself to do it. Caring about people was a waste of time. They all died in the end.

"I'm fine," he said.

None of them commented on the gruff tone of his voice or the fact that he brushed his hand over his eyes. Jennifer backed out of the way with an exaggerated caution that suggested she expected him to leap at the Hellphyr as soon as the coast was clear.

He shook the chain, urging the creature forward, ignoring the urge to do just that.

# CHAPTER TWENTY-THREE

The constant barrage of emotions threatened to overwhelm Topaz once again, but this time, she was able to resist. Her concern for her companions helped her stay strong in the face of Johnny's grief, Jennifer's loss, and Satana's fear of her own dark impulses. Still, the situation was dire. At this rate, Lucifer wouldn't need to defeat them. They'd all end up huddled in a depressed pile on a random street corner.

She needed to cheer them up. Their biggest strength was their ability to work together, but that would do them no good against Lucifer if they were all too busy doubting themselves. They'd hate her for being the annoying ray of sunshine, but she was used to that. Once, Satana had thrown a pan at her for singing too early in the morning. It hadn't bothered her. She had excellent reflexes.

For all her hotheadedness, Satana was usually the easiest mark. The demoness rebounded quickly from her dark moments, probably because she had so many of them. She'd gotten good at pulling herself out of the doldrums, especially with the help of her handy neighborhood empath. So Topaz sidled over to her, sliding an arm around her waist as they followed the Hellphyr down the street.

Satana looked at her like she'd sprouted an extra head.

"What?" she asked.

"You've been really quiet," Topaz observed.

"Just trying to avoid going full demon and biting everyone's heads off."

"Come on," said Topaz, giving her a psychic nudge. "You did what was necessary to save us. I'd argue that it's the least demonic thing you could have done."

"Are you blind? It's one thing to change forms, but I can't believe how big I got. That was like my demon form times a million. You don't get much more demonic than growing to twelve feet tall and turning red."

"You didn't turn red," Topaz said.

"Details, details." Satana waved a hand. "Just leave me alone for a while, OK? I never realized I could do that, and that's going to take some getting used to. I need to deal with this on my own."

Topaz gave her a quick squeeze and withdrew. She didn't take the rejection personally. After all, Satana had a point. Topaz couldn't understand what she was going through. Even though she could sense the conflicting instincts that sometimes threatened to tear the half-demon apart, she'd never experienced them herself. She didn't want to, either.

She dropped back to walk with Jennifer, whose attention was torn between the Hellphyr and the Tome. She'd strapped the magical book to her chest to leave her hands free, but she might as well not have bothered. Her arms had been wrapped around it ever since they'd left the house, like it was a precious baby she needed to protect from the world at large.

"You OK?" asked Topaz.

"Fine," Jennifer replied in the briefest of speeches. "I'm willing to listen, but not really interested in talking right now."

Topaz debated pushing the subject, but she didn't want to risk unsettling the sorceress further. Plus, she'd said she was going to respect boundaries, and ignoring that promise would do more harm than good.

"OK. But I'm here when you're ready," she said.

With some reluctance, she moved on to Johnny. Since they barely knew each other, she didn't know how he'd handle her offer of help. Some people got defensive when she knew things she shouldn't, even if she hadn't gone looking for them in the first place. Better to face that problem head on, she'd found.

"Hey," she said. "Can I talk to you?"

He startled, her words drawing him back from somewhere deep inside him. It took him a moment to orient himself, checking on the Hellphyr and only then turning his attention to her. His expression was neutral, but his eyes were drawn with a pain he tried in vain to hide. As if that would do any good with the likes of her around.

"What's up?" he asked.

"I have to apologize," she began. "Normally, I'm good at filtering things out. Psychics overhear things, you know, especially when they're just coming into their powers. I've gotten good at blocking things out, but the stress got to me, and my shields couldn't handle the pressure."

"Sorry to hear that," he replied cautiously. "But I don't see what that has to do with me."

"I make it a policy not to rummage through people's private business without permission. No one would want me around if I threw their thoughts and feelings into their faces all the time, you know? But I couldn't block it all out, and I have some idea of what you're going through right now. I wanted to own up to that and see if I could help."

"You see what I'm thinking? You know about…" He swallowed hard and forced himself to say the words, "About my kids?"

"Not everything. But the things you feel strongest about, yeah. That little girl reminded you of your daughter, right?"

Johnny nodded once.

"I don't really want to talk about that. Not now," he said.

"I understand that." They walked on in silence for a while. The rhythmic jingle of the chain seemed loud in the quiet. Then she said, "I lost my family, too, you know."

"Yeah?"

"I mean, it's different. I never knew them. But still, sometimes I used to pretend they were coming to pick me up. I'd get ready and pack a bag even though I knew it wasn't true. That's a childish fantasy, isn't it?"

"No," he said. "It's not."

"Maybe not. But anyway, I wanted to make you the same offer I've made to Satana and Jen. I don't go muddling around in people's heads without permission, and I refuse to make big changes. Stealing memories, no matter how bad they are, is just…" She shuddered. "I couldn't live with myself later. But I can make things a little easier to face, if ever you need the help."

He didn't even stop to consider it.

"Thanks, but no thanks," he said.

"It's OK. I wouldn't trust me either after I pried in your head."

"No, that's not it." He paused, searching for the right words to explain. "I saw a show on TV once about cowboys. Even when they're home, they sleep on the floor so that when they go out into the field with their cattle, they won't miss their nice, cushy beds. They'll still be able to sleep. You're offering me a nice, cushy bed."

"So, if you take it, it's just making it harder for you to deal when I take the bed away?"

"Exactly."

"That only makes sense if you have to go back out there. If you could get used to sleeping in the bed every night, maybe it wouldn't be an issue."

"I don't think we'll be walking long enough for you to fix all my problems," he said, his lips curling into an unaccustomed smile.

She laughed.

"Touché," she said. Then she sighed. "I just wish I could cheer everyone up. My shields are back up, but it still feels like I'm wading through a pool full of depression and sulfur."

"Sulfur?" She drew his attention to the possessed statue, and he nodded. "Ah," he continued. "You can smell them, too?"

"Just the Hellphyr. My magic fuels its body. I could probably track it if it got away, but that's not an experiment I'd like to conduct."

"No, I don't blame you there." He sighed, running a hand over his hair. "As for the other thing, I think you've got to let people work through their emotions on their own. They have a right to feel what they're feeling."

"Yeah, but going to face Lucifer while you're going through

an existential crisis does not strike me as the best of ideas. I can't afford to let you all stew."

"You got a point there. But I don't know what to do about it."

"How did you used to cheer up your kids?"

"I tickled them. You're welcome to try it, but not on me."

They both gave a half-smile.

"OK, how did they cheer you up?" she asked.

He fell silent, lost in his memories. Whatever he was thinking of made him shake his head in fond bemusement, a wave of love pulsing out from him, so strong that it washed over Topaz's reestablished mental defenses.

"When she was little, Emma used to sing at me. Not to me, at me. It was more like shouting, really. She'd yell the lyrics right into my face. Very inspirationally."

"What did she sing?" asked Topaz, bemused.

"Her favorite was 'Jingle Bells,' because she said it's a happy song. Let me tell you, it's hard to be upset when a four year-old is screaming Christmas carols in your face in the middle of July."

The mental image delighted her. It was hard to look at Johnny the same way now that she'd heard that. At first, he'd been just like she'd imagined: gruff and businesslike, the kind of guy who would always be driven by his duties and never stop to smell the roses. But this mental image cast him in a new light.

"I bet you were a good dad," she said.

"Not half as good as they deserved."

The unconditional love in his voice brought tears to her eyes. It was the kind of thing she'd always imagined her father would say, if ever she got to talk to him. If he was still alive, he had to think about her as much as she did him. He had to love her regardless of the time and distance that separated them. She wasn't willing to consider the alternative.

As great as this bonding moment was, Topaz had to concede that it was a step backward in her efforts to cheer everyone up before they went toe to toe with the King of Hell himself. She was supposed to be lifting everyone else's spirits, not letting them knock her off balance with strong emotional responses. But she'd exhausted every idea she had.

Every idea except one.

Before she could second-guess herself, she threw her head back and started belting out "Jingle Bells" as loud as she could. She couldn't carry a tune in a paper bag, so it wasn't the best rendition. Her voice wobbled and croaked, the rhythm lurching along as closely as she could remember. She wasn't certain of the words. She'd celebrated Christmas a few times over the years, but sometimes she was just too busy and other times she didn't have anyone to celebrate with. One year, she'd spent the entire day watching sitcoms and eating Chinese takeout with Wong. That had probably been her favorite Christmas of all.

Johnny watched her for a moment, his expression wavering as he tried to decide how to react. But finally, he grabbed onto her face and said, "No, you're doing it wrong. Like this."

He proceeded to shout the words right into her face, grinning like a maniac. Over his shoulder, Topaz could see Satana and Jennifer, standing stock-still on the sidewalk, staring at them like they'd both lost their marbles. Satana made a big show of clapping her hands over her ears.

Topaz joined in, shouting with all her might. To her immense surprise, it actually worked. She couldn't be upset while doing something this stupid, and Johnny's maniacal grin dissolved into something more genuine as they sang. As the lyrics wound to an end, Topaz couldn't help it. She hugged him.

Johnny patted her on the shoulder just once before releasing her, but she still felt like she'd accomplished something big.

"See? You got it," he said. "I think you and Em would have liked each other."

"I think so, too," she replied.

"Have you both had a mental breakdown?" asked Satana, smirking.

"Do you need to ask?" Jennifer interjected.

"Johnny was teaching me how his kid used to cheer him up," Topaz explained. "And I think she was a genius. It even worked on the three of you."

Satana opened her mouth to argue and then shut it with a clack. Jennifer took a long, hard look at her cousin before she nodded.

"Yeah," she said. "Logic doesn't work on our family, does it? We're too stubborn."

He chuffed. "I can't argue with that."

"Shall we go defeat the Lord of Darkness?" asked Jennifer.

"Only if I can shout Christmas carols into his face," countered Johnny.

They all snickered, with varying degrees of nervousness. But as they continued their long walk across town, they all kept humming "Jingle Bells."

# CHAPTER TWENTY-FOUR

Try as she might, Satana couldn't shake the obnoxious earworm. She hummed that stupid Christmas carol as they crossed the railroad tracks leading to Salem's small industrial park. She tried with all her might to replace it with another tune – anything would do – as they turned onto the gravel path leading to the fairground. But nothing seemed to work until she caught sight of what she hoped was their final destination. The song finally let go its stranglehold on her attention as she looked around the county fairground.

Across the long expanse of the gravel parking lot sat a cluster of dingy RVs and pickups with sleeper trailers, illuminated by an insufficient ring of streetlights. Dusk had fallen fast – and early. Either they'd been walking longer than she'd thought, or Lucifer's hand was at work here.

In the fairground beyond, the drooping sun outlined the shape of an enormous Ferris wheel. Next to it, a haunted house stretched its spires up into the sky, a long blank pennant at the tippy top flapping lazily in the weak breeze. The surrounding area was dotted with rides in various stages of construction, shuttered food trailers, and shelled-out game tents. The place looked deserted, without a single light burning in the RVs and nary a person in sight.

"You think this is it?" asked Satana.

"Seems like Lucifer's style," Johnny admitted. "He'd get a kick out of murdering unsuspecting folks in the funhouse."

"Good, because my feet hurt."

"What do we do now?" asked Topaz.

"Do?" Johnny arched a brow. "We find him, and we kill him. Follow the dog and be ready for anything. It's not rocket science."

"Sorry. That was probably a stupid question," Topaz said.

"Nah, I was harsh. He's close by. I can sense him, and it's making me edgy." He paused. "It's making Zarathos *really* edgy. He wants out."

"You want help?"

Topaz held out her hand, and to Satana's surprise, Johnny took it. The furrow between his eyes lessened but didn't disappear entirely. Topaz might not take away the struggle, but at least she took the edge off.

Speaking of taking the edge off, Satana needed to kill something. Something demonic. Something that would help her prove once and for all that she had chosen her side in the battle for her soul. To herself, if to no one else.

Clenching her fists, she led the way across the parking lot toward the carnival. Brightly colored flyers on every lamppost advertised the Cirque du Night, opening over the weekend, with "rides, treats, and a death-defying vampire stage show suitable for ages thirteen and older!" Under normal circumstances, this was the kind of shlock that Satana loved, but right now, she wasn't in the mood to appreciate it properly.

She transformed as they drew closer. A shivery, tickling sensation ran over her body as she dropped the glamour that hid her horns, hooves, and claws from overly excitable mortals. If any of the circus people did happen to look out the windows of their RVs, maybe the sight would convince them to stay hidden inside. Either that, or they'd try to recruit her for their stage show.

Even after the transformation was completed, the back of her neck prickled, making her look back over her shoulder in paranoia. Lucifer had to know they were coming, and he wouldn't be waiting patiently for their arrival. He'd prepared some kind of surprise for them, and she had enough experience with the denizens of Hell to dread what it would be. But whatever it was, it would hit her first.

Her and Johnny, anyway. Topaz had offered him what support she could, and now he drew even with her, the Hellphyr tugging eagerly at the end of its chain. The demon's body rippled with excitement, straining at the seams of the illusion. Jennifer waved a hand, dropping the façade and allowing the golden form of the statue to shine through once more. The demon shook its metallic body like a dog just out of the bath and leaped forward again, its eager flight halted once more by Johnny's firm grip on the chain.

The Ghost Rider had a hold of himself now. His jaw was set with determination, and his eyes held a steely glint as they met Satana's. The two of them took point without any discussion necessary. Out of the four of them, they'd faced Hell over and over again, and they knew what to expect. They knew they could survive it.

They pushed through the turnstiles and past the darkened ticket booths, entering the grounds. Here, the bulk of the trailers and tents blocked out most of the light from the RV lot, shrouding everything in shadow. Every corner was a dark pool, perfect for obscuring demons hungry for their blood. Satana tensed, trying to sniff out any potential predators, but the place confused her senses. The very air reeked of Hell.

"Where to?" murmured Jennifer.

Satana shook her head, looking at Johnny. But his brow furrowed in a confusion that mirrored her own.

"The entire place stinks," he said. "There isn't a spot here that hasn't been demon-touched. I can't get a read on anything. Stay alert."

Satana straightened her shoulders, pushing away the cloying dread that tried to sap away her mental strength before the battle. Her father played these mind games with her all the time, and they used to work all too well. She'd allowed him to jerk her chain, leading her along like they led the Hellphyr. But she was no dumb demon driven by intuition and hunger. She wouldn't let Hell win. Not this time.

"We've got this," she said.

She'd never been great at pep talks. Actually, this was her first attempt at one. Topaz usually held the corner on the cheering front, but her lips had gone bloodless with fear, and she seemed inches away from bolting. Who knew what her highly attuned empathic senses were picking up? She was probably awash in demonic hungers at this very moment, and that would shake anybody with half a heart.

Under those circumstances, Satana's one-sentence encouragement shouldn't have accomplished anything, but the others knew how hard it was for her to drop her shields and speak from her soul. Topaz straightened, meeting her eyes, and nodded.

"Yeah," she said, swallowing hard. "We've got this."

Jennifer hugged the Tome tighter to her chest. "I still can't believe you talked me into this, but there isn't anyone I'd rather be here with. And that includes you, Johnny. I'm sorry this happened, but I'm glad we finally had a chance to set aside our differences."

"Yeah." His voice was rough. "Like I said before, you're family. We might not always agree, but you can count on me if you're ever in too deep. That goes for all three of you."

A wave of contentment and belonging washed over Satana, and at first, she tried to resist it as she always had. After her long years in Hell, any vulnerability terrified her. She'd fought tooth and nail not to care about anyone except for herself, but her annoying coven mates had refused to take no for an answer. She'd spent all these years refusing to acknowledge the connections between them, and now that they were threatened, she realized how precious they were. She would give anything to keep them.

She wouldn't be bursting out into song like some people, but for the first time in her entire life, she found herself going into a fight more concerned for others than for herself.

"Shall we?" she asked, trying to pretend like this was all no big deal.

Johnny nodded. "I think Jen's eager to get this guy back in his book." He indicated the Hellphyr, who sat quietly, staring off into the darkness. Satana followed the creature's gaze, but she neither saw nor sensed anything. "He's too well behaved for my liking."

"Agreed," said Jennifer. "Let's end this."

Johnny shook the chain, rousing the Hellphyr back into action and leading them further onto the carnival grounds.

The entire circus was horror themed. Instead of darts, patrons would throw little bats at balloons to win stuffed crows or bat masks. All the food vendors had pithy, monster-themed names like "Midnight Snack" and "Love at First Bite". The darkened Ferris wheel had black painted carriages with plastic wings rising from the back of each seat. Although the falling night had gone still and quiet, the seats still swung to and fro in some unfelt current, creaking ominously. Darkness cloaked it all, the sun falling behind the trees like a film on fast-forward.

With every passing moment, Satana grew tenser. A pit of foreboding built in her stomach, sapping away the resolve that her emotions had built within her. She still wouldn't falter – she was too stubborn for that – but somehow, she knew they were destined to fail. It would be smarter just to give up and go home, back behind the safety of their shields.

"Looks like there's no one here," Jennifer said in shaky tones. "Darn."

"The fear you're feeling is just a mental trick," Topaz put in through stiff lips that refused to work right. "Child's play."

"Can you counter it?" asked Johnny. "It's ticking me off."

The empath focused for a moment, and the cloying sensation of dread lessened its hold for a moment, but then it came back in full force. Topaz squeezed her eyes shut, her face screwed up in concentration as she redoubled her efforts.

The haunted house flared to life, bathing the area around them in light and noise.

As if on cue, the Hellphyr bolted.

# CHAPTER TWENTY-FIVE

Johnny Blaze and fear did not get along. When he'd first become the Ghost Rider, he'd been more frightened than he'd wanted to admit. He was scared of the unknown force that took him over. Scared of the ease with which he grew to accept it. Of what that might mean for his ability to live a normal life. But as time went on, he learned to live with what he'd become. This curse was his cross to bear, and he couldn't reject it no matter how much he wanted to. He'd tried it. It hadn't gone well.

Now he was more frightened than he'd been in a long time. The wave of inexplicable dread only served to make him angry. He was scanning the area for something to pummel when the House of Horrors blared to life. Red-tinted floodlights snapped on, bathing Johnny and the witches in scarlet. White searchlights emitted a searing glow, tracing random patterns on the ground and temporarily messing with his night vision. Animatronic ghosts lurched into motion, dancing behind the windows on a continuous loop. The loudspeakers flanking the front doors wheezed to life, booming out an invitation to enter in sepulchral tones.

The Hellphyr surged forward, taking advantage of his momentary surprise. Johnny's attention might have been elsewhere, but he wasn't stupid enough to relax his grip on the chain. He would have held on just fine if disaster hadn't struck. Satana took one of the searchlights right in the eyes and backed away hurriedly, tripping over a thick power cord that stretched across the pathway.

She knocked into Johnny, knocking him off balance. The Hellphyr leaped forward. The chain slid free of his leather-gloved grip.

"No!" yelled Johnny.

Within him, Zarathos surged, eager to smite the wicked. Johnny didn't need the distraction, not now. Struggling for control of his own body, he threw himself forward. Unfortunately, Satana had the same idea. Half-blinded, she lurched forward at exactly the same time, their hands outstretched to grab the chain. They collided, knocking each other off course, and the Hellphyr slipped through their fingers.

It darted up the metal ramp leading into the House of Horrors. The chain rattled against the hard surface, and metal boomed as the heavy golden statue ate up the ground in long, bounding strides. Moving as quickly as its borrowed body would allow, it disappeared into the carnival attraction.

There was no time to place blame, even if it needed to be placed. Johnny scrambled to his feet, squinting in the glare, and ran after it.

Behind him, Jennifer yelled, "You two go in the entrance. Topaz and I will take the exit, and we'll trap it in the middle."

Johnny needed no further urging. He tore into the haunted house at full speed, Satana hot on his heels. The tight entryway hall made an abrupt right a few steps in, but a quick shove off the wall reoriented him without losing too much speed. The agile maneuver backfired on him. He hit a series of rollers on the ground at a full run, losing control and cartwheeling his arms in a desperate bid for balance. The rollers flung him forward, nearly dropping him on his tailbone. At the end of the hallway, some unseen machine suspended in the darkness above him blasted cold air into his face. An animatronic clown with faded paint and an obscene leer popped out of a slot in the wall, its limp arms flinging into his face with the force of its movement. Startled, he hauled back and punched it. Plastic cracked under the blow, cutting his skin.

"That isn't a demon." Satana shoved past him without slowing, her hips brushing against his in the close quarters. "Do you need flashcards?"

Instead of a coherent response, all he could manage was a growl. His hand hurt, and if they didn't get that demon back, there would be more pain. A lot more. He should have known that releasing the Hellphyr was a bad idea, but he'd been so desperate to get to Lucifer that he'd been blind. His plans had a tendency to go wrong. Always had and always would. At some point, he'd have to start accounting for that, or more people would get hurt.

Of course, now wasn't the time for such maudlin thoughts, not when he had a demon to catch. He hurried after Satana, rubbing his aching knuckles.

The interior of the House of Horror was dimly lit. The ground wobbled beneath his feet, threatening to pitch him back to the ground at a moment's notice. He squinted, trying to see where to put his feet using the shafts of light that filtered down from high above. Satana went down to one knee, hitting the ground with a loud metallic bang. He pushed past her, determined to get to the demon first. After all, this was his fault. He'd dropped the chain. He would pick it up again before someone got hurt.

She grabbed him by the arm, hauling herself up but slowing him down in the process.

"Me first," she said.

"No."

He shook her free, unwilling to waste time in an argument over chivalry, and pushed through a half-open metal door with a surprising heft to it. Its surface was dented where the Hellphyr had hit it.

"It's my fault the demon's out," said Satana.

"I dropped the chain," he responded before slamming face first into a clear plastic partition. The empty bench behind it suggested that during normal operating hours an employee would sit there, ready to jump out at unsuspecting patrons and scare the crap out of them. He didn't like to be frightened, but it would have saved him the pain. Tears sprang to his eyes. "Ow. I hate haunted houses."

"Sorry about your schnoz," she said, and to his surprise, she sounded like she meant it. She passed him again. "Where in the heck did the Hellphyr go? Could we have passed it? Ow!"

She slammed into another Plexiglas partition and swore at length.

"No, it definitely went through that door back there. How big is this place?" Johnny groped ahead of him in the darkness, unwilling to bark his injured nose on another unseen obstacle. "Jen? Topaz? You got him?" he shouted.

There was no answer. That more than anything spurred him on. The House of Horrors hadn't looked like a small attraction from the outside, but if he shouted at full volume, they ought to be able to hear him. The lack of response, combined with their failure to find the Hellphyr, made him worried. He rushed forward, his hands encountering another plastic partition, but this time he managed to avoid impacting himself on it. Satana was right beside him, her jaw tight with tension.

"Are they OK?" he asked.

He didn't know how the witches worked exactly, but they were linked to each other. Maybe Satana could use her witchy Spidey-sense to find them.

"I think I'd know if they died, but otherwise, I have no clue," she responded. "And I don't like it. If you transformed, would you light everything on fire? We need illumination. The Hellphyr has to be hiding; if it was running through this place at full tilt, it would have run into the others by now."

Johnny nodded. "If it's hiding, it's hunting. And no, I won't light everything on fire. Not if I don't want to."

"Well, then," she said, "fire it up."

The two of them paused, crammed into a small space between two partitions. He grabbed her by the arm to hold her in place. She turned, arching one perfect brow, and for the first time, he became aware of the fact that she was very female, and a succubus, and they were pressed together in the small space. His face flushed, and even though it was too dark for her to notice, her lips quirked.

"Sorry," he said. "I don't get too close to people these days. I barely see my girl."

She shook her head, waving away the apology. "Just change."

He shifted. He couldn't remember a time when someone had watched his transformation at close range with such frank curiosity. The process wasn't the prettiest thing to witness, but Satana seemed transfixed by the sight of his flesh melting from his bones. As the flames rushed up from his collar, she put her hand to his cheek. The Ghost Rider turned its head into her touch for the briefest of moments. Then it pulled away, intent on the hunt once more.

"Aren't you gonna tell me I'm an unclean devil and threaten to send me back to Hell where I belong?" asked Satana, echoing Johnny's unspoken thoughts.

"*No*," said the Rider. "*We are partners.*"

The only answer was shocked silence. The Ghost Rider grinned. He had given the succubus something to think on, and maybe that would be enough to tip the scales in the direction of her human half in the future. If not, he would do his duty, but he wouldn't relish it. Johnny would mourn, and although Zarathos had a much longer and more rational view of the greater scheme of things, the spirit did not want souls to fall. More fallen souls meant more work for him, and someday, he would rest.

That day wasn't today.

"*Come*," he said. "*We hunt.*"

# CHAPTER TWENTY-SIX

Jennifer Kale couldn't believe this was happening. She'd had one job – to keep the Hellphyr contained – and not only had she failed, but she'd given the demon a body instead. When she died and went to the afterlife, she was going to get the world's worst tongue-lashing from the rest of her family. That was a stupid thing to be obsessed over given the circumstances, but it was easier to think about her grandmother's hot temper and old-fashioned insults than it was to think about the dead bodies that would pile up as a result of her mistake.

Her heart thumped in fast-forward as she and Topaz pushed through the exit doors into the House of Horrors. The three-story monstrosity was big enough that Johnny and Satana would probably defeat the demon before they got close enough to help. But if the Hellphyr ran for it, she had to be ready to throw down. She'd put it back into the *Tome of Zhered-Na*, whether they'd found Lucifer and Magda by then or not. She couldn't risk losing control of it again. Whatever happened, she refused to end the evening with more blood on her hands. That was unacceptable.

Or so she told herself. But the reassurances failed to drown out the chorus of self-recrimination that ran in an endless loop through her mind, making her knees shake.

Topaz picked up on her tumultuous feelings, because nothing was ever private when the empath was around. She tried to be respectful about it, but sometimes Jennifer felt like she might as well write her stronger emotions on her forehead with a Sharpie and get it over with. She tried not to hold that against her fellow witch, but sometimes she just wanted to have her existential crises in private.

Jennifer glanced over her shoulder, worried that maybe she'd thought that a little too loud, but Topaz didn't even notice. She was too busy keeping a constant eye out for the demon, just like Jennifer ought to be doing.

More than a little ashamed, Jennifer wrenched her attention back to the matter at hand. The first room was a maze of empty prison cells suspended over a shaking floor. She clutched the bars as she made her painstaking way into the space, but maintaining her balance was difficult. Her mind kept circling back to the same litany of troubles, worrying at them like a cut on the inside of her cheek that she couldn't manage to leave alone. Over the past couple of days, she'd found it increasingly more difficult to focus, and that unsettled her. She'd always been good at getting the job done. In their coven and at home, she was the one who kept conversations on track and made sure the essentials happened, balancing between Satana's humorous ruthlessness and Topaz's emotional empathy with ease. But she'd lost the knack, and she didn't know why.

"Yes, you do," said Topaz, breaking the illusion that she couldn't hear Jennifer's thoughts.

"Come on, 'Paz. You promised to quit listening in all the time," Jennifer said, exasperated.

"I wasn't. But you practically shouted that. I couldn't help overhearing." Topaz winced, pinching the bridge of her nose. "And I'm sorry. I'm struggling, too, you know."

"Yeah? Why is that?"

"Because for the first time, we've both realized we could lose what we've built here, and that's damned scary," said Topaz.

Jennifer flicked a glance at her, but Topaz remained stoic.

"You've been swearing a lot over the past couple of days. I think you might have set a new record," Jennifer said.

"Yeah, well," Topaz shrugged. "It seems justified given the circumstances. That's a dead end."

"What?"

Topaz pointed. "Go left instead of right. That way is a dead end."

At the end of the room, a long hallway stretched off into the darkness. When Jennifer stepped inside, a plate on the floor triggered a blood-curdling scream that made her jump. But she hurried on regardless, pushing through a patch of rubbery tubes suspended from floor to ceiling. Their flabby suckers, coated in a slime that she didn't want to contemplate, stuck to her skin before she shook them free with a grimace.

A closed metal door stood at the end of the hallway. At first, Jennifer assumed it was a hollow, painted veneer, just like everything else in this place. But to her surprise, the latch was cold metal that chilled her hand when she tried it.

"Locked," she said, frowning.

"Just kick it open," suggested Topaz.

In response, Jennifer tapped it with the toe of her tennis shoe, eliciting a deep boom.

"Even on my best day, I couldn't kick that down," she said.

"I wouldn't use magic. Not yet. No need to advertise our presence."

"Agreed."

Jennifer put her ear to the door but heard nothing. Either the others hadn't found the Hellphyr, or the door was solid enough to block the noise of their combat. Neither option appealed to her.

"Well, at least we know the Hellphyr isn't in this part of the house," said Topaz, trying for optimism.

Jennifer nodded, her hand still resting on the door. The more she thought about it, the less she liked its presence here. She'd been in plenty of carnival attractions. When she was a teenager, she'd worked the county fair, serving fried Twinkies and funnel cakes to harried moms with flocks of hungry children all day, and riding the rides all night. Back then, she'd loved anything that flipped her world upside down or defied gravity, and she'd never refused a dare. Back then, her powers had made her feel invincible.

Now she'd been around the block enough times not to take anything for granted, and the presence of this door concerned her. Carnival rides were made as light as possible to save on the gas required to haul them from site to site. Installing a heavy door in the middle of a haunted house didn't add up. She could see replacing the entry and exit doors with something a little sturdier to deter vandals, but this location made no sense. The more she thought about it, the less she liked it.

She crouched down to get a closer look, but the light wasn't sufficient at all. Normally, she'd rely on her magic here, but that was out. After a moment, she smacked her head in exasperation, pulling out her cell phone. She should have thought of that in the first place. The phone's flashlight would have saved her all of that groping around in the dark, but she'd gotten so used to relying on her magic that she often forgot about mundane things like phones.

"What are you doing?" asked Topaz.

"Checking to see if this door is a recent installation. It looks like it might be. Those look pretty fresh," Jennifer said, indicating the hinges.

Topaz leaned over, tilting her head to and fro as she checked it out.

"OK. So what?" she asked.

In short sentences, Jennifer explained her theory about the door. As she spoke, Topaz's expression darkened.

"You're right," she said. "It's shady. Unless they're just slamming it to scare people. I bet it would make a loud noise."

"Possibly, but there are much lighter ways to make that noise. It's not worth the cost, and at a carnival, penny pinching is practically a religion."

Jennifer looked around, shining the bright, narrow beam from her phone around. The short hallway leading up to the door was covered in greasy handprints. Were they deliberate decorative choices, or had someone been locked up in here? She couldn't tell, and she didn't like the uncertainty.

"I think we should get out of here," she said, shining the light directly into Topaz's eyes by accident. "Whoops. Sorry."

Topaz threw her hands up a second too late, blinking furiously.

"Yeah," she said, "but you'll have to go first, because now I'm blind as a bat."

Muttering an apology, Jennifer took point. She kept the light on, searching the space for anything else fishy. As an added bonus, it made navigating the maze of bars much easier. That fact failed to relax her. She was too busy worrying to notice. What if the upgrades to the House of Horrors had been designed to hold the Hellphyr? Lucifer wanted the demon for nefarious but unknown purposes. If he'd lured them to the carnival with the hopes of capturing the possessed statue, they'd walked right into the trap.

"Oh no," she moaned as the full implications of this train of logic came crashing down on her.

"What?" demanded Topaz, jerking to attention. "What's wrong?"

"We need to find the others. Right now."

But it was too late. Jennifer could hear footsteps. From the sounds of it, a lot of people were entering the House of Horrors. She wanted to hope that they were regular old circus employees, but who works on a haunted house in the middle of the night? Their presence wasn't a coincidence. It couldn't be.

Topaz stiffened.

"Turn off the light!" she hissed.

Jennifer did as requested, closing her eyes to reorient her night vision. Together, they began to creep backwards through the cellblock maze, trying to put some obstacles between them and their unseen visitors.

"How many?" she whispered.

Topaz frowned, concentrating hard, and then shook her

head. "Five, I think? They're not right. I can't read their minds. There's nothing there."

"More of Lucifer's puppets, then." Jennifer's jaw tightened. "I'm scared. What if I did the wrong thing by summoning the Hellphyr? What if those premonitions were real after all, and we just walked into a trap?"

"Then we'll face it together," Topaz replied gently.

But the reassurance didn't have its desired effect. The more Jennifer thought about it, the more upset she got. Adrenaline filled her limbs with furious energy, making her hands tremble. She was tired of second-guessing herself. Tired of questioning every move. Of being jerked around like a puppet on a string. Lucifer wanted the book? He could come get it. She would show him why it wasn't wise to mess with a Kale. She contemplated the Tome strapped to her chest but decided not to bother with fancy spells and complicated incantations. She felt like throwing down old school.

Jennifer Kale was angry, and there would be hell to pay.

# CHAPTER TWENTY-SEVEN

Satana had only been inside the haunted house for a little while, but she was already eager to leave. Not that the place was scary. She'd seen phone commercials more frightening than this place. But the childish décor combined with the genuine low-grade stench of Hell that coated the entire fairground turned her stomach in new and interesting ways.

Time stretched like taffy. Every second the Hellphyr remained loose increased the chance that it would escape them for good, and Satana didn't want to see how Jennifer handled that. As a result of her growing worry, each second felt like an eternity.

The Ghost Rider's flaming skull helped to dispel the gloom that clustered in the darkened corridors, but it still wasn't easy to see in here. At its current size, the Hellphyr could hide in some out of the way corner, wait for them to pass by, and then sneak out unseen. They had to find it quickly, before Lucifer struck, but they also had to move slow and deliberate to avoid passing it by mistake.

"Can you sense it now?" she asked. "The Hellphyr?"

*"It is still here somewhere."*

The Rider turned its empty eye sockets to her. She stared into their flaming depths, wondering what it would be like to be pinned by its Penance Stare. It turned its enemies' sins against them, and she had racked up quite a list of them in her life. Some had been done against her will, but that didn't matter. They stained her soul regardless of the circumstances.

The possibility that he could turn on her at any moment should have frightened her, but the Rider had already spared her once. Besides, she didn't think that Johnny would be on board with killing her, especially not while they were working together to defeat a greater evil. But she couldn't count on that forever. Better to find the Hellphyr and get Johnny back just in case.

"Well, can't you track it?" she asked.

*"Your magic tethers it to its body. You should be able to find it."*

"If I use my magic, Lucifer will know we're here."

The Rider tilted its head, and Satana got the impression that it was thinking, even though she had no features to base the assumption on.

*"He knows,"* said the Rider.

Satana jerked to attention. "Are you sure? Crap. I can't hear Jennifer and Topaz, can you? Jen? Topaz?" She shouted their names and heard nothing in response. "We need to find them."

*"Capture the demon. They can take care of themselves."*

"You're a jerk, you know that?" The Ghost Rider just grinned at her, and finally Satana sighed. He was right; they were perfectly capable. Her panic ebbed, only to be replaced by the flush of embarrassment. She'd overreacted. "Oh, fine," she said. "You really think I should use my magic?"

*"Yes."*

Although Zarathos sounded pretty certain, Satana still tried to keep her magic down to a trickle rather than a deluge. Hopefully she could avoid triggering a confrontation with the lord of Hell before they were ready. Separating into two groups had sounded like a great idea at the time, but the possibility of confronting Lucifer without her coven mates by her side made her twitchy.

The trickle of power rushed through her body, brightening her surroundings. She sensed the pulsing life energy that powered the Hellphyr's body just up ahead and sagged with relief. Beyond that, the bright forms of her fellow witches blazed with light and power. Something was wrong.

Jennifer and Topaz were under attack. They needed her.

"The Hellphyr's right up there," she said, baring her teeth. "We need to snag it, take that door down fast, and rejoin the others. They've got company."

The Ghost Rider nodded. *"Lead the way,"* it said. *"The demon won't escape me again. I will send it back to Hell."*

Jennifer might not like that, but it sounded like a terrific idea to Satana. Demons in books could be let out by accident – or due to manipulation, as Andy Kale had discovered. Marduk's interest in the demon hadn't slipped her mind either. Any arrangement that kept the Hellphyr well out of Daddy's hands would get Satana's vote, hands down.

She resisted the urge to open up and just blast the creature back to Hell where it belonged. Although that would have been very fulfilling, draining herself before the big, inevitable showdown with Lucifer wasn't smart. Plus, she could hurt the others by accident. Satana's magic was like a loaded gun, and she needed to use it safely. She would never point a weapon at a target without intending to destroy it, or without being aware of what was behind it in the unlikely event that she missed.

So she couldn't let loose, no matter how much she wanted to. Instead, she kept a stranglehold on her magic, channeling the barest trickle necessary to keep tabs on the Hellphyr. She crept forward for a few steps before she realized how ridiculous it was to try to sneak up on her prey with a giant flaming skeleton at her side. The Rider wasn't the most subtle creature in the world. He had many skills, but stealth wasn't one of them.

She led him through a room full of creepy dolls and up a short flight of rickety stairs. The Hellphyr was just ahead, in a room full of shadows and darkness. It had chosen its hiding spot well. Even though Satana knew it was there, she still couldn't make it out in the black. She pointed. Once the Rider got in there, he'd light things up well enough that she wouldn't trip over something in the dark. She'd done that once already, and she didn't intend to repeat the mistake.

The Ghost Rider squeezed its skeletal hands into fists with something like glee. It needed no further encouragement. It stomped into the dark room, eager to face down Hell and live to tell the tale once again. Satana followed close on the spirit's heels. Normally, she'd be out front, taking all the damage and keeping her fellow witches safe from harm. Her ego tried to push her forward just to prove that she hadn't lost her edge, but she resisted the pull with surprising ease. Her instincts weren't usually so easy to overcome. Maybe she was getting wiser in her old age.

The glow from the Rider's flames didn't spread far, but it illuminated a small spherical space. Enough for Satana to see black-painted floors and no tripping hazards, at least not in the middle of the room. It was a long room, bigger than she'd realized. But her keen ears picked up the unmistakable sound of something moving down at the end. It had to be the Hellphyr.

The Rider heard it, too. He lunged forward, bony fingers outstretched and eager. The flames illuminated the golden glow of the Hellphyr's puppet body for one short second, and for a moment, the whole thing seemed like it would be all too easy. The Ghost Rider would grab onto the demon, or its chain, and recapture it again.

The Rider's bony fingers slid over the smooth surface of the lion dog statue, unable to find purchase. The Hellphyr reared up on its hind legs, swiping at the leather-clad skeleton but failing to connect. Satana circled around as they struggled, hoping to get at the thing from behind while it was distracted. If they could box it in, it would be less likely to escape.

Bone bounced off metal with a hollow *tink* as the Ghost Rider tried once again to grab onto the statue. The Hellphyr swung again, connecting this time, but the Rider didn't so much as flinch under the heavy blow. Instead, it reached out again. Not at the statue this time. It grabbed onto the length of chain that still hung from the demon's neck. As soon as its bony hand touched the links, they burst into flames.

The Hellphyr screeched in pain and anger, tossing its head. The Rider tugged on the chain, holding the bucking creature in place, unmoved by its expressions of pain and fury. Satana smirked.

"You know," she said, "I'm starting to think that the Hellphyr doesn't deserve its reputation. I could have captured this thing with one hand tied behind my back, in a blindfold, with a hangover."

Zarathos grinned at her.

"*I make things easy,*" it said.

Satana rolled her eyes. If she had to guess, neither of them deserved the credit here. Now that she'd had multiple opportunities to see the Hellphyr at work, she understood it better. It required surprise and stealth to grow powerful enough to be a threat. Controlling it right out of the book was easy, although the first slip-up would be your last. But understanding this didn't mean she was going to let him take all the credit.

"Egotistical much? If you're going to hog all the credit, I'll have to make a necklace out of your finger bones."

The Ghost Rider threw back its head, laughing aloud. The sound rolled over Satana like a cold wind at night, making her shiver. But underneath the instinctive fear ran a current of triumph. She'd known spirits like Zarathos during her time in Hell. They didn't laugh. Anything unrelated to their all-encompassing purpose barely even registered with them. Making the Rider laugh was an accomplishment.

Johnny might be worried about Zarathos, but Satana thought everything would be OK, and she wasn't the optimistic sort. The spirit might be changing, but that didn't have to be a bad thing. It had learned to laugh. Maybe Johnny was rubbing off on Zarathos as much as the spirit rubbed off on him. Just yesterday, Satana wouldn't have said that such a thing was possible. A balanced partnership could never be achieved; there would always be a struggle between the Rider's two competing sides.

But if she could reach some level of peace with herself, Johnny could, too.

At the end of the chain, the Hellphyr swelled with a sudden magical power. The blinding flare swallowed its golden figure, making bright spots dance behind Satana's eyes. She threw up her hands, peeking out through slitted fingers as the demon's body swelled to enormous dimensions. It shouldn't have been able to do that. They'd layered on extra protections after the last time. Something wasn't right here. There was some other magic at work, something familiar...

The Hellphyr loomed over the Rider. As it grew, it returned to its usual form, the one Satana sometimes saw in her dreams. It hunched beneath the low ceiling, an eight-foot monstrosity with a wide mouth full of teeth as long as her fingers. Wickedly hooked claws grasped at the air. Desiccated flesh clung to the creature's long limbs, giving it a rotted, undead appearance. So it pretty much looked like one of Satana's childhood neighbors, but Jennifer hadn't had that experience. She'd stood before the creature as it spoke to her in her brother's voice, and her grief at his death had almost undone them all. Not that Satana could have done anything about it. She'd been too busy fighting her father.

But this time, she'd get to throw down. She and the Ghost Rider together would make mincemeat of this demon. Jen might be sad not to be a part of the fight, but she'd understand. Satana would kill it for her.

She tensed, gathering all her strength for a leap that would carry her onto the creature's back while its attention was on the Rider.

# CHAPTER TWENTY-EIGHT

Topaz didn't like what her senses were telling her. As the sounds of movement drew closer, she'd tried to pick up any signs of conscious thought in their pursuers, but she found nothing except an eerie silence in their heads. They thought nothing. Felt nothing. Topaz had fought zombies with more substance than this. At least the undead were driven by hunger or their master's will. These things didn't even have those limited motivations. They were like clockwork automatons. They would continue on the course that had been set for them, but nothing more.

She shivered. What an awful thing to do to someone.

The motion attracted Jennifer's attention. She shot a concerned look in the empath's direction.

"What are you picking up?" she asked.

"They're alive, but there's no one home. I've never seen anything like it."

"Is there any way to free them?"

"Maybe, if I could figure out where their minds are hiding. I'd need more time than we've got, though."

Jennifer's teeth flashed in a humorless smile.

"I can buy you time," she said. "The hallway will keep them from mobbing us. I should be able to hold them here if you're willing to try."

Topaz hesitated. She had no way of knowing what awaited her in their minds. It could be a trap that would suck her in, too. But if she didn't help these people, they might be stuck like this forever. Who knew what kind of torment they were enduring at this moment? They might be locked away inside, powerless to control their own bodies. She couldn't leave them to that fate.

"It'll attract the attention of whoever did this to them," she said.

"If they've sent their goons after us, they know we're here already," Jennifer said.

Although they were being vague, both of them knew what was really going on here without needing to belabor the point. Lucifer had been playing with Magda's powers, and this peek at her abilities made Topaz worried. If they didn't stop Lucifer, he'd be able to create an army of mind-wiped people who would do his bidding without question. Topaz had never been to Hell, and based on Satana's expression whenever she talked about it, the empath had no desire to go. If he wasn't stopped, Lucifer would make Earth just as bad. Heck, with that level of mental magic, he would make it worse.

Topaz squared her shoulders as the empty-headed goons finally came into view. She'd expected them to shuffle like zombies, their blank stares and glassy eyes empty of anything resembling reason. But they didn't appear zombie-like at all, and somehow that made it even more frightening. They could have walked down any street, and no one would have known that they were being driven like remote-control cars by an evil sorcerer who also happened to be the King of Hell.

Of course, because they were circus people, they would have stood out in the average crowd. A gawky young man with a protruding Adam's apple was dressed up like an old-school vampire, complete with a black cape trimmed in red. The wrinkled old Black woman next to him looked like a swamp witch, complete with leaves and bracken in her afro, and a strip of muddied fabric running along the bottom of her black dress. A pair of tall, pale twins were dressed in identical Victorian suits with skull brooches at the necks. Leading them all was an evil clown, its makeup streaked with lines of deep red that may or may not have been actual blood.

Topaz turned her attention to the old woman as Jennifer stepped forward to meet them, summoning up a purple glow of magic that surrounded her like a halo. Senior citizens tended to have strong minds full of memories that a good psychic could grab hold of. Out of the five of them, Topaz thought she'd have the best chance of success with the older woman. Plus, there was always the chance that the witchy outfit wasn't just a costume. If the woman had any magical talent at all, it might help her fight back against the mind control.

"Stay back!" Jennifer ordered. "I don't want to hurt you."

But the carnival folk continued on, slack-faced, like they hadn't heard a word. Their lack of response made shivers run up Topaz's spine. For the first time, she realized how angry she was. How dare Lucifer take people's free will? How dare he strip away their choices? She'd never put much thought into what Hell must really be like; whenever she'd thought of what Satana had endured during her long years there, she'd mostly imagined fire and other elements of physical torture. Of course that had bothered her, because Satana was her friend.

But for the first time, Topaz realized that physical pain couldn't begin to compare with having your free will stripped away from you. Satana had been stuck in Hell for no reason other than the accident of her birth. She'd been half-mortal her entire life, but before she joined the coven, she'd never had the opportunity to choose between her two sides. When she'd finally had the opportunity, she'd chosen to do the right thing, and how much strength must that have taken after a life full of torture, manipulation, and back-stabbing?

Now Lucifer had taken these people's choices from them, just like Satana's father had taken hers. Just like Topaz's abductors had done to her on the day that they pulled her from her family in their selfish desire to claim her magic for their own. They had all been mental slaves in one way or another, and Topaz couldn't stand it any longer. Someone had to do something.

She was that someone.

The group reached Jennifer, reaching out to grab her. The sorceress implored them to back away, but their empty eyes and grasping hands didn't bode well. The vampire took her by the arm, and she responded with the smallest discharge of magical power that she could manage. Just a zap. His lips drew back from his teeth in a silent snarl, and he took a single step backwards.

The entire group paused as one, as if they were responding to some unspoken instructions beamed straight into their heads. Then they surged forward again, trying to pin Jennifer down. She pushed at them with her magic, trying to drive them backwards without hurting them.

"I won't be able to hold them long," she said. "Whatever you're going to do, you'd better make it quick."

Topaz nodded. She gathered up all her pain and rage and regret, forging them into a lance of magical power and flinging it at the swamp witch. The lance would forge a link between their minds, allowing Topaz to combat whatever magical power had taken over their brains. Normally, she didn't like to fight, but right now, she was eager for it. She had gifts, and for years, she'd kept them under wraps, trusting the voices that told her to focus on saving the world. But she couldn't ignore her instincts any longer. Everyone deserved to know that someone would come for them during their darkest hour.

Jennifer's purpose was to keep the Hellphyr contained. Johnny hunted down the fragments of Lucifer's soul. Satana would stand against her father until the day she died. But Topaz had never had a purpose, not really. She'd just followed her coven mates, supporting them in their fights and making their struggles hers. But it didn't have to be that way. Someone needed to fight for the forgotten victims. The collateral damage. People like her who had always been relegated to the background but still suffered, nonetheless. She would do that.

Bolstered by her roiling emotions, her mental lance pierced the shields around the woman's mind like a knife through butter. The immense emptiness inside made Topaz even angrier. Lucifer had wiped their minds clean, replacing conscious thought with an endless litany of booming instructions, running on a loop that didn't allow the victims a moment to reconsider.

"*Bring them to me. Bring them to me,*" it said.

The words hummed with power. Despite her considerable

mental skills, Topaz struggled to resist the compelling urge that engulfed her. She wanted to obey. Listening would be so much easier; she wouldn't have to worry about anything ever again. The voice would take care of her.

But it would imprison her once again in a world where she couldn't choose what happened to her. Where she could do nothing but follow along like a good little apprentice. She deserved better than that.

Over the past few years, she'd honed her mental skills. But she'd always avoided using her mind as a weapon. She could lobotomize someone with a glance if she wanted to, but no one deserved that. Knowing that possibility, she'd always exercised extreme caution. The most she'd ever done was to put someone to sleep against their will, and although sleep did no lasting damage, she still wondered if she'd done the right thing.

For the first time in her entire life, she let loose and struck hard. The King of Hell didn't deserve her mercy. He stole people's minds from them, making them into empty slaves. He would mind-wipe the world if he could get away with it. But he wouldn't.

Topaz struck with the fury of someone who had lost everything. Someone who knew what it was like to be unable to control your own body or mind. Someone who had come out the other side despite impossible odds. She had never been to Hell, but she'd gone through it. And she had had enough.

Her magical power flared out in an uncontrolled wave of mental destruction. It filled the empty space in the swamp witch's mind, grabbing onto the voice and following it back to its source. It struck hard, cutting the voice off in mid-sentence.

Topaz had the vague impression of surprise before the walls slammed down, cutting off her mental contact.

She had struck Lucifer, the King of Hell himself. She had hurt him. Triumph welled inside her. She'd heard of facing one's demons before, but she'd really gone above and beyond that.

As her magic faded, receding back into her, she could sense the smallest of figures tucked away in the corner of the swamp witch's mind. This woman wore a housedress and a flowered apron, her hair neatly twisted into a bun. She peeked out from behind gnarled fingers as Topaz approached.

"Are you OK?" asked the empath.

"What's happening?" asked the woman, trembling with fear. "Is he gone?"

"He's gone. You can come back now. I'll help you, and then I'll get out of the way."

The woman snorted. "Sure you will."

"I promise. But I don't want to go until you come out of your shell. Nature abhors a vacuum. If you leave the space empty, something will come and fill it."

The woman straightened, dropping her hands just far enough to peer over them.

"This isn't a dream," she declared. "It's all real, isn't it?"

"It is. But when you come back to yourself, there's no harm in convincing yourself that it was all a hallucination. The mind sometimes needs that kind of reassurance."

"No, I want to remember. After all these years of pretending, now I know that magic is real." The woman's face lit up with wonder. "I play at being a witch, but you are one. Admit it."

"I am."

Topaz swelled with pride. She'd always answered admiration with modesty, secure in her belief that others deserved respect more than she did. After all, she'd always followed and never led. Always questioned and never answered. Even when she'd taken charge of the coven, she'd always exercised the lightest touch possible. She'd told herself that she needed to do so, because it was so easy to misuse psychic powers in a way that would harm everyone involved. But for the first time, she allowed herself to accept recognition for what she'd done.

"Thank you," said the woman. "I'm not sure what brought you here, but I'm glad for it. Things have been bad. We've been locked up in the House of Horrors for days."

"Well, you're free now. What's your name?"

"Aggie. And you are?"

"I'm Topaz. And I'm sorry to say it, but things are about to get worse. I'll release the rest of your people, and then you've got to get them out of here."

"No." Aggie's head shake was automatic and firm. "The Cirque is my home. You wouldn't just leave your home, would you? Things like that are worth fighting for."

"But do you know how to fight?" asked Topaz. She tried to gentle her voice, knowing all the while that it wouldn't completely take the sting out of what she had to say. "You play at being a witch, but can you wield magic? Can you use a weapon? Can you block out the mental attacks?"

Aggie's face fell further and further with each question. "No, but…"

"I understand," said Topaz. "I know what it's like to feel helpless. It's awful. But if you and your friends stay here, you'll just get brainwashed again. Then we've got to fight you and the person – the *thing* – who's doing this. It'll make things worse, not better."

"So I'm useless," said Aggie, bitterly. "If you win, maybe I can bake some cookies. How terrific for me. I finally discover that magic is real and then get put on the shelf. I can't even watch. Do you have any idea how frustrating that is?"

"Look, I'll make you a deal. You lead the rest of the employees out of here. They'll listen to you, and I don't have the time to have this conversation again. Take them into town. Go to Mystic Energies. That's my shop. There's a key underneath the third pot on the right beside the back door. Lock yourselves in and stay there until I come for you. After this is all over, we can sit down and talk. I'll answer what questions I can." Topaz smiled a little. "You don't have to make cookies, although I wouldn't mind if you did."

Aggie's face split in a wide smile. "You've got a deal, missy. Now get out of my head. It's starting to feel a mite crowded in here."

"I'd be glad to."

A sensation of vertigo rushed over Topaz as she returned to her body. Feeling raced back into her extremities, and for one moment, she was aware of every part of her physical being. She could feel her fingernails growing, and the molecules of air traveling in and out of her lungs, and the rhythmic rush and lull of her blood through her veins. Everything worked in perfect concert, and it was beautiful beyond imagining. Over the next few seconds, the hyperawareness faded away, leaving her breathless in its wake.

Jennifer still stood between her and their attackers from the carnival, but the brainwashed employees didn't move. The sorceress still clung to the bright glow of her magic, ready for anything. She glanced at Topaz as she began to stir, and the tense rigidity of her shoulders relaxed as the empath stretched.

"Are we good?" Jennifer asked.

Topaz didn't answer right away. She walked straight over to Aggie. The old woman's eyelids fluttered and then opened to find Topaz staring her in the face. A momentary confusion flickered in her eyes, but it didn't last. As full awareness returned to her, Aggie took one of Topaz's hands in her gnarled ones.

"Thank you," said the old woman.

"I'm glad you're OK," replied Topaz. "Do you remember what we talked about? You need to get out of here as fast as you can. All of you."

Aggie nodded and turned to her companions. The twins clung to each other, and tears tracked through the evil clown's makeup. She patted him on the shoulder.

"It's OK, love," she said.

"Aggie, what happened?" asked the clown. "Was I sleepwalking again? I think I..." He broke down, sobbing.

"Oh, give me a break!" snapped the vampire. "Can we do this without your hysterics?"

Aggie turned on him, her lips pursed in disapproval. He rolled his eyes. It didn't take psychic powers to pick up on his general disdain for everyone in the room. Even the ones he hadn't met yet. As a result of her powers, Topaz knew very well that most people had reasons for even the poorest of behaviors, and she tried to like everyone. But she disliked the vampire instantly. He was a jerk down to the core.

"You aren't helping, Phil," said Aggie.

"Yeah, well, I'm leaving. Maybe you don't mind getting locked up like an animal and… and drugged. But I do. I'm packing my bags and getting out of here," said Phil the vampire.

"You can't go back to your trailer," said Topaz.

Phil scowled at her.

"Yeah, and I listen to what strangers tell me to do. How stupid do you think I am? For all I know, you're the one who locked me up and drugged me."

"I didn't."

"So who did, then?"

"Magda Kale."

He flinched. "No. No way. Magda's not that kind of person. Besides, she loves me."

Topaz winced. She hadn't realized that Magda was part of the carnival, but of course that made sense. From the looks of things, it had just arrived in town, which explained why they hadn't sensed Lucifer's presence at first. Once he'd realized the *Tome of Zhered-Na* was nearby, he must have begun to prepare. He'd been waiting for them all this time.

Her stomach sank. They'd been played from the start. Her coven. Johnny. Magda herself. Whatever had happened here, it wasn't her fault, and her loved ones needed to know that.

"Magda isn't herself. She's been… drugged, too," said Topaz.

Phil considered this for a moment before shaking his head. "No. I don't believe you. I can't. And I don't know what kind of nonsense you're up to, but I won't risk my good reputation to be a part of it."

"What good reputation?" the left twin said at a pitch that pretended to be a whisper but was really meant to carry.

"Shut up, you inbred traitor," said Phil.

"Who are you calling inbred?" demanded the right twin, holding up his fists.

"Now, that's enough," said Aggie, stepping between them.

Topaz had to do something. She took a deep breath, picturing waves lapping on the side of a boat during a lazy day on the river. Her family clustered around her, quietly resting under the warm afternoon sun. Peace and contentment spread over her, and she exhaled deeply, allowing it to spread a blanket of comfort over the small area.

But the argument raged on. Aggie's voice got a little quieter, and the clown's trembling trailed off, but the carnival employees kept on shouting. Their brainwashing had rattled them hard, and their fear and confusion was too strong for her gentle suggestion to have much effect. They were resisting the influence as best as they could, if only by instinct. After all, they'd just been through the unspeakable. Topaz didn't know what Lucifer had made them do, but based on the clown's reaction, the truth would only disturb her.

"You can't talk about this here," she said, trying to cut through the argument with reason. "You're in danger. Follow Aggie to safety. I'll come as soon as I can and explain everything."

"You seem to know an awful lot about what's going on here. Are you the one who did all this?" Phil demanded, focusing all his ire on her. "Do you have any idea what we've been through? I *bit* someone!" The twins laughed, and he whirled on them, his fists clenched. "It's not funny!"

A wave of sympathy washed over Topaz. Phil might be a jerk, but no one deserved what Lucifer had done to these people. Not even him. She reached out to put a hand on his shoulder, but he shook her away, his eyes going wide in fear.

"Don't touch me!" he exclaimed.

She held up her hands, trying her best to diffuse the situation. Meanwhile, the seconds ticked along. Her unease grew with every passing moment, churning her insides. This was all taking too long. Too many things could go wrong with the Hellphyr and Lucifer both in play. But she couldn't just leave these people to suffer.

Jennifer stiffened. She'd been watching the chaos in silence, not because she didn't care about such things, but because she trusted Topaz to handle them. Just like Topaz would give way to her in matters of deep sorcery. But now she pulled out the Tome, moving with a haste that made Topaz sick with worry.

"What's wrong?" the empath demanded.

"I don't know. The Hellphyr is working some kind of magic. Can't you feel it? It shouldn't be able to do that," Jennifer responded.

Topaz hadn't noticed a thing, and that concerned her. Her magic linked the Hellphyr with its new body and fueled its every move. She should have realized the moment something went wrong, but she'd had her shields up in full force. Her desperation to avoid another empathic slip had blocked out all warnings. As soon as she relaxed them, she could sense it, too: a swell of sickening, hellish magic just on the other side of the door. Her mouth began to water, and her stomach churned as the urge to vomit took her over. But she shut that down with a twist of magic. She had no time for hysterics or physical weakness. Satana and Johnny needed their help.

If only that heavy door didn't stand between them.

"Does anyone have the key for this door?" she asked in a burst of inspiration.

"We were locked in here, remember?" said Aggie. "If we'd had the key, we would have used it."

Jennifer loosened the straps that held the *Tome of Zhered-Na* to her body. The ancient book came free, and she clutched it with shaking hands.

"Jen?" asked Topaz. "You OK?"

"I need to put the Hellphyr back before something awful happens. I wonder if the ritual would work through this door," said the sorceress, opening the book.

Her nervousness made her careless. Jennifer was usually the slow and deliberate sort who either had the page number memorized or took a deep dive into the table of contents whenever she consulted one of her magical books. But this time, she flipped the pages to and fro, cursing all the while, unable to find the information she needed. The longer she searched, the more her hands shook.

"Where is it?" she demanded.

The book overbalanced and toppled toward the ground. Jennifer snatched at it, desperate to protect the ancient cover and delicate pages, but she didn't move fast enough.

"*I'll take that!*"

The disembodied voice took them all by surprise. The clown let out a surprisingly high shriek. Phil swore. A wave of horror overtook Topaz as she realized why that voice was familiar. She'd only met Satana's father once, but she'd recognize his self-satisfied tones anywhere.

The *Tome of Zhered-Na* disappeared.

Jennifer's hand swiped through the empty space where it had been just a moment before. She fell to her knees in its absence, scrabbling desperately at the air as if she might make it reappear if she just searched hard enough. But it was gone.

Topaz couldn't believe her eyes, but she couldn't deny the wave of horror and grief that washed over her. Was it Jennifer's? Hers? She didn't know, but it didn't matter. A quick scan confirmed her worst fears. She could sense nothing.

The book was gone.

She dropped to her knees next to her friend. Jennifer resisted at first, but soon sank into her comforting arms and cried.

# CHAPTER TWENTY-NINE

Satana launched into the air, claws outstretched. The Hellphyr still hadn't noticed her. The slavering demon was locked in a stare down with the Ghost Rider. Satana wasn't sure which one she'd put her money on. Demons didn't back down from a challenge – not if they wanted to make it through a single day in Hell – but the Ghost Rider couldn't blink even if he wanted to. If she didn't do something, they'd be there all night.

It all happened so fast. She braced herself for impact, imagining the satisfying thrill of her claws sinking into demonic flesh. The tips of her nails grazed the back of the Hellphyr's neck. It tensed, realizing a moment too late that it had an enemy at its back. But then, before she could tear out its throat, someone grabbed her from behind, arresting her forward motion and squeezing all the air from her lungs. Before she could react, she was flung across the room, slamming against the wall and sliding down to the floor.

The impact stunned her for a moment, but she recovered quickly. Survival in Hell depended on being able to carry on fighting despite the pain, and she'd become an expert at moving on autopilot even when her mind still reeled from a blow. She rolled to her feet, positioning herself in a defensive crouch even as she struggled for breath.

Her father stood before her, the *Tome of Zhered-Na* dangling from one hand. As soon as she saw his face, the pieces slid together with sickening ease. That familiar magic that had strengthened the Hellphyr at exactly the wrong moment? It had been her father all along. He'd been trying to create an opening to get the book, and it had worked.

He hadn't bothered with the disguise this time. Instead, he loomed over her, his head brushing the ceiling. His ruby red skin glistened in the dim light, and his devilish face wore a twisted smile of self-satisfaction. He dipped his head to her, the tips of his curled horns gouging lines into the ceiling. At moments like this, she was reminded of how much she hated her horns. They were just like his.

"I told you, daughter," he said.

His voice was honey over gravel. The Hellphyr broke off on stalking Johnny and turned to stare at Marduk, bowing its head as if before a new master. Satana had never been sure why Lucifer and her father wanted the book so badly, but now she understood. Once Jennifer had summoned the demon, anyone with enough magical power could take control so long as they possessed the book. The Kale blood was necessary to open the portal, but after that, anyone could step in. Marduk held up the Tome, wiggling it as he grinned. The demon's eyes followed every movement with baleful hatred. Johnny stepped off to one side as if to see better, but Satana noticed how his hand crept up behind his head, fingers grazing the holster of the shotgun strapped to his back. He was angling for a clear shot. If the marksman had been anyone but the Ghost Rider, she would have chalked the effort up as futile, but Johnny might be able to hurt her father.

It might be their only chance of surviving this. Marduk's control of the Hellphyr changed everything. He could disappear at any moment, taking the demon and the book along with him. So what kept him here now? He wanted something, and if she wanted to buy time, she had to make sure that he got it.

"Told me what, pops?" she asked, angling for information.

"I told you I'd get the Tome. You should have joined me while you had the chance," he purred.

"The Hellphyr seems thrilled."

"Not yet, but it will be."

Marduk glanced at the demon with an air of disturbing fondness. The Hellphyr didn't move a muscle. Its attention remained locked on the book, desperate to destroy its prison once and for all. Unleashed, it would rain down fear and death on the mystics of the world. She had to keep that from happening. Marduk would have learned his lesson; now that he had the Tome, he wouldn't risk discovery by the likes of Doctor Strange. He'd nurture the Hellphyr's growing power in secret, picking victims at random and moving around from place to place so it would be more difficult to find him. By the time the Sorcerer Supreme discovered the threat, the Hellphyr would be too strong for even him to stop. Once it devoured Strange's magic, the demon's power would be strong enough to defeat Lucifer himself.

The thought made Satana pause. Was that Marduk's ultimate end game? He'd always had delusions of grandeur. For the longest time, she'd thought he was Satan, and Marduk had encouraged the misapprehension by "naming her after him." He'd always snatched at any opportunity to expand his power, and she had no reason to believe that had changed.

Satana welcomed the insight but had no idea what to do with the information. She could accuse Marduk, but if anything, he'd take pride in his scheming. The most she could hope for was to gain a little time while he bragged. She began to pace, putting on a show of how upset she was.

"Funny finding you and Lucifer in the same place," she said. "That's a real coincidence."

"Perhaps we've both come to see you. Pay a little social visit."

"That's a load of rubbish, and you know it."

He grinned. "What can I say, my little lotus petal? You attract powerful men."

"Still not buying it."

"I'll have to try something else, then. I could appeal to your familial loyalty, perhaps?" He tapped a finger on his chin in mock thought. "Never mind. You don't have any."

Satana rolled her eyes, but her heart wasn't really in it. Her agitated pacing had been a ruse. She'd stopped on the far side of the room, giving her a better vantage point and pulling Marduk's attention away from the Hellphyr and the Ghost Rider. From his forgotten spot behind the demon, Johnny began to draw his shotgun. He'd been moving in slow degrees this whole time, trying to avoid attracting attention.

This would be the difficult moment. The gun would make noise, and she had to keep all focus on her. She would have to make a scene.

"Familial loyalty?" she said, injecting a little extra heat into her voice. "It's awful ironic for you to call me out on that, isn't it, Daddy?"

"But, my darling daughter, you act as if I don't care!" he exclaimed, putting a hand to his heart.

"Good parents don't put their kids in cage matches."

"You and Daimon would have both died long ago if not for my training. Tell me I'm wrong. Go ahead."

She feigned hesitation, or at least that's what she intended. But to her surprise and disgust, she found that the feeling rang true. Marduk's guidance had made her tough. What little parenting he'd offered had been self-serving; he hadn't hesitated to make use of his skilled daughter who was desperate to win his affections and buffeted by instincts she barely understood and couldn't control. But still, she wouldn't have survived without him.

He grinned, taking a step toward her. Looking up at him made her feel like that little girl once more. She remembered the coppery tang of blood in her mouth and the ache of muscles abused almost to breaking point. The sting of sweat as it dripped into her eyes and trickled into the rents torn in her skin by her father's demonic enemies. She'd crouched at his feet, just a step or two from feral, while he'd patted her head like a good dog.

Then, almost as if he was reading her mind, he reached down and did just that.

*Pat. Pat. Pat.*

Over his shoulder, Johnny aimed the gun at her father's back. Her breath ran ragged as all her emotions squeezed her tight. She had wanted to shoot Marduk for years. She'd fought him with every ounce of her being. If she'd been asked, she would have said that she hated him more than anyone else on Earth, and it wouldn't have been a lie. But inexplicably, she didn't want him to die. Or at the very least, she wanted it to be by her hand.

Satana did not want to love her father. Marduk was too monstrous to deserve it, and he certainly didn't offer her such devotion in return. But she couldn't help it. She hated herself for it, but that didn't change how she felt.

She pressed her lips shut to hold back the cry of alarm that wanted to escape them. If she warned him off, they would never defeat the Hellphyr and get the book back. The book! It still dangled from Marduk's hand, his casual grasp giving no indication of the object's power. If Johnny blasted him to pieces, the book would go, too. Johnny would probably be able to banish the Hellphyr, but all the spells and knowledge in the Tome would be lost forever.

Satana couldn't spare the time to think. She launched herself at her father, unsure of whether or not she was trying to save the book or just using it as an excuse to save him. He swatted at her like she was an annoying gnat buzzing around his head. His oversized hand connected with her shoulder, spinning her around like a top.

*Blam!*

The shotgun fired, spraying fire and metal over her shoulder, barely missing them both. Marduk stiffened, his head snapping around to look over his shoulder in surprise. He hadn't survived this long by underestimating his enemies. He would teleport out of here any moment now, taking the book with him. After that, it wouldn't matter what battles they won; they would have lost the war. Satana had lost too many times in her life, and she wasn't about to do it again.

She poured all her power into her body, her size increasing with such speed that her skin tore. Even though her magic healed the damage immediately, pain ripped through her and white spots danced behind her eyes. She held on to consciousness with every ounce of willpower she possessed. Now she was Marduk's size, or maybe even a bit bigger. Now, she had the strength to take the book from him.

While his attention was still caught by Johnny's surprise attack, she grabbed onto the *Tome of Zhered-Na* and tore it from his grasp.

Marduk had a temper. Satana had been the subject of his anger many times before. Sometimes his fury had hit her like a physical blow, driving the air from her body. Sometimes she'd cowered behind his throne of stone and bones, desperate to escape his attention when he was looking for a victim to vent his ire upon. Other times, she'd challenged him, standing up to him like any teenager with an abusive parent. But, over time, she'd learned that defying him only made it worse in the end.

But now she was a grown woman who understood her strength in a way that she never had before. She had proven to everyone – but especially herself – that she could stand on her own two feet. She'd taken charge of her own destiny.

Still, she cowered before his fury. It took her back to her youth, when he had infatuated and terrified her in equal measure, when her world had revolved around pleasing him. It was one thing to try to match the Hellphyr in size and strength. It was another thing entirely to go toe to toe with a furious Marduk. Now, he couldn't have been more displeased. His eyes blazed with fury, and when he leaned forward to shout in her face, the wall shook with the brutal force of his voice.

"Give me the *Tome of Zhered-Na!*" he ordered.

She almost did it. Her hands spasmed, desperate in their need to follow his bidding. She had to force them to clutch the book to her, but her will faltered under the immense pressure of his demands. His demonic magic enclosed her in a capsule of fear and regret, sucking her in before she could even attempt to counter. Memories assaulted her, an endless litany of times that she'd tried to defy him and ended up paying the price. She couldn't stand to pay any more. She had nothing left.

Nothing except for the Tome. Maybe if she gave it to him, he would let her live.

But when she focused on the magical book, something strange happened. She could feel its connection to the Kales. Jennifer stood just on the other side of that stupid metal door, and through the book, Satana could sense her desperation to do something. The sorceress was worried about her.

Jennifer loved her like a sister.

Satana had a brother, and she would protect him if he ever needed her, but she was also more than a little tempted to drive a blade into his back. Daimon dealt with his demonic side in a different way than she did, and he'd been lucky enough to escape their father's notice as often as he had. Anyone would have resented that. As a result, their relationship was complicated.

But she had none of that history with Jennifer. They'd fought; sometimes side by side and sometimes with each other. They'd spent evenings watching cheesy horror movies and gorging on popcorn. They'd debated magical theories and moral dilemmas. They'd bonded as only family can, bickering like sisters.

In a flash of insight, Satana knew exactly what to do.

"Johnny!" she yelled. "The door."

Marduk blurted out a single curse word before he lunged toward the book, making one last desperate effort to get his hands on it. She swung with all her might, landing an open-handed slap to his cheek, as she held the book out of his reach. His head snapped back, taking her by surprise. Over the years, she'd scuffled with her father many times, but she'd never managed to hurt him.

He staggered backwards, his eyes widening as he realized what had happened. She took a step forward, ready to press her advantage. She would end this once and for all. She could walk the streets of Salem without worrying that he'd pop out from behind a tree and attempt to haul her back to Hell. The thought of true freedom, after all these years, danced behind her eyes. But before she could land the killing blow, his figure flickered and disappeared.

A flaming skull emerged from the billowing smoke as the Ghost Rider approached her, its gun at the ready.

"Shoot the door!" she urged again. "I'll get the book to Jennifer!"

She held the book up so the Rider could see it. As she did, her heart sank. How stupid could she be? Marduk would take advantage of her carelessness and teleport in to grab the book from her. With a convulsive movement, she pulled the precious magical Tome back to her body, shielding it as best she could. But her father failed to appear.

Maybe she'd really beaten him? Hope swelled within her, beautiful and dangerous. She couldn't afford to underestimate her father, but she couldn't keep from wondering.

The Ghost Rider took aim at the door. The spirit cut a

striking figure, its flaming head and hands casting an orange glow as grey curls of smoke wound around its motorcycle boots and up the legs of its jeans. As Satana gaped, fire swirled along the length of the gun, merging it with its bearer. From the far side of the room, flames flared bright, outlining the figure in stark relief, a killer in perfect form, suspended in the moment between life and death.

Her friends were on the other side of that door! Satana had lost sight of that fact, caught in an admiration she would never admit aloud. She squeezed the book tight, trying to send a message through its link to Jennifer. She had some minor psychic talent, but she'd never done much with it. Most people who got a glimpse inside her head ended up gibbering on the floor. The unaccustomed mental effort drained her, but she had to warn her fellow witches despite the strangely soundproof walls.

*Blam!*

The shotgun discharged again, filling the small space with thunder and flame. The blast struck the metal door, engulfing it in Hellfire. With a whoosh, it went up in flames.

# CHAPTER THIRTY

The disappearance of the *Tome of Zhered-Na* finally lit a fire under the carnival employees. Eyes wide with fear, they tabled their endless bickering and fled. Not that Jennifer really noticed. After her initial panicked attempts to track the book had come up empty, she found it difficult to focus on anything at all.

As the scurrying footfalls of the performers faded, Jennifer sagged to the ground. Despair hunched her shoulders and stole her breath. She needed to do something, but it all seemed so futile. Marduk was probably in Hell by now. Even if she managed to track him, she would be at a disadvantage confronting him in his territory. If he took control of the Hellphyr and unleashed it on them? It would be a suicide mission.

The Book of Zhered-Na was gone. Without it, what was she? Just your average sorceress who had failed in her family's sacred duty. She'd let the Hellphyr loose, and now everyone would die because of her shortcomings.

"That's enough of that," said Topaz, unaccountably stern.

Jennifer grumbled at her.

"Maybe you do have a right to feel sorry for yourself," Topaz went on, pretending that Jennifer had managed to say some words. "But that doesn't do us any good. Marduk has the Tome now, and we've got to get it back."

"Oh, why hadn't I thought of that?" Jennifer asked.

Bitterness saturated her voice, filling her with instantaneous shame. Topaz didn't deserve such treatment. Just another thing for Jennifer to feel guilty over.

"I'm not trying to insult your intelligence," Topaz protested, flushing. "I'm just trying to sum things up."

"Well, thanks for telling me what I already know. It's not like I haven't spent the past few years studying this book."

"Look, I know you're angry, but–"

"Get out of my head!" Jennifer snarled, drowning her terror and shame in a welcome rush of anger. She sat up, poking the empath in the sternum.

But Topaz didn't rise to the bait, which only ticked Jennifer off more. The empath sighed with a superior air that made Jennifer want to punch her in the face.

"Honey, I wish I could," said Topaz.

"Then get out! I don't want you poking around in my memories anyway!"

The anger smothered all of Jennifer's misgivings and fears in a blissful haze. She poured herself into it, whipping herself up into a mental frenzy. Topaz had this innocent act going on, and Jennifer had bought it for too long. But being nice wasn't the same as being kind. Topaz wouldn't know kindness if it bit her on the behind.

"If I'm not wanted, then I won't help!" exclaimed Topaz.

Any misgivings Jennifer might have had about her behavior

were drowned in a wave of indignation. She ignored the pain that twisted the empath's mouth and the hitch in her voice.

"Good!" she exclaimed. "I'm going to find the Hellphyr. Toddle off after your friends if you want. I don't care."

She spun on one foot without waiting for a response, heading for the exit with a growing sense of single-minded determination. Maybe Johnny could track down the Hellphyr. Maybe Satana would have some idea of what her father wanted with the Tome. They could help her, but Topaz, with all her new age mysticism and tea blends, could offer nothing.

After traversing the haunted house multiple times, she should have been able to find her way through, but her distraction worked against her, ruining her angry exit. She had to backtrack twice. Topaz made no remark, and when Jennifer glanced at her, tears tracked her cheeks. Of course they did. Topaz had always been too soft. But still, a pang of misgiving settled in the pit of Jennifer's stomach. Maybe she'd been cruel. But Topaz couldn't understand where Jennifer was coming from. She thought of things in black and white, while Jennifer knew that the truth was always tinted in shades of grey.

If Jennifer had managed to keep her emotions under control, things might not have gotten so bad. But they were about to get worse. If she hadn't bitten the empath's head off, if she hadn't been so upset and off balance, one of them would have picked up on the mental warning earlier. But her emotions were in a jumble; her thoughts raced faster than she could follow, vacillating between anger and regret with a speed that left her reeling.

As a result, she didn't pick up on Satana's warning until the very last minute. But as she left the cells – and Topaz – behind, it hit her with an almost concussive force, driving her back a step. At that moment, awareness of the *Tome of Zhered-Na* flared inside her once again, making her limbs go weak with relief. The pleasant emotion would only be short-lived, because it was followed by a warning so intense that it drove the breath from her lungs.

"Topaz, get down!"

She tried to shout, but her voice came out as a weak and inaudible squeak. She ran for it, desperate to prevent the unknown tragedy from happening. Even though she knew she couldn't make it in time, she tried anyway. It wasn't enough. She made it two steps before the door exploded with fire and fury. The blast sucked all the air from the room, knocking her to the ground despite the fact that she stood all the way on the other side. Bits of burning metal pelted her face, singeing her skin.

Topaz had been standing right next to that door.

Jennifer's heart leaped. She ignored the flaming motes and bits of debris that pattered around her, tenting a hand over her eyes as she tried to penetrate the haze of orange-tinted smoke that spread across the room with an alarming rapidity. Unseen flames crackled and hissed. A piece of metal gave way with a tortured screech, clattering to the ground. The empath was nowhere in sight.

"Topaz?" she called.

The smoke stung her throat, and she dropped to her knees, overcome by a sudden fit of coughing. Her lungs spasmed, working overtime for oxygen. She pulled the thin fabric of her t-shirt up to cover her mouth, but it didn't help as much as she'd hoped.

Magic. Why wasn't she using her magic? The blast must have addled her wits if she'd forgotten that. With some effort, she forced her exhausted body to tap into the well of power at her core. Dark witches sucked magic out of the world around them, but she would never stoop to such lows. She alone fueled her abilities, and all the stress and strain had depleted her reserves. It didn't bode well for their chances of taking on Lucifer, but she shoved that thought away. Losing Topaz would be much worse.

"Jennifer!" Satana called.

"Over here!" said Jennifer, gasping for air. "Hurry! Topaz is down!"

An angry roar shook the building. It reverberated up through Jennifer's shoes and twisted her insides. She would have recognized the Hellphyr anywhere. She heard its bellow in her dreams.

"Take the book! I'll find Topaz," said Satana.

What book? She couldn't be referring to the *Tome of Zhered-Na*. Marduk would have cut and run as soon as he had it. Hope coursed through her veins. Maybe he hadn't. After all, he couldn't use it while Jennifer still lived. It would be in his best interest to stay and finish her off. But could Satana have gone toe to toe with him and won? She didn't dare to believe it, but she wanted to. Oh, how she wanted to.

A dark shape arced across the room, cutting through the haze. Jennifer would have known it anywhere. She had traced its cover a million times. After her brother's death, she'd sat by the fire, overcome by the temptation to burn it and release her family from their curse, no matter what the cost. At the time, she would have even welcomed death at the hands of the Hellphyr itself. She would have said she deserved such an ending, and maybe that was true, but it was also a cop out. It saved her from having to atone for her mistakes. She needed to survive. Johnny and Satana counted on her, and she had an apology to make to Topaz. Those things she'd said – the things she'd thought – were a testament to her despair, not a true reflection of her beliefs. Topaz needed to know that.

The *Tome of Zhered-Na* dropped down a few feet to her left. If not for the maze of bars that filled the room, she could have caught it. Instead, she lunged toward it and smacked a bar with her head. Her eyes watered from the pain, but she continued on blindly, following the magical signature of the book. She didn't know how Satana had gotten it back, but she wasn't going to stop to ask questions now. She had to banish the demon before Marduk stole the book again, because he wouldn't make the same mistake twice.

As if summoned by the thought, Marduk came lunging out of the haze at her, scrambling for the book. He wore his demonic form, his carmine skin glistening in the fiery smoke. Satana came tearing after him, maneuvering with difficulty through the maze and grabbing onto his ankle. They slammed against each other, struggling for dominance. Jennifer took advantage of the delay and squirmed past, desperate to reach the book first. She thrust her arm between the next set of bars, hoping that it was close enough to reach. But her fingers just barely grazed the cover.

The Hellphyr bellowed again. Smoke still poured from the burning carnival attraction, so she couldn't see the demon, but its fury was palpable. A shotgun fired, its report deafening in the small space. The demon shrieked, its anger unabated.

Johnny must be holding it off, but he wouldn't be able to do so for long.

Snarling, Marduk lunged forward again, ignoring his daughter in his desperation to get his hands on the Tome once more. His clawed hand closed on Jennifer's ankle. He pulled her backwards, her torso scraping along the dirty floor. Her skin stung, pebbles and dirt embedding into the tender skin. She rolled over and lashed out with all her might, kicking him in the face. His head snapped back with satisfying rapidity, but the grin he gave her was less than reassuring.

His fist slammed into her gut. She coughed, her eyes stinging. Everything hurt, but she had to ignore it. She needed the Tome.

Satana crawled up Marduk's back, her face twisted with demonic fury, and thrust her claws into his spine. Black, brackish blood went flying, and this time, Marduk couldn't ignore it. He bucked like an angry horse, but Satana held on, slashing and stabbing with everything she had.

The demon bellowed again, spurring Jennifer back into action despite her pain. She crawled forward on bruised knees, slipping around the final set of bars that separated her from the book. When her fingers closed around its cover, relief settled over her, releasing her shoulders and allowing her to take one deep breath despite the pain and smoke. Regardless of what happened next, at least she hadn't completely failed.

She had only done this once before, but the words to the spell that bound the Hellphyr to the Tome came easily to her. The archaic language flowed off her tongue like she'd been born speaking it, and it brought with it a power that strengthened her voice despite the abuse her throat had taken. The Hellphyr emerged out of the smoke, its hellish visage thrashing in fury.

Bars bent and metal screeched as it muscled its way toward her.

When it spoke, it used her brother's voice yet again. She should have been used to it by now, but those wheedling tones still tore at her heart.

"*Come on, Jenny,*" it said. "*Let me go free. We could be together again.*"

She paused, just for a moment. But she couldn't fall into that trap again, no matter how much she wanted to. Andy was gone, and the only thing the Hellphyr could offer her was a cheap carbon copy. It wouldn't be the boy she'd grown up riding tricycles with, nor the sometimes infuriating young man he'd become.

Regardless, she had to let him go. After all these years, she still hadn't been able to do it. Sure, she'd struck the killing blow, sending him and his demonic possessor to their respective afterlives. She'd mourned. Then she'd carried around the guilt for years, chastising herself for all the things she could have done differently. If only she'd found out about the demon sooner, she could have warned him. If only she hadn't been so busy bickering with Satana and Topaz, they could have helped. If only she'd loaned him the money he'd asked for, maybe he wouldn't have taken Marduk's job offer.

She'd wallowed in blame. Somehow, it made her feel better.

But it wasn't her fault. She knew it logically; she'd known it all along. Andy had made his own choices, as had Marduk and Satana and Doctor Strange. It was time to stop tormenting herself. Time to stop indulging in her grief and get on with her life, the way her brother would want her to do.

"You're not Andy," she said, clutching the book tight. "My brother is gone."

"*But I'm right here!*" The demon wailed, twisting her brother's mouth into torturous shapes. "*You locked me away with the Hellphyr, and it's driving me crazy. Please don't send me back there again.*"

She could see clearly now. Andy would never ask her to do such a thing. He'd always been the self-effacing type, the first one to give up his seat on the bus, the one who would take the smallest slice of pizza, the guy who would give his umbrella to an old lady during a storm. Heck, once he'd given away *Jennifer's* umbrella. At the time, she'd been furious. For the first time since his death, she could remember that and smile.

"You're not my brother," she said.

She resumed chanting, her voice growing in power. Tendrils of violet magic swirled from her mouth, halting the Hellphyr's approach. They twined around him, creating unbreakable bonds. The demon thrashed against them anyway, howling and cursing her name in a hundred different tongues. Andy's voice cried out in desperate pain, but still, she continued on.

A magical wind whipped her hair around her head, dissipating the smoke and extinguishing the fire. It tore the book from her hands, opening the cover. The *Tome of Zhered-Na* floated in the air above her head, well out of her reach, linked to her by a million threads of magic. Every word written in its pages filled her mind, and for one split second of complete clarity, she understood them all. Worlds of magical power opened themselves up to her. She could sense the magical underpinnings of the universe, the ancient currents of power that undergirded all creation. The universe unfurled before her like a buffet, ripe for consumption.

There were so many things to see, so many dimensions to

explore, but she had a job to do. She focused her power, tearing a hole in the very fabric of reality, breaking through to the realm of empty space that served as the Hellphyr's prison. The demon swelled inside its magical bonds, making one last ditch effort to escape. But she held it fast, pulling it toward her to look it in the eye one last time.

"Don't *ever* wear my brother's face again," she said.

Its red eyes blazed with fear as it gazed deep into her soul and the well of power that it had tapped, even for a moment. For the first time ever, the Hellphyr dropped its gaze before a superior predator.

With a flash of magic and a gust of wind, the demon vanished.

# CHAPTER THIRTY-ONE

The fires of vengeance lashed at the Ghost Rider as the Hellphyr turned its back on him, drawn toward the sorceress Jennifer Kale like a moth to a flame. The Rider knew how this confrontation would end. Although the Hellphyr would put up a fight, the Kale blood vow would not be denied. Jennifer would banish the demon back into the *Tome of Zhered-Na*.

It was the Rider's last opportunity to send the demon back to Hell where it belonged. He paused, torn between his two sides. Zarathos needed vengeance like humans needed oxygen; it fueled him. Resisting the urge filled him with a buzzing discomfort. But Johnny trusted Jennifer's skill. He wouldn't even contemplate interfering, and the conflict between the two threatened to tear them apart.

"*Marduk,*" the Rider said aloud.

That was one thing they could agree on, and the thought of getting their hands on the elder demon united them once again. Eager with anticipation, the Ghost Rider swept the room with its flaming eyes. If Johnny had been ascendant, the smoky room would have made his weak mortal eyes water and his lungs spasm, but Zarathos came from a realm of fire and suffered no ill effects. The Rider's gaze penetrated the hazy air without much difficulty, but failed to locate its prey.

Satana must have truly beaten her father. The Rider was overcome with a begrudging admiration tinged with the slightest regret. Although he'd been denied the satisfaction of burning Marduk to ash, he couldn't be dissatisfied with the outcome.

*They acquitted themselves well*, said Zarathos. His voice echoed in the caverns of their shared mind.

*I told you so*, replied Johnny. *Leave them be.*

*It would be easier to banish the Hellphyr now, but I will grant this boon on one condition.*

*Name it*, said Johnny, cautious.

*If the Tome ever passes to another member of the Kale family who proves unworthy, we will hunt down the Hellphyr and dispatch it for good.*

*Done*, Johnny replied. *Gladly.*

*You seem surprised*, said Zarathos.

*This is the first time you've ever compromised*, said Johnny. *You're changing.*

There was no answer to that, just a vague sensation of shock. Before they could pursue the matter further, a gasping noise on the ground drew the Rider's attention. Topaz was curled up in a ball at his feet.

Transforming quickly, Johnny fell to his knees beside her, turning her over with gentle reluctance. Burns covered her exposed skin, and the odor of charred flesh hung heavy in the air. This was his fault. Maybe he hadn't intended to hurt her. Maybe he couldn't always think things through clearly when he assumed the form of the Rider, but none of that mattered. At the end of the day, he was responsible for what he had done. After so much killing, one more death shouldn't bother him, but the thought of losing her hit him like a lance to the chest. Just a short while ago, she'd been shouting Christmas carols into his face, and now she was dying.

He had no idea what to do about it, and his uselessness stung. Were the burns killing her? Did she have internal injuries? He had no clue. She breathed in short, pained gasps, and no one's complexion should be such a leaden grey. He didn't like that at all, but maybe it was just the smoke. After all, he could barely see.

A wind came up then, as if bidden by his thought, blowing the smoke away. The fires raging at random spots around the room went out, smothered in a blanket of oxygen. He took a deep, cleansing breath, hoping that Topaz would do the same. She didn't. If anything, she looked worse.

"Heal yourself!" he urged, crouching over her. His voice was hoarse with irritation and emotion. "Come on, you know how to do this."

With wordless pain, she shook her head. He didn't know what was going on with her or what pain she carried around in her heart. But he knew despair when he saw it. He'd walked those roads plenty of times before.

"You're not alone," he said. "Whatever's got you down, your coven will face it together. I'll come along, too, although that's probably a point in favor of unconsciousness if anything. I'll even flame up if you need it."

He took her hand in his. Her fingers squeezed his, ever so weakly.

"Come on," he urged. "What do I have to do? Sing? I'll do it."

He didn't know what else to do. With every passing moment, her form grew more still, and he knew what would happen if he didn't talk her into trying. If she didn't want to live, no amount of medicine would help her even if he'd had the skill. Maybe the other witches could help, but they had their hands full with the Hellphyr. He couldn't risk distracting them during their ritual.

He leaned down close to her, his face flushing in embarrassment. What good would singing do anyway? She needed someone who knew magic, or at least how to find a pulse. As the Ghost Rider, Johnny's body could recover from just about any injury. As a result, he'd begun to forget what it was like to be hurt, what to do, how it felt. The first time one of his kids had asked for a Band Aid, he'd panicked. Just like he was doing now.

But singing was all he could think of to do, so that's what he did. Topaz was stronger than most people gave her credit for; he had the perspective to see that. She would heal herself if only he could rouse her. Maybe she'd crawl out of the depths of unconsciousness just to shut him up.

The first line of the song came out of his mouth, wobbly and out of tune. His grief-stricken mind couldn't dredge up the rest of the lyrics after "Jingle Bells," so he kept repeating that line over and over again. He whispered it into her ear, cradling her head in his arms. The position made him feel uncomfortably vulnerable. He didn't even let Dixie get this close. But to shirk away from it was unthinkable.

"The next line is 'Jingle all the way'," she murmured.

She didn't move a muscle, and for one heart-stopping moment, he wondered if he'd imagined it. But then she stirred in his arms, the smallest of motions cut short by an abrupt inhalation of pain. He froze.

"Am I hurting you?" he asked.

"I'm resetting my bones. Please don't move." Her voice grew quieter. "It's nice to be held."

It was nice to be close to someone without feeling the weight of expectation pressing down on him, but he never would have admitted that aloud. Instead, he said, "I promise not to get fresh."

Her lips twisted into what might have been a grimace or a smile. He couldn't tell.

"No more singing, either. Please," she said.

"No singing," he agreed. "I'd consider it a favor if you didn't tell anyone about that."

Her eyelids flickered. When she opened them, her right eye was filled with bright red blood that faded away as he watched, leaving only warm brown behind. The tension in her jaw relaxed by slow degrees as her burns healed, new skin replacing the charred flesh.

"Why not?" she said.

"It would ruin my rep. The Ghost Rider rides fast and fights hard. He doesn't mangle Christmas carols. It's just not done."

"Well then, it was kind of you to break the rules for me. I'm better now. Let me up."

He backed away with more reluctance than he was comfortable with. He wasn't interested in Topaz. He barely knew her, and he wasn't stupid enough to get romantically involved with a witch. But being close to someone without a ton of relationship expectations hovering over his shoulder soothed him. He had a complicated non-relationship with his siblings, who had left with his mother when he was young, but he imagined that if they'd stayed around, their relationship might have resembled the strange connection he had with Topaz. It felt something like home.

But Johnny Blaze couldn't afford that luxury. The curse he carried wouldn't allow it. No matter how brotherly his intentions were, the outcome would be poor. The best thing he could do for family was stay away, so he made the resolution right then and there that he would leave just as soon as his task was complete. But for the first time, he might just look back in regret as he hit the road.

He pushed the maudlin thought away and helped Topaz to her feet just as Jennifer and Satana came rushing over, fear etched onto their faces. Satana was covered in soot and dirt but had returned to her normal dimensions and somehow managed to make the grunge look good. Jennifer had the air of someone who had been to Hell and back. Johnny knew it well.

"I thought you were dead!" Jennifer said, hugging Topaz with panicky relief. "I thought you were hit in the blast."

Satana wrapped her arms around them both without a word. She didn't need to say anything. Her uncharacteristic affection spoke volumes on its own.

Johnny watched the three of them for a moment before looking away with a sense of discomfort. All that naked emotion was too much for him to bear. Deep down, he longed for it, but he had made his choice. So, while the witches enjoyed their reunion, he took a look around.

The House of Horrors had been all but destroyed. The hungry flames had devoured most of the cheap, flimsy walls. Some of the bars had melted clean through, and globules of cooling metal hardened on the remaining pieces. Sometimes, he'd wondered exactly how hot Hellfire was, but when he saw the aftermath of one of his empowered shotgun blasts, he had to concede that the exact temperature didn't matter. It was hot enough to do the job.

The door had been obliterated, but one large sheet sat on the ground a short distance from the witches. The existence of that door still bothered Johnny. Its newness meant that it had been installed after Lucifer's arrival, and the King of Hell didn't do things on a whim. He'd had some kind of plan, and Johnny could only hope that he'd thrown a wrench into it.

Marduk's disappearance still worried him, too. He scanned the area once more, searching for any signs of the demon's current location, but he noticed nothing out of the ordinary. Everything was blanketed in the sense of residual evil that hung about the entire place.

"Sorry to interrupt," he said, "but I've got to ask. Anybody know what happened to Marduk?"

The witches unclenched, although Jennifer kept one hand on Topaz's shoulder like she worried the empath might blow away. Satana took a moment to glance around the area just like Johnny had before she responded.

"He took his sorry butt back to Hell is my guess," she said.

"A guess isn't good enough." He paused and then added, "No offense meant."

"None taken," she replied with surprising good humor. Her pleasure in their success had blunted her rough edges. "I'm pretty confident. If he'd had the juice for it, he would have tried to snatch the book when I threw it to Jen."

"I was surprised when he didn't," admitted the sorceress.

"He's a high-level demon. It takes a lot to drain him," Johnny observed.

Satana pinked, her cheeks flushing with pleasure.

"I've never managed it before. But I had motivation," she said, feigning modesty.

"You're so full of it," said Jennifer.

The succubus threw her head back in laughter, but she didn't deny the accusation. Instead, based on her delighted expression, she'd decided to take it as a compliment.

"Oh, you're right," she said. "I'll be bragging about this for years."

But she didn't brag. Instead, she fell silent, a satisfied smile curving her lips. Winning that battle had meant something to her. She wouldn't cheapen it with empty talk, but she'd carry around the triumph for the rest of her life. Johnny could understand that. During his first few days in Hell, everything had seemed so hopeless. The demons that tormented him had power he could never match, and even his Rider abilities weren't enough to protect him from those numbers. They were legion. He'd tried so many times to escape, but Lucifer had always been two steps ahead of him. After they'd beaten him and thrown him back into his prison enough times, escape seemed like an impossibility. They were too powerful, and he was nothing. If he hadn't made it out when he did, he would have lost all hope.

Of course, now he knew that Lucifer had wanted him to break out of Hell all along, just so he could hitch a ride down to Earth. Not for the first time, Johnny wondered if he would have escaped without Lucifer's assistance, or if he would be stuck there forever, hopeless and helpless and tortured by his memories for all eternity. The thought made him shudder.

Satana had survived that. She'd grown up without the knowledge that true kindness existed, and people could offer help without ulterior motives. Her father had moved her around like a chess piece on a board, deploying her as he saw fit. For the first time, she'd realized that she could stand up against him. That she could refuse to play his games and choose something different for herself.

When he'd arrived, Johnny had worried about her. He'd assumed that Zarathos would try to send her to Hell the moment the spirit took over, but it had stayed its hand. Now Johnny understood why. It must have seen that potential in her, the choice she had made to embrace her human side over the demonic one, even before she knew it herself. Someday, she might choose differently, but they'd cross that bridge when they came to it.

He sighed. "Well, I'm sorry to break up the celebration, but we ought to go."

Murmurs of agreement greeted this statement, and they turned as one to pick their way through the burnt debris toward the exit. As they did so, Johnny edged toward Topaz in what he hoped was a subtle way.

"You OK?" he asked out of the corner of his mouth, trying not to attract attention.

"Yeah. Why?" she asked, surprised.

"You're quiet. I just figured..."

She smiled a little. "Just thinking is all."

"Because if I need to sing again…"

"Please don't. Promise me you'll never do that again."

He grinned, reassured by the playful pleading in her voice and the impish grin that curled her lips. For a moment, he considered telling her how he'd felt when he held her in his arms, but the moment passed before he could work up the courage. Maybe the empath already knew, but he wasn't the type of man to bring it up, no matter how much he ought to.

Jennifer tapped him on the shoulder, drawing his attention. She carried herself with a new confidence after their most recent encounter. She'd never been the wilting violet type, but now he would have described her as more at home in her skin without being able to articulate exactly what made him say that.

"Yeah?" he asked.

"Is it always like this?" she asked. "Hunting Lucifer? We've already been through the wringer, and we haven't even seen him."

"It's always unexpected. He likes keeping me off kilter. When I started hunting down the fragments, I expected a lot of blood and carnage, and I got that. He liked putting me into positions where I had to choose between taking him down or saving a bunch of innocent people, and then when I'd save the people, he'd end up killing them anyway. It was…" He swallowed. "Tough."

"I bet." She put her hand on his shoulder.

"But after the first hundred fragments or so, things changed. He got creative."

"That doesn't sound like a good thing."

"Not really. Maybe. Depends on how you look at it, I guess." He paused, considering how to explain. It was tough to put the workings of a demonic mind – and this mind in particular – into words that a human could understand. The fact that he could begin to comprehend it didn't bode well for his overall sanity. "He's playing with me."

"Definitely not good."

"Not for me, but if it means fewer buses blow up, I'll take it. But there's more to it than that. Lucifer's no dummy. He plays the long game. If he's messing with me, there's a reason for it. I was too blind to see that in Hell, but I'm beginning to wrap my head around it. We should get moving."

"What does he want?" Jennifer asked, her forehead creased with worry. "Let's go that way. The floor doesn't look too sturdy over here."

Johnny nodded, leading the way through the rubble. He tested each step before he took it, using his steel-toed boots to nudge bits of burning metal out of the way. The other two witches stuck close, listening to their conversation without interruption. The confrontation with the Hellphyr had weirded them out or worn them out. Either way, they weren't doing much talking.

"Freedom. Power. The usual. But he's already reached his limits in Hell. If he wants more, he has to branch out. I think that's why he's been pulling my chain all this time. He's been manipulating me for years, and I never got it until now. I'm not a complete idiot, I swear."

"I don't think you're an idiot. He got me, too, with those premonitions. I still don't know for sure whether they were legit or not, but I suspect not. Like you said, he plays the long game. Our lives are comparatively short, so we're not used to thinking like that."

"No, I guess not." Johnny rubbed his chin, deep in thought. "But I wish I could figure out what he wants now. Like you said, his actions don't make sense. He's got all this magical power from your cousin or whatever she is, but he's barely using it. He doesn't do things on a whim. He's got some reason for it. Maybe he was holding off to see if he could get the book from you first? I don't know, and I don't like it."

"What was the last fragment like? Maybe comparing them might help."

"Yeah, not so much. The last one didn't make sense either. He possesses an Army officer and then sits around until I'm in town. Then he steals a tank and drives it through a fence. He makes a few vague threats, and then I blow him to smithereens. It's a waste of a good tank, and the fragment to boot. He doesn't have many left. Why would he do that?"

"Well, logically speaking, I can think of a few options." She ticked them off on her fingers. "One, he had something nasty planned, and you stopped it. Two, he's playing the long game again, and the stunt with the tank set you up for something later. Three, he's messing with your head again."

"Explain," Johnny said, frowning.

"Think about it. You've banished hundreds of these fragments already. I don't want to know the details, but I bet it's been nasty. Lots of carnage, chaos, and despair. Am I right?"

Johnny closed his eyes. Usually, he did a good job of blocking out the things he saw as the Ghost Rider. He could go to bed knowing that he'd done his part to keep those atrocities from happening again, and that had been enough. But Lucifer had upped the ante. Over the past month or so, he'd seen more death than he had in his entire life put together. As hard as he tried to lock them away, sometimes the images trickled out to taint his dreams.

"Yeah," he said quietly. "You're right."

"Well, I don't think anyone ever gets used to that, not even you. But you've got to get numb at some point, don't you?"

"That's not a bad way to put it," Johnny sighed. "I know sometimes I come off like an uncaring bonehead, but it's not that way. You just... run out of gas eventually. Everyone does."

"That must be awful. I'm sorry."

"Eh, somebody's got to do it. Might as well be me, the uncaring bonehead."

Jennifer opened her mouth to argue, but one look at the flinty expression in Johnny's eyes convinced her to table the topic for now. That was good. Johnny couldn't allow her to chip away at his defenses right before he came face to face with Lucifer once more. Especially if she was right about Lucifer's long game. The theory made sense. He had something up his sleeve, and Johnny would have to figure out what it was.

"Well, maybe he's letting your own worries work against you," said Jennifer. "That was my point."

"Come again?"

"Maybe Lucifer really did make the last one easy. He knows you're getting numb to all the carnage. He's got to throw you off balance for these last few fragments in the hopes that he'll win that last battle. So, he takes the Army guy, who could have created a bloodbath, and he does nothing with it. Because if you're worried about that, if you're distracted by what happened last time, you'll be a little less able to stand up against this one. Maybe he's trying to throw you off your game."

"Could be." Johnny sighed again. "I hate this. For all I know, the next fragment will be near a military base, and I'll get arrested and court martialed as soon as I show my face there."

"Why would they arrest you?"

"I blew up a tank, remember?"

"Well, I'll ready some bail money just in case."

"I don't think they let you bail people out of military jail, Jen. I've watched a lot of TV, and I'm pretty sure that's not how that works."

"Well, then, we'll just have to break you out," she said, her eyes flashing.

As they'd talked, Johnny's spirits had sunk further and further. But for some reason, this statement buoyed them. Dixie would bail him out if he got tossed into jail, but he'd be willing to bet that getting thrown into the stockade would end their relationship before he could even make his case. That wasn't a ding against her. She had her own problems to deal with, and he didn't expect her to go the extra mile for him so early on in the relationship. But sometimes he'd missed having a ride or die.

"Thanks," he said.

His voice came out rough with emotion, and he didn't dare look back at Jennifer because his eyes were watering from all the damn smoke. He ought to say more, but he didn't know what. Thankfully, she understood anyway.

"We've got your back, Johnny. Until you do something boneheaded, that is," she said with a smile in her voice.

"Heh," he chuckled. "Gimme five minutes, and I can probably oblige."

# CHAPTER THIRTY-TWO

As she exited the House of Horrors, Topaz took a deep breath of fresh air and tried to relax. She hadn't realized exactly how smoky the haunted house had been until she'd left it, and distant hissing and popping suggested that things still smoldered in the darkness. She'd spent most of the walk struggling to breathe, and the rest of it worried that the place would fall down on their heads. It wasn't the sturdiest construction, aside from that stupid door that had nearly killed her.

She didn't want to think about that, though. She didn't want to think about anything but sucking down clean air and trying not to cough. They would have to fight Lucifer any minute now, and she could use all the oxygen she could get in the meantime. Despite all the magic she'd poured into healing her broken body, it felt like rubber bands encased her chest, making every inhalation painful. Her ribs had been pulverized, and fixing them had taxed even her considerable powers.

Johnny and Jennifer didn't bother with any attempt at stealth. After lighting the place on fire, anyone on the grounds knew they were here. But Topaz still didn't know what had happened to the rest of the employees. She should have asked Aggie earlier, but she'd been so distracted that she hadn't thought of it at the time. She pulled out her phone, but it was fried. She wouldn't be making any calls from that charred brick any time soon. She leaned against the side of a funnel cake trailer and tried not to worry. Everything would be fine. Normally, she had no problem maintaining a sunny outlook, but the words rang false this time.

"What's wrong?"

Satana marched over with a familiar mulish expression. Topaz was exhausted just looking at it. She didn't have the energy for a debate with the succubus, but Satana rarely took no for an answer.

"I'm fine," said Topaz, pasting on a smile. "Just winded."

"You are the worst liar in the world. Never play poker."

"You always say that."

"Well, you haven't gotten any better. I could give you some tips if you want."

"If they'll make people leave me alone, I'll take them."

Topaz leaned her head back and closed her eyes, hoping that Satana would take the hint. But subtlety had never been the half-demon's strong suit.

"I'm not leaving you alone until you tell me what's wrong."

"What makes you think there's a problem?"

"You're quiet."

"I'm always quiet. You talk enough for all three of us."

"Touché. But this is different. You don't feel right. What happened in there?"

Topaz half-opened her eyes and instantly regretted it. Satana stared at her with a frown, her muscles tense with worry. That only made Topaz feel guilty, and the worst part was that she had no idea what was wrong. She and Jennifer had gotten into that argument, but people argued all the time. She'd always been able to set it aside. People said things they didn't mean. Spurred on by pain and fear, they thought things they would never say out loud. She heard more of them than she would have liked, and she'd always been able to meet them with empathy and understanding. Time after time, she'd put aside her own feelings to help them deal with theirs, and she'd never resented it. After all, it was her choice. She did it because she wanted to.

None of that had changed, but everything had changed, and Topaz didn't understand why. She didn't hold Jennifer's words against her. The sorceress had been dealing with all the emotions surrounding the Hellphyr's escape, and that had forced her to come to terms once and for all with her feelings about her brother's death. Any empath in a thousand-mile radius could have picked that up, because she'd been so agitated that she'd broadcast her emotions at high volume. Topaz couldn't avoid hearing them no matter how hard she tried.

Topaz had never had any problem dealing with things like this. But something had knocked her off kilter, and she didn't understand what. She didn't like it. But how could she ask for help when she didn't even know what the problem was? And how could Satana even begin to understand? The succubus wanted to be human more than anything, and she'd done a pretty good job of it, but her demonic impulses would never go away. Topaz couldn't begin to explain how it felt to give and give of yourself until you felt like a scooped-out melon with nothing left and no way to keep going. She wanted to collapse onto the ground and sit there for hours. Doing nothing. Saying nothing. Somewhere completely alone where no one needed her for anything.

Some of her conflicted emotions must have shown on her face, or maybe the silence worried Satana, because the succubus took her by the shoulders.

"You're freaking me out." Satana stared into her eyes, and Topaz expected to see the red glimmer in her pupils that betrayed her temper, but the demoness's gaze was clear and blue. "What. Is. Wrong?"

"I'm fine," said Topaz.

She wasn't.

Satana began to growl but cut herself off before building up much in the way of volume or momentum. She took a deep breath, still maintaining her grip on Topaz, and tried again.

"You're not," she said. "And we both know it. If you need me to mind my own business, say so. But don't ask me to pretend that nothing is wrong or that I don't care."

It cost Satana a lot to say that, and Topaz knew it. The bald statement touched her, driving away some of the deep sadness that had filled her for reasons she didn't understand. But it didn't strike at the core of it, and Topaz had no desire to look deeper and figure out why. She would put one foot in front of the other until the job was done. Then and only then would she sit down and figure out what was bothering her. Any other approach would make them all vulnerable. Who would hold everyone together if she was falling apart?

"We have a job to do," she said. "Maybe we can talk later, though."

Some of the worry bled off Satana's face. She released Topaz, wiping off her hands as if she'd just completed a difficult task. Emotional empathy probably fell into that category for Satana, come to think of it.

"That's a deal. If you're really upset, maybe I'll even drink some of your tea without complaining," she said.

"Will wonders never cease." replied Topaz.

"Don't push your luck."

Satana backed off, made content by the promise. But for all her acting, Topaz didn't feel any less on edge. Something had changed, and she wished she had a handy empath who could take her hand and help her to face it. But the helper couldn't be the helped.

She would just have to face it alone.

# CHAPTER THIRTY-THREE

Johnny Blaze didn't like talking. Most days, he'd go into a diner for a cup of joe and some breakfast and leave a half-hour later with a full stomach and a headache from all the endless yammering. People plopped down next to him at the counter, desperate to talk about the weather, their sciatica, or their mother-in-law. They held shouted conversations with the waitress or screamed into their cell phones. If you asked Johnny, all that jibber-jabber didn't amount to much of anything. It gave folks an excuse not to think, and that wasn't necessarily a good thing. Not thinking tended to get people in trouble, and before you knew it, they'd be staring up at the Ghost Rider with the same expression of horrified comprehension and regret they all wore at the end. Even the baddest gang members and serial killers looked like that, just for a moment. Sometimes he thought it was a gift from the Rider – one moment of clarity before an eternity of Hell – but it was probably a curse.

Most things were.

As much as he hated empty chatter, he had to admit that the talk with Jennifer had helped. He hadn't even realized he'd needed it until they'd finished talking, but a weight had been lifted from his shoulders that he hadn't known he was carrying. He'd been worrying at the puzzle of Lucifer's behavior for weeks now, as each fragment got less overtly brutal and more dangerously complex. But she'd laid it all out in simple terms that made sense to him. Lucifer had ulterior motives. Johnny wasn't going to successfully psychoanalyze the Prince of Darkness, so worrying about them was fruitless. If anyone had a chance at success, he did, but it was an impossible task.

But the witches noticed things he didn't. He'd be interested to hear what they thought of Lucifer's approach once all was said and done. Maybe they could chat over a plate of eggs and bacon at the local greasy spoon. Now that Johnny had started thinking about food, his stomach growled.

Jennifer overheard it, and she smiled as she surveyed the carnival ground, but the pleasant expression faded as she took in their surroundings. Nothing moved in the darkness. No one came running toward the still-smoldering House of Horrors with a bucket of water or a cell phone to dial nine-one-one. No dogs barked in the quiet. The place felt more like a morgue than a fairground. Johnny had the eerie sensation that there was no one alive for miles around, even though he had no way of knowing that. He could sense evildoers just fine, but normal people eluded his radar.

Which explained a lot about his failure to maintain relationships, come to think of it.

"Where to?" asked Jennifer. "If we go through each of these

tents one by one, we'll be here forever. This place creeps me out."

Johnny agreed. He didn't relish the possibility of walking the entire place, pulling back tent flaps and peeking into darkened RVs and trailers. Although he thought it deserted, he could be wrong, and then they'd end up getting thrown in the slammer. He'd spent plenty of nights in a holding cell, and he knew what happened in there. Someone would pick a fight with him, and they'd get more than they bargained for. He didn't have the time for that nonsense.

If he wanted to end this, he needed to start thinking like Lucifer. On the surface, that seemed like an awful idea, but what other choice did he have? The demon had been playing games with him all along, sowing doubt and desperation, and it had worked out great so far. All his actions had a purpose. Johnny just had to figure out what it was.

More importantly, he needed to know how to stop it. Ever since he'd found out about the fragments, he'd just assumed that he'd fight his way through until the end. Every one of the fragments would be an exercise in pain and death. Johnny could deal with that; he'd done so for most of his life. But games weren't his forte. He needed to get over himself and figure out how to play before it was game over.

"He'll want something big," he said aloud. "Lucifer won't murder just one person when he can kill twenty and really make us squirm. So he's probably got the rest of the performers stashed somewhere. He likes forcing me to choose between killing him and saving the innocent. He thinks it's hilarious."

"Well, that's not going to happen this time," said Jennifer, her jaw tensing. "You've got backup today. We'll take care of the carnival people if you can take down the Prince of Darkness. Yeah?"

Her eyes skimmed over the other two witches. Satana nodded, cracking her knuckles. Topaz also agreed, but her slumped shoulders suggested how much that healing had taken out of her. Johnny would have been concerned if he hadn't noticed how Satana flanked the empath, ever so casually stopping just a step or two ahead of her, ready to intercept any threats that came her way. The succubus knew what she was doing. She must have worked security details before.

He decided not to draw any attention to it. The problem was taken care of, and that was all that mattered.

"Sounds like a plan," he said. "Although I'll need help countering Magda's magic. I'm not sure if it'll affect me with Lucifer at the helm. I'm pretty tough, but Lucifer's no weakling. With Magda's power at his disposal, he'll be a lot to handle."

"I'll take care of that," said Jennifer. "Topaz and Satana can get any hostages to safety, and then they'll assist."

"You think you're up to it?" he asked. "No offense. I don't really know how these things work, and she must have been powerful to lock you out like she did during that spell you cast."

Jennifer licked her lips, visibly steeling herself.

"I'm the most powerful Kale alive," she said. "The Tome chose me for a reason. Besides, I was holding back."

"You were?" Satana arched a brow.

"Not on purpose," Jennifer clarified. "But I think it's time I went off the chain."

"I like the sound of that. It's very sexy," said the succubus, giving her a thumbs up.

Johnny nodded in agreement, scanning the grounds. Lucifer would want a big structure. A nice wooded area would have worked, but the fairground sat at the back of a small industrial park, and the plant life around here was limited to a line of scraggly trees around the border of the grounds. Beyond was a long stretch of empty parking lots broken by wilting clumps of weeds. But at the far end of the grounds, on the other side of the super slide and the black painted carousel, a large dark shape caught his eye.

A circus tent. He didn't know how he hadn't noticed it before, except that it was tucked off into the corner, shielded from view behind the slide. But he still should have noticed a structure that large. Perspective, maybe? Or lack of illumination? That side of the grounds was so dark that he could barely make out the outline of the structure against the sky. The slide blocked what little light had made it that far, cloaking the entire tent in darkness.

As far as locations for a showdown went, it was perfect. He pointed wordlessly, and the three witches squinted in that direction until they could see it, too.

"How did we miss that?" asked Satana, shaking her head. "I know I was distracted by the Hellphyr, but I'm not usually that oblivious."

"It was cloaked," said Topaz. "You can see the remnants of the spell if you look around the edges. See?"

Jennifer pursed her lips as she surveyed the large, striped tent. It was at least two stories tall, with a long pennant at the top that flipped and flopped in the light breeze.

"She's good, if she managed to hide something that big," she said.

"You still think you can take her?" asked Satana.

Jennifer's teeth flashed in the darkness. "I'm looking forward to it. I could use something to hit."

"That's my line," said Satana.

She tried to pretend amusement, but if anything, she grew tenser. The demoness looked from Topaz to Jennifer and back again as if torn between them. Johnny didn't like that. If even Satana was worried about her companions, then they were in worse shape than he'd realized. He hoped he didn't have to sing again. It would be nice if none of them died, either.

Worrying about it wasn't making this any easier. He began to walk toward the main tent, his boots crunching in the gravel. The three witches flanked him, stalking through the shadows like ghosts of vengeance. Zarathos stirred deep inside him, eager to get on with the show, but Johnny spoke to him silently, urging patience.

*Not yet,* he thought.

"*Let me out, and I will find the Prince of Lies,*" Zarathos promised. "*We will burn him together.*"

*You'll get your chance soon enough. But I need to see. I need to understand.*

"*There is no understanding evil. To attempt it is to fall.*"

*You know full well that's bull. I walk the line every day, and I haven't fallen off it yet. Let me walk it a little longer before you light it on fire,* Johnny urged.

"*Why?*"

*Because whatever I discover might help us survive the final fragment.*

Zarathos had no answer for that, and Johnny clenched his fist in triumph. Satana looked his way, her brow furrowed in confusion, and he forced himself to relax. But he'd get himself a pastry when they finally made it to a diner. Zarathos never let him have the last word, and now he'd done it twice in a row. He'd earned a baked good or two.

# CHAPTER THIRTY-FOUR

As their small group crossed the fairground toward the big tent, Jennifer kept tripping over things. The sub-par lighting, combined with the on-the-ground clutter, made even a slow walk treacherous. Every few steps, another cord stretched across the path. Some had been carefully taped to the ground, but most hadn't, and they didn't lay flat. After catching her toes on the fourth one, she wanted to scream.

Under different circumstances, she would have used her magic to light the way. Lucifer had to know they were here, but she still didn't think it was wise to advertise what direction they came from and when. Besides, she only had so much juice to work with. Over the past twenty-four hours, she'd cast a taxing spell from the *Tome of Zhered-Na* and banished the Hellphyr. She'd taken a few beatings and doled out one or two herself. If she'd been a black witch, it wouldn't have mattered. She could have sucked power from any living things nearby and cast magic indefinitely – or at least until the Ghost Rider sent her to Hell in penance for her sins. But she would never do such a thing. Even the thought of using a willing battery made her cringe.

No, she would power her own magic until the end, and that meant playing it safe. Lucifer wouldn't hesitate to suck the world dry during the fight. With an infinite amount of power at his fingertips, he would be difficult to beat. She couldn't afford to waste energy maintaining a light or adjusting her eyes to see in the dark. Satana or Johnny would warn them if danger approached, so it was merely an inconvenience. She'd just have to deal with it.

So she stumbled around, trying not to make too much noise in the process. Topaz was just as blind as she was, and the two of them found each other in the dark. They linked arms, hoping to steady each other, but ended up making it worse instead.

Satana's glowing red eyes turned toward them after one particularly noisy stumble. It was eerie to see them floating in the pitch blackness. Then the eyes rolled in exasperation. Jennifer would have snickered aloud if they weren't trying to be at least semi-quiet.

The darkness clung to her. The more she thought about it, the more unnatural it appeared. The inadequate glow from the lights in the RV park was mostly blocked by some of the larger structures, and there was no moon tonight, but she should at least be able to make out the outline of her hand right in front of her face. But she couldn't even see the stars. Overhead stretched a blanket of inky blackness, too deep and unbroken to be natural.

It was a magical cloak of some kind, but not worth poking at. Lucifer could have used it to sneak up on them, but if he'd wanted to take them unawares, he would have done it by now. He wanted them to survive long enough to see what he'd planned for them, and to take malicious glee in their reaction.

There would be no knives in the back until then. That thought reassured her slightly, but she'd begun to see what Johnny was talking about. The weird choices on Lucifer's part really unsettled her.

Jennifer kept up the unspoken dialogue in her head as they approached the tent. Her emotions vacillated wildly from optimism to fatalism and back again with every step. It nearly gave her whiplash. Or maybe her head just hurt because of the low-hanging banner she ran into.

"Is that the entrance?" Satana said.

She kept her voice low, but it still carried in the deep silence. For the first time, Jennifer realized how quiet it was. The Florida nights were usually full of sound as crickets advertised their presence to prospective mates and frogs croaked out their satisfaction with their late-night meals. But she could hear nothing. No rustle of tiny feet attracted by the smell of the food trailers, no peep of night insects. Not a single owl. In contrast, their fumbling progress was deafening. As a group, no one would commend them on their stealth.

"Yeah," said Johnny. "This way."

The two of them led the way into the black. Jennifer and Topaz followed, trying to step only where they stepped, but still managed to trip on things en route. It was getting embarrassing.

They walked for a few seconds in silence before their two guides stopped. Jennifer nearly ran into Satana's back before righting herself, her fingertips on the succubus's shoulder. She peered about but was unable to see a thing. Her heart thumped with adrenaline as she waited for something to leap out of the black at them, but it didn't happen.

"Where are we?" Topaz whispered.

"In the tent, I think," replied Satana. "But it's so dark in here that I can barely see. I was in an oubliette that was this dark once." She shuddered, her shoulder quivering under Jennifer's hand. "I don't like it."

"Should I transform?" asked Johnny. "Brighten things up a bit?"

*"That won't be necessary."*

The voice wrapped itself around Jennifer's spine and squeezed. Her lungs spasmed, trying to draw breath through a torso stiff with fear. It was the pleasant alto of a young woman and the voice of a predator all at once, the deep bass tones mingling with the higher ones to create an eerie blend.

The lights came on, blazing and bright. She threw up her arm to no avail. After the long minutes spent in pitch blackness, her pupils couldn't stand the light. It seared through her eyes and into her brain like liquid fire. The headache was sudden and debilitating, and it knocked her to her knees.

Acting on instinct, she released all the magic she'd held curled inside of her, driving away the unnatural light and reestablishing her equilibrium. The pain ebbed with excruciating slowness, but she had no time to dwell on that. She pushed herself back up to her feet, feeling a trickle of wetness down her face. At first, she thought tears of pain leaked from her eyes, but when she wiped her cheeks, her hand came away stained red with blood.

Topaz cried red tears, too, her face drawn with pain and fear, but she stood steady at Jennifer's shoulder. Satana had taken her demon form, her glossy skin hiding any bloody tears from view. But her grimace said it all. The blast of light had hurt her, too.

Johnny hadn't so much as faltered. He stood in front of them, shielding them with his body, his head thrown back in defiance as he looked around the room. Appreciation and shame flooded Jennifer in turn. She shouldn't be surprised by his protective instincts, not now that she'd gotten to know him a little better. But she was. She was still getting used to not thinking of him as a mindless goon, slave to the spirit he carried around in his head. But he'd achieved something of a balance with the Ghost Rider, and that took strength. She should quit underestimating him.

Her strength returned, Jennifer stepped up next to him. Satana already flanked him on the other side, and not a second later, Topaz joined them. Johnny didn't even blink. His attention was too engrossed with the person silhouetted against the entrance on the far side of the tent.

They stood on the hard-packed dirt floor of the big top, a wide and open performance area stretching out before them. Stacks of crates suggested some construction still under way, but most of the structure had been built. Metal bleachers surrounded the performance area, their upper seats still cloaked in darkness. Harnesses dangled down overhead, silks and trapeze bars swaying beneath them in the still air. A trio of decorative wooden bats hung at the back of the tent, their wings casting monstrous shadows on the canvas.

Magda Kale stepped out into the light that pooled on the hard-packed dirt of the performance area. Although they'd never met, she was immediately recognizable. An aura of power clung to her, like an invisible cloak that swirled around her as she moved. Jennifer surveyed her with interest. They weren't closely related, although Jen hadn't had the time to spend with her family tree to work out the exact relationship. But the weakness of their blood link was secondary to the magic that flowed through them both. That was all too familiar, and her heart leaped as it wound tendrils around her body. If only they'd met while Magda was still alive. Before Lucifer had slipped into her body like it was just another set of clothing and used it for violence. It would have been nice to talk shop with someone who spoke her exact language, and Jennifer found herself mourning a relationship she'd never had the opportunity to enjoy.

Magda stepped forward into the light and smiled, her face alight with self-satisfaction. She was a petite woman in her late twenties with an athletic build born of hours of intense training. Her black leotard, hung with a lacy skirt, showed off the definition in her pale limbs, the long muscles of an acrobat bunched along arms and shoulders. Dark hair with a deep widow's peak framed her face. Her dark eyes glittered, and her red painted mouth curled in satisfaction as she looked them over.

"It's about time," she said, her mouth still producing two voices at once. The effect was chilling. "I was getting bored."

"Then go back to Hell," Johnny replied. "I'm sure you'll have plenty to do there. If you don't return soon, you might not have a throne left."

Magda arched a brow.

"Are you implying a coup?" she asked.

"That, or one of your brilliant underlings will burn the whole place down."

Magda considered, tapping her finger on her chin. "Maybe," she allowed. "But my throne is fireproof. At the very least, it'll still stand. Besides, when I am the King of Earth, I'll no longer need my throne in Hell."

Johnny scowled. "Should have known you'd say that."

"Aren't you going to introduce me to your friends?"

Magda surveyed the witches, and as her eyes met Jennifer's, they seemed to grow to fill the room. An immense intelligence and power lurked behind that gaze. It weighed her soul and dismissed its value in the blink of an eye, monstrous in its inhumanity. If she had ever doubted Johnny's story, she believed in it fully now. This could be no one but the Prince of Darkness himself. No one could meet that gaze and doubt that he was here, and he was hungry.

Magda Kale's body might still walk the Earth. Her magic might survive. But the only personality in that body belonged to Lucifer, and the fallen angel knew nothing of mercy or care. He would obliterate the world in his interminable hunger for power.

"Why should I bother?" asked Johnny. "We all know how this is going to end. Why don't we get on with the part where we fight and you die?"

"Can you blame me for wanting to stay here just a while longer? The demons of Hell aren't much for conversation, and we don't even get a cell signal down there," replied Lucifer.

Without waiting for a response, he turned toward Topaz and smiled. It was not a pleasant expression. Magda's canine teeth had been surgically capped to make them more vampiric, and they poked at her lower lip. Maybe she'd done it to make her circus act more convincing, or maybe Lucifer had had them altered for reasons Jennifer didn't want to contemplate.

"Well, aren't you a pretty one. Topaz, is it?" he said.

The empath nodded, her expression distant. She had to be concentrating with all her might to maintain the mental shields that protected her from his psyche. Jennifer didn't want to think about what the inside of Lucifer's mind looked like. That way lay madness. In Topaz's shoes, she would have done the same.

"Boring, though." Lucifer turned away from her without a second glance, and Topaz blanched. Jennifer wondered what that was all about. Lucifer's disapproval was something to celebrate, in her opinion. His gaze shifted to her, and she would have given anything to avoid it. It missed nothing, ferreting out every fault, every mistake and regret, and filing them away for use later. "Miss Kale! It's so nice to meet our cousin at last," he said, feigning delight.

"You're not my cousin."

"It's like a family reunion," the demon continued, ignoring her. "You, me, and the bonehead. I am positively verklempt." He mimed wiping away a tear. "Should we take a photo to commemorate the occasion?"

"You're not my cousin," Jennifer repeated, biting out the words. "You're just taking her body for a pleasure cruise."

"And what a pleasurable ride it is," said Lucifer. "I look forward to showing you what I can do with it momentarily. But before that, I have one last relative to greet. Satana is from the other side of my family tree, you know." He clapped Magda's hands, rubbing them together with evident relish. "My dear. You are a sight for sore eyes."

The mulish expression faded from Satana's face, only to be replaced with utter confusion.

"What?" she asked.

"I know we haven't seen eye to eye in the past, but that's your father's doing. Honestly, I'd like to rip his head off and nail it to the nearest wall. Modern art is so *au courant*, isn't it?"

"If anyone's going to rip off Marduk's head, it's me. I have dibs."

He grinned, showing Magda's fangs again.

"I cannot argue with one so beautiful. But if it's beheading you're looking for, I can help you with that. He's injured. It would be in both of our best interests if someone were to press the advantage and take him out before he can recover."

"How giving of you," said Satana. "But I'm not that stupid."

"Oh, I'm not going to deny that I would greatly benefit from such a thing. Marduk's death would help us both. Besides, if I throw you this bone, you won't try to kill me just yet, and I get to enjoy a little more time on this nice green Earth. I like to ride the Ferris wheel, you know. It's almost like flying."

"Right. That's all you've been doing, all this time. You haven't been imprisoning all the circus employees in the House of Horrors or anything. Not you. You're a model citizen."

He spread his hands. "You got me. But that isn't so bad, is it? I could have done much worse. I could have blown them to smithereens. Isn't that such a glorious word? Smithereens."

Satana's forehead furrowed as she tried to make sense of his twisty conversation. Jennifer didn't like how this was going at all. Lucifer might play at honesty and collaboration, but ultimately, he only served himself. Out of all of them, the succubus should have known that the best, but after everything that had happened, Jennifer couldn't blame her for wanting to believe him.

"You might play at redemption," she said. "But it's just an act. We can all see right through you, can't we, Satana?"

The demoness stiffened, a spark lighting in her eyes.

"Oh, yeah. I see it. And I don't like being manipulated," she said.

"How is it manipulation if I'm clear about my motives, hm? I like it here. With every passing day, I grow to like it more. But Johnny Boy has gotten it into his head that I've got to be snuffed out. I'll admit that he was right at first. It was a bloodbath."

Lucifer shook his head, oozing shame. Jennifer checked to see how Satana was reacting to this farce and was reassured to see the skepticism written all over her face. Johnny laughed outright, low and mocking.

"I'm still right," he said. "You can't fool me."

"See what I mean?" Lucifer sighed. "He can't be reasoned with. But is it really so difficult to believe that I've changed?"

"It would be an awful coincidence, don't you think? After thousands of years, you've suddenly seen the light?" Jennifer shook her head. "I don't buy it."

"Ah, but that was thousands of years stuck in Hell, resenting humans for their freedom. But now I'm free, too, and of course something that monumental would change my outlook on things. Look, I'm not going to try to sell you on the idea that I've completely redeemed myself. I have no intention of working a day in my life. I'll cheat and steal to my heart's content. I want to gorge myself on excellent food and sleep on a cushy bed. Perhaps I might be selfish and egotistical and greedy, but is that really so bad? It sounds quite human to me."

"So you'll just give up on the killing?" asked Jennifer.

He shrugged Magda's shoulders. "It was fun while it lasted, but it's not exactly a long-term plan, is it? If I want to stay here,

I need to play nice with the other kids. It's taken some time to learn that, but I'm a fast study."

Despite herself, Jennifer felt a pang of misgiving. The argument hung together well, but she didn't want to believe it. Was that just her biases working against her, or was she right to automatically distrust the King of Lies? The fact that she genuinely had to ask herself that question made her flush in shame.

Satana had come to the same conclusion. She shook her head, hard and firm.

"Nope," she said. "You're just trying to muddy the waters."

"My actions bear out my claims, though. It would be one thing if I just put on a show of spiritual growth, but I'm taking action. Johnny's seen it, even though he hasn't figured out what it means. I could have blown that military base to smithereens, right, Johnny? After all, I had a tank! Thousands of people would have died, and he would have had a hard time getting on base to stop me. I could have racked up quite the body count. But I didn't."

"I see your game now," said Johnny, scowling. "It won't work."

Lucifer turned his back on the Ghost Rider, making a direct appeal to the three witches.

"Never mind him," he said. "He'll only hear what he wants to. But let me ask you, what would it take to convince you that I just want to live out my life – Magda's life – in peace? I could have killed all the carnival employees, but I didn't. I could have melted your brains when you tried to scry me, but I didn't. In fact, I let you extinguish those pesky demons and didn't lift a finger. I could have sent all the employees out onto the streets of Salem to burn and kill, but I didn't do that either. Instead, I waited for you to come to me so we could talk."

"We almost died!" Topaz exclaimed out of the blue. She stepped forward, hands clenched into fists. "In the House of Horrors, I nearly lost my life. And it's your fault."

"No, it isn't. I didn't make you release the Hellphyr, nor was it my fault that you all lost control of it. If anyone's to blame for that chaos, it's the four of you, but I'm happy to shunt it all onto Marduk if it makes you feel better. He manipulated you into it, after all."

Satana growled. "He didn't manipulate me. I was on to him from the start."

"Were you?" Lucifer arched a brow. "That's nice to hear. So how did he almost manage to steal the *Tome of Zhered-Na*, if he didn't successfully manipulate you into a vulnerable position? I'd love to hear it."

"I... He didn't..." Satana spluttered.

"We'd be idiots to tell you that," said Jennifer. "Maybe mistakes were made, but we're trying to do the right thing here."

"So am I," replied Lucifer. "Like I said, I believe Marduk is to blame. But I've done nothing wrong as Magda. I've done the bare minimum to defend myself, and nothing more."

"Brainwashing is wrong," said Topaz.

"And I eventually realized that it would be a deal breaker and let them go. I won't say I'm not still learning about this whole morality thing, but isn't that the point? Think about it, my friends. You could be the ones who redeemed the Prince of Darkness himself. What a coup. We could go on the talk show circuit." He paused. "That was a joke."

"Where are the rest of the employees?" Johnny asked abruptly.

Lucifer blinked.

"Come again?" he asked.

"It takes more than five people to run this place. Where are the rest of them?"

"Oh, they're around here somewhere. You think I know? They're not the most organized group I've ever seen. Working with them is a bit like herding cats," Lucifer replied in airy tones.

"So they all just happened to leave the grounds at the same time, and you don't know where they are? What a coincidence." Johnny turned to the witches. "I hope you're not buying this crap. Because it's a load of BS."

"I'm not," said Topaz, folding her arms and scowling.

Jennifer shook her head but said nothing. She wanted to believe it. Perhaps not as much as Satana clearly did, but she couldn't deny the urge. It was less about the glory of redeeming Lucifer than it was about avoiding a fight with him. Although she believed in her coven and in Johnny's skills, this was the King of Hell. Even winning would hurt, and she'd been hurt enough.

Johnny looked from Jennifer to Satana and back again, his eyes narrowed. He clearly didn't like what he saw. He turned to Lucifer, who watched them all with Magda's dark and glittering eyes.

"You're having a blast, aren't you?" asked Johnny.

"It's a heck of a lot better than Hell, I can tell you. Come on, Johnny. Can't we let bygones be bygones? I'll promise not to kill anyone, and you can head back to the house with your friends and have a cookout. Enjoy the normal life for a while. Then, if you want, you can take out the rest of my fragments, although I will make you the same promise for them as I do for Magda. I won't kill. In fact, I'll bring the rest of the fragments to you and let you destroy them if you'll agree to let this one go. I'm not going to lie to you and say I'll live a blameless life, but who does?"

Johnny shook his head, grumbling under his breath. Jennifer couldn't make out the words, but she didn't have to. His agitation was palpable. Could Lucifer be right about Johnny? She couldn't help but wonder if it would be smarter to strike a bargain. Perhaps there was some way to magically ensure that Lucifer kept to his promise. Besides, if he lied or cheated, it was up to other people whether or not they wanted to believe him. She didn't like the idea of standing in the way of anyone's free will, even if what they ultimately did was wrong in her opinion.

She met Satana's eyes. If her tortured expression was any indication, the demoness was conflicted, too. Jennifer waffled back and forth, trying to decide what to do. Lucifer could only be trusted to follow his own self-interest, but if his self-interest aligned with hers, would it be a mistake to go along with it? Would that put her in debt to him? Or could she make this bargain and leave knowing that she'd saved lives? She didn't know the right thing to do, and anxiety twisted her insides as she mulled it over.

"He's hiding something from us," Topaz murmured. "I can feel it."

Lucifer whirled to face her. Magda's body was light on its feet, and he made the movement look like the first step of a dance without music, one that was cut off way too short. He edged closer, holding his hands out in invitation.

"Would you like to see what I'm hiding?" he asked. "Come on in, little psychic. I'll show you everything."

Topaz shuddered. A trickle of blood inched its way out of

her left nostril, the only testament to a mental war that Jennifer could barely sense. But now that she knew to look, she could see the tension in every limb as the empath fought against the demon's mental onslaught.

"Did you try to read Lucifer's mind?" Satana demanded, her voice rising to a screech. "Are you insane?!"

Topaz shuddered, the trickle turning into a red gush that coated her face. She swayed, and Jennifer caught her by the arm, holding her upright.

"Lucifer, leave her alone, or else," said the sorceress.

"Not my fault," said Lucifer. "Sorry, though."

Johnny pointed at him with a smoking hand, a testament to his struggle to contain his temper. Slow curls of steam began to rise from his shoulders, too, framing him in a hazy cloud of fury.

"I knew it was all a lie," he growled. "And now you'll pay the price."

Lucifer clucked his tongue. "I didn't do anything. You said it yourself, Johnny; she shouldn't look into my head. It's a cesspool. But you can't blame me if she chose to do it anyway."

"That's how you're gonna play it, huh?" asked Satana, cracking her knuckles. "Plausible deniability? If people around you are getting hurt, and you're manipulating them into it, you're still at fault. Come on. I tried that excuse to justify my actions when I was five. Can't you do better than that?"

Magda's face twisted with anger for just a moment before Lucifer regained control of his emotions.

"You'd better stop while you're ahead, girl," he said.

"What's on the bleachers?" asked Topaz.

The psychic's voice fluttered weakly, and blood coated her

face and clothes, but her eyes were flinty. She clenched her fists, digging bloody gouges into her palms without even registering the pain. Jennifer tightened her grip, steadying the empath. Satana stepped in front of them, guarding them with her body.

Lucifer sighed.

"Are you sure you don't want to deal?" he asked.

"Go to Hell," said Satana.

"Oh well," he said. "I tried."

He raised Magda's arms in a dramatic gesture. Although she wasn't a tall woman, she had presence. Maybe she'd always had it – after all, she worked for a circus – or maybe Lucifer just had a knack for theatrics. Probably a combination of both. Either way, Jennifer's eyes were glued to the petite figure at the other end of the ring. Something would happen now. It wouldn't be good.

Lucifer threw Magda's head back and dropped her arms as if letting go of some heavy burden he'd been lugging around for hours. Jennifer's ears popped as the ambient pressure in the tent plummeted. She hadn't even noticed the cloying closeness until it was gone. Now the music of the night crept in from the outside, the whistles and cheeps of nighttime bugs, the hoot of an owl on the hunt. Light filled the corners of the tent, illuminating the areas that had been cloaked in darkness.

The bleachers went up higher than she'd realized. The clinging darkness had obscured the top half, which was crowded with blank-eyed people in costume. They'd found the rest of the employees. Jennifer wasn't sure whether to be relieved or worried. Lucifer hadn't killed them, just like he'd said, but his obfuscation worried her. He wouldn't have hidden them if he really intended honesty and peace.

She took a step toward the closest group, intending to check on their general wellbeing when Topaz grabbed her by the upper arm, squeezing hard. Jennifer hissed in pain, following the empath's stricken gaze. A protest about the rough handling died on her lips as she saw what had alarmed Topaz so much.

About twenty people stood frozen high above them on platforms and tightropes, their eyes empty of all rational thought.

"That can't be good," Jennifer said, hiding her growing panic under a casual veneer. In total, there had to be over a hundred employees here. How could the four of them stand against so many?

"That's it," said Johnny, pulling out his chain. "Enough conversation. Let's dance."

Fire licked the length of the chain as Johnny transformed in a whoosh of heat. Normally, he changed in gradual stages, the flames moving with steady deliberation over his exposed skin. But this time, he went up like a pile of dry tinder, his power fueled by his rage.

"I thought you'd never ask," Lucifer said in Magda's voice. "Get him."

# CHAPTER THIRTY-FIVE

The Ghost Rider whipped his chain, building up momentum for a strike as the witches stood at the ready. Lucifer just smiled, clapping his hands like he was watching one of his favorite shows. He didn't appear worried in the slightest, and that gave Topaz pause. She had no desire to read his mind again; the brief glimpse she'd gotten would haunt her for the rest of her days. Besides, she didn't need her empathic abilities to know that he had something up his sleeve. She might be naïve, but she wasn't stupid.

Without a word from their master, the circus folk spilled off the bleachers with surprising speed. They moved in silence, the bang of their feet on the metal the only sound as they swarmed. Topaz glanced up at the rafters, but thankfully the people there remained still. She returned her attention to the rushing crowd, picking one man at the front, an elderly chap in a nondescript pair of overalls, and leaped into his mind, hoping to free him from Lucifer's influence. But the space was empty, and the same tricks she'd used to free Aggie and her friends didn't work this time. If the man's awareness slumbered anywhere nearby, she couldn't find it. She withdrew with a queasy sensation growing in the pit of her stomach. Lucifer had kept a few tricks up Magda's sleeve, and that didn't bode well at all.

But there was no time to explain this to the others. Within seconds, the Ghost Rider was engulfed in a crowd of people. They clustered close, making no attempt to grab him. As they packed in tight, his chain came to a gradual stop. Lucifer had been smart. With their minds and souls on vacation, the Rider couldn't use his Penance Stare. He had no way to judge whether or not each person deserved to burn. Zarathos might be on a single-minded mission to send Lucifer back to Hell, but it wouldn't attack innocent people.

Lucifer cracked Magda's knuckles, stretching elaborately. On either side of Topaz, her coven mates tensed. They would have to stall him until Johnny could get loose and send him back to Hell, and it wouldn't be easy. Topaz was no slouch when it came to battle, but she didn't relish it like Satana did, or study for it as Jennifer did. She knew her role here, and she stepped into it without needing to ask.

She spread her awareness among her allies, linking them in a psychic net. As her mental power spread, she became aware of Satana's eagerness and Jennifer's caution. Both were as familiar to her as her own face, and so she absorbed them without difficulty. But she didn't know Johnny very well, and when her neural net touched him for the first time, an alien awareness looked back at her.

*"If it's domination you seek, go elsewhere,"* Zarathos thought at her, its voice echoing in her mind.

"Coordination, not domination," she corrected.

*"Explain."*

"Through this link, we can each sense if one of our allies is in trouble and come to their aid. We can fight together, without words that will alert Lucifer."

*"Intelligent. I will accept."*

A wave of begrudging respect rushed through their connection. Topaz got the sense that Zarathos didn't respect many people, nor did he customarily work with others, so his approval meant something. Pride welled within her as she completed the circle, drawing the Rider in. Satana and Jennifer both started as awareness of the spirit's mind seeped into their bones, and Jennifer gave her a side-eyed glance of astonishment. But Topaz knew she'd done the right thing.

The Rider couldn't move without hurting someone. Bodies pinned him in on all sides, and perhaps a more agile person could have squirmed through the tight crowd, but he was more of a brute force kind of guy. He tried to shove his way through, but the employees pushed back, packing together so tightly that they couldn't even fall over. It would take him some time to free himself. The link assured them all that he didn't need assistance, but he was out of commission for the moment.

That left the witches. The three of them turned in unison to face Lucifer. His smile widened as they realized the full implications of the Rider's detainment. They stood face to face with the King of Hell, the Prince of Lies, the Morningstar, and they would have to stand up to him alone.

"You could still run," he said. Now he used Magda's voice alone, the alto soothing and intimate. It was the kind of voice that made you want to listen. She must have been very persuasive while she was alive. "I'd let you go."

Waves of disapproval came from all corners, uniting them in purpose.

"No," said Jennifer.

"No," said Topaz.

"Hell no," said Satana. "How stupid do you think we are?"

"Very stupid," replied Lucifer. "But I'm not complaining. I've been wanting to take Magda for a spin."

He turned, grabbing onto a thick length of silk that dangled from the rafters. The crimson fabric swayed as he began to climb. Sinewy muscles bunched and pulled the acrobat's slight figure up off the ground swiftly. She'd been strong, but Topaz didn't think she'd moved with such spiderlike agility before. The scuttling motion appeared more insectoid than human, and the sight of it ran chills down her spine.

Satana took a single step forward, eager to pursue. She glanced over her shoulder, wafting concern through their link.

"I can climb up, but I can't take you with me," she said.

"Go," Jennifer urged without a pause. "We'll provide ground support."

The succubus needed no further urging. She dashed across the floor and grabbed onto the burgundy silk, two long strands of it that swung from a single mount high up in the rafters. Magda was already halfway up a deep purple silk that swung next to it, her arms churning. She paused to look down, her eyes wild.

"Come on up!" she shouted. "The air's great!"

As Satana began to climb, Jennifer summoned up a purple globe of power, holding it at the ready. Topaz followed suit, edging away. Lucifer wouldn't be able to block them both. She had a clear shot, and the urge to take it was overwhelming. They could end this fight before it began. But Lucifer wouldn't have climbed up there if he wasn't confident in his ability to shield himself from any distance attacks. It would be better to conserve her power for the right moment and strike him when he was distracted.

He reached the platform high above, jumping off the silk with a light bounce that betrayed a long history of climbing and no fear of heights whatsoever. Topaz envied Magda that skill. She'd learned to fly under Doctor Strange's tutelage, but it turned out that heights made her sick.

Lucifer leaned down, cupping Magda's hands to her mouth.

"Hello, down there!" he yelled.

Topaz and Jennifer exchanged glances but didn't respond.

"I hope you enjoy our show!" he continued.

With equal amounts of drama and relish, he pointed to the frozen people up in the rafters. The lights intensified, and dramatic music blared from the speakers. Topaz didn't know if he controlled the electronics with magic, or if he'd left one of his flunkies with just enough will to work the light board. It didn't matter anyway.

One boy on the end near the trapeze took a single step forward.

"No!" she yelled.

He was maybe twenty years old, with a clean-shaven face and a deep cleft in his chin. His eyes fixed on something unseen off in the distance, heedless of the small platform he stood on or the hundreds of feet to the ground. Topaz unleashed every bit of mental power at her disposal, trying to wake him up, to grab onto some wisp of thought that she could use to pull him back to himself. But she found nothing. Her mental calls echoed infinitely in his mind, as if she shouted into an abyss.

Without a blink or a moment's hesitation, the young man took another step. His foot encountered nothing but air.

He plummeted toward the ground as Lucifer applauded.

# CHAPTER THIRTY-SIX

Satana climbed the silk swiftly. Like Magda, she threw form out the window and just pulled herself higher and higher off the ground, her arms churning. Humans used a variety of tricks to make up for their lack of strength, coating their hands with rosin and wrapping their feet in the fabric to give them leverage as they ascended, and Satana had gone through the motions in aerial class, but she didn't bother with the ruse now. Her supernatural strength allowed her to skip such assistance. All subtlety had been thrown out the window. The only important thing was to win.

She'd taken a few classes during a bored period about two years ago. She'd mastered pole dancing in a matter of weeks, but the silks hadn't been her strong suit. She'd lacked the patience necessary to remember the various wraps and drops, whereas she could just muscle her way through the pole classes, making up for her lack of training with superhuman strength. Luckily, she didn't need to do any fancy moves today. She just had to ascend quickly, and she could do that.

She'd just joined Lucifer on the platform when someone

jumped. At first, she didn't realize what had happened. The young man had been standing on another platform a few yards away, and all she saw was a flicker of movement out of the corner of her eye. But Jennifer's horrified scream drew her attention to the plummeting body. Desperate horror flooded Satana, quickly replaced with a wave of mingled relief and pain as Topaz caught the falling performer, boosting her strength with a momentary surge of magical power.

Now Lucifer's plan became clear. He would hurl these innocent people to their deaths as a distraction. Torn between saving the circus folk and fighting him, they could lose.

Not on Satana's watch. Although his mind was thousands of years old, even Lucifer had his limits. She would test them. If she kept him busy enough, he wouldn't have the time to order those people to their deaths.

Also, it would be fun.

She dashed at him, claws outstretched. Magda only came up to her shoulder, but her build suggested long hours of physical exertion, augmented by her magic and Lucifer's extensive power. Satana had never faced an opponent so formidable. As she launched herself into the air, fear and worry coursed through the coven's mental link, but to her surprise, she found that she wasn't afraid. Lucifer might be dangerous, but defeating him would be easy compared to overcoming her fear of her father. She'd done that. She could do this, too.

Magda's lips twisted, revealing her fangs. The moment that Satana's claws grazed the acrobat's gauzy clothing, she took a single step backwards. Her foot met nothing but air.

Lucifer fell.

As he toppled backwards, Satana swore that he crooked

one of Magda's fingers at her in a come-hither gesture. She didn't even bother to hope that he'd splattered on the ground; someone so egotistical wouldn't commit suicide. But Lucifer was deathless. He could only be defeated, and if she wanted to do that, she'd have to follow him.

She dropped to her belly and looked over the edge. Lucifer had grabbed onto the silk as he fell, halting his descent with a move that would have torn a normal person's shoulder right out of the socket. He hung there, one-handed, and gestured to her as if inviting her to take a nice walk outside.

She hesitated. Confidence was one thing, but tussling with the King of Hell while suspended twenty feet off the ground on a piece of fabric didn't seem wise. She could just blast him and be done with it. She raised her hands, summoning up a ball of red energy about the size of a golf ball. It crackled as it grew, sucking power from the marrow of her bones. She had enough fury to fuel a thousand of them. That wouldn't be a problem.

But she'd forgotten the hostages in the rafters. No sooner did she realize it than two more stepped off the ledge. She sent an instantaneous warning to Jennifer and Topaz, which was answered with a wave of reassurance. They would save the jumpers, but it was up to her to bring Lucifer down. She'd learned this lesson, though. Blasting him with magic wouldn't kill him, even if they all attacked at once, but it just might send twenty people to their deaths. He wanted her to join him on the silks, and he would make her pay in lives for every moment she kept him waiting.

The prospect of aerial combat concerned and excited her in turn. She took a deep breath and lowered herself onto the silk once more. Although she had the strength to drop down like

Lucifer had, she couldn't guarantee when she'd be able to catch hold of the fabric, which spun slowly from its rigging. If she fell further than she wanted, Lucifer would gut her like a fish.

So she descended gradually instead, dropping down a few feet and wrapping her legs. It had been so long that she wasn't sure she had it right, and split silks were unforgiving. If she lost her grip, she'd be a goner.

"Come on," said Lucifer, impatience tinging his polyphonic voice. "I'm getting tired of waiting, little succubus, and my boredom is fatal."

Another performer stepped off her platform, her hoop skirt flaring like a bell as she dropped like a stone toward the ground.

"Patience is a virtue, grasshopper," replied Satana.

He growled, the insult hitting home. Then she released the silk that anchored her in place, opening her legs in a split and spinning toward the ground. The fabric unwound from her body as she descended, her senses reeling. While her demonic blood spared her from a variety of human ills, vertigo wasn't one of them, and she was out of practice on the silks. During her first class, she nearly threw up, but it got easier with time. Too bad she hadn't kept up with it.

She'd intended to stop next to Lucifer so they could battle hand to hand on equal footing, but she must have miscounted in her rush to wrap the silks around her body. She came to an abrupt stop, hanging upside down just above Lucifer's head. For a moment, their eyes met in shock and confusion. The blood rushed to Satana's face, filling it with heat and pressure, but flipping upright would leave her back exposed to attack. She would just have to beat him before being inverted became too painful to bear.

Although they hung in midair, they brawled like two street toughs. Lucifer swiveled, one knee anchored in loops of fabric, and kicked her in the face. She snapped backwards, trying to absorb the blow, but it made her already spinning head swim. She grabbed Magda by the hair, pulling the possessed acrobat's face into her forehead. Bone crunched and blood flew as the impact broke Magda's nose, but of course Lucifer didn't so much as blink. He was just taking the body for a ride, after all, and he felt no pain. But he could be incapacitated. He could be delayed long enough for the Ghost Rider to join the fray and end this before more people died.

Satana spun wildly, the silks absorbing the momentum of their struggle. As she turned to face Lucifer again, she hit him with a red blast of magic that sent him whirling and bought her time to right herself. But as soon as she flipped upright, a return blast of magic walloped her on the side of the head.

Her grip loosened, and she fell, spinning in dizzying circles. In desperation, she snatched out, frantic to grab onto something to halt her fall before she splatted on the ground. Her flailing legs caught the purple silk, and she clamped down as hard as she could, her teeth slamming down on her tongue as her fall came to an abrupt stop.

It hurt, but she was in a better position now. Now they were on the same silk, which thankfully held both of their weight. If Satana climbed up underneath him, Lucifer could only stomp at her fingers, without much force behind the blow. But Satana had claws, and she wasn't afraid to use them. By the time she was done, Lucifer could kiss Magda's Achilles tendons goodbye.

She climbed swiftly, her lips stretched by a wicked smile. Lucifer saw her coming, but there was nowhere to go but up.

So he anchored Magda's right hand in loops of fabric, locking her feet into position. Satana recognized the move. Once he'd anchored himself properly, Lucifer would drop down a few feet, trying to knock her loose.

She didn't give him the opportunity. She reached his feet and freed her hand from the delicate fabric before manifesting her claws. One rip in the stretchy silk could mean the death of her. She clawed at Magda's ankles, drawing blood. Lucifer snarled, kicking at her, but to no avail. Grinning, she grabbed on and dug deep, her claws rending the flesh.

She would have torn Magda's foot off if she'd had the chance. But before she could, something grabbed her by the ankle and yanked, pulling her off balance. The silken fabric slithered over her skin like a snake, animated by Magda's magic. It grabbed hold with an unnatural dexterity, heedless of her attempts to kick free. She snatched at the silks, trying to rip herself away. But her claws snagged the fabric that held her high off the ground, tearing it until only the tiniest piece supported her weight. With alarming speed, it frayed under the pressure. Desperately, she grabbed at the intact fabric above her, knowing she only had milliseconds before she fell.

Lucifer kicked at her hands, knocking them loose.

She should have fallen to the ground. But the red silk held her aloft by her ankle. At first, she couldn't believe her luck, and she wondered if she had her fellow witches to thank for the save. Then the silk lifted her up with apparent ease to look Lucifer in the eye. Blood spatter from her ruined nose spread across Magda's cheeks, but he grinned anyway, showing her fangs.

"Now I have you right where I want you," he said.

"Afraid to fight fair, aren't you?" she spat.

Lucifer clucked Magda's tongue. "Come now, child. You don't expect me to fall for such juvenile trash talk, do you?"

"What next, then? You haven't beaten me yet."

"Oh, yes, I have."

With a dry slither, the silk that entwined her feet began to work its way free. She pulled herself up, every muscle in her body tensing to lift her torso up and try to grasp at the retreating fabric, but she couldn't get a grip on it. The silk released her.

She plummeted toward the ground.

# CHAPTER THIRTY-SEVEN

The Ghost Rider tried to push his way through the crowd without harming them. They crushed him, pressing together with such force that some of them gasped for breath. But not a flicker of intelligence showed in their eyes, even as they suffocated themselves to death.

But his efforts got the Rider nowhere. Sure, he managed a few steps, but the crowd moved with him, smashing his arms to his sides. He couldn't draw his weapons. If he was mortal, he would have struggled for breath, too, but the Rider's power fueled Johnny's weak mortal body without the need for such things. What he did need was to free himself and join the fight. But he couldn't move. The blank-eyed performers pressed against his flame-covered hands, staring into his empty eye sockets.

He couldn't damn them, but maybe a little pain would wake them up. He concentrated, allowing the flames to burn them a little, hoping to drive them back. The air filled with a sickening sweet stench, but the plump, middle-aged woman before him didn't bat an eyelid as her flesh sizzled.

Well, that didn't work. He wormed his hand downwards, inch by painstaking inch. The tips of his phalanges brushed against the cold metal of the chain. He twisted, contorting his body nearly to its breaking point, desperate for those last few millimeters that would make all the difference.

Somewhere deep inside, Zarathos wondered why he even cared. Most of the performers would be unworthy. He should burn them all and engage Lucifer before the demon could escape. Nothing else mattered. But something stayed his hand. Exasperated, he tuned in to Johnny's voice, listening for the inevitable litany of reminders. Once, in a rare moment of humor, Johnny had shown him the film *Pinocchio*, pointing out the cricket and saying, "That's me, when you've got the wheel." Then he'd laughed. Zarathos didn't understand mortal humor, but the comparison was solid. Whenever Zarathos took control, Johnny kept up a steady stream of can'ts and don'ts.

But he was quiet, and as Zarathos wormed the chain free of the pressing crowd, he thought that over. Perhaps he was getting too soft, too human, after all his time spent on this plane. With a start, he realized that he thought of himself as male now, even though spirits had no use for things like gender. Such distinctions served no purpose. His only purpose was to bring justice and vengeance upon the sinners of the world. But over slow stages, the work had changed him.

When Johnny took over again, he would put some thought to this. He would scourge the human weakness from his being and return to his true form – single-minded and merciless in his pursuit of his mission. For now, he slid the chain free and wondered at the pointless humanity of it all.

But he still did it.

The chain finally slid free, and he lashed it out overhead with an expert flick of the wrist, whipping it like a helicopter blade. The metal whistled through the air, coming to life with a roar of flames. Bodies pressed on him with increased agitation. The performers grabbed at his sleeves and collar, trying in vain to hold him in place. Their zombie-like stares pinned him.

As soon as the chain had built up sufficient speed, he whipped it toward a dangling trapeze on the other end of the tent. The metal hit it with the force of a rocket, nearly tearing the structure from its moorings. But it held, and the Ghost Rider began to climb free of the crowd. The fiery metal discouraged the brainwashed circus folk from tearing down the chain, although they tried anyway, hissing in pain as the Hellfire burnt gouges in their skin. Desperate hands tugged at his body and tore one of the belt loops from his jeans. But he ignored them, ascending quickly along the length of the chain. Finally, he was free.

He paused to take stock of the fight. Satana had acquitted herself well. She and Lucifer hung suspended over the arena on long lengths of fabric, exchanging blows. The other two witches had their hands full fighting a small group of about ten performers. The struggle kept them just busy enough, distracting them from the true target.

But the Rider would end this, once and for all. He reached the trapeze, holding on with one hand with supernatural ease, and shook the chain free. Satana provided an excellent distraction. Lucifer wouldn't know what hit him; all Zarathos had to do was wait for a clear shot. He swung the chain into motion, building up momentum for the strike.

The fabric moved of its own volition, manipulated by

magical currents that the Ghost Rider couldn't see. He could only watch as it yanked Satana free, dangling her upside down and shaking her with teeth-rattling vigor. Now was the time to strike, but the fabric held her up before Lucifer, shielding him. The chain would have to go through Satana in order to hit Lucifer, and that wouldn't do at all.

The fabric loosened as Satana struggled. The Rider watched, torn between duty and pity, between his mortal side and the urges of the immortal spirit that rode him, as she tried to delay the inevitable. He could catch her partway down, or he could take the opportunity to strike out at Lucifer and end this once and for all.

The chain whipped around overhead as the Rider's two sides warred for domination. The flames flickered; the chain faltered.

Satana fell.

# CHAPTER THIRTY-EIGHT

Jennifer Kale let loose a clinging gout of magic that enveloped the lithe acrobat that clung to her back, pulling her free. She was getting tired. The performers just kept coming, their mindless attacks zombie-like in their desperate hunger. They bit; they clung; they tried to climb inside her and wear her body like a suit. That's what it felt like, anyway.

Topaz had tried to put them to sleep, but their minds couldn't be quieted. There were no minds there to calm. So the two witches worked in efficient unison, catching the performers as they fell to the ground and then dropping them when they tried to bite. She kept an eye on Satana while she fought, but the succubus held her own against the King of Hell, striking a series of furious blows that made Jennifer want to cheer if only she'd had the breath to spare.

A hulk of a man lumbered toward her, his fists clenched. He cocked a meaty fist back, telegraphing his every move. Jennifer waited, light on her feet, until the strongman began his swing. Then she darted inside his defenses, the blow whistling through her ponytail, and struck a quick uppercut into his gut, her hand blazing with red magical energy. The magic lent her strikes the oomph that her muscles couldn't, and her attacker's air whistled out of his lungs. But she was already moving, landing a brutal spin-kick to his ribs and turning to follow up with the flat palm to his throat that would end this once and for all.

But she'd forgotten herself. This man was at Lucifer's mercy, one of his puppets. Maybe he was a good person or maybe not. But Jennifer had no right to kill him, not while he couldn't even control his limbs.

She pulled the strike at the last instant. For one breathless moment, she enjoyed the wave of relief that coursed over her. Then a hand the size of a canned ham came barreling into the side of her face. The force of the blow spun her around as pain rocketed through her head and stars danced behind her watering eyes. She blinked quickly, trying to regain her vision before he pounded her into a pulp, but her eyes didn't want to cooperate. They wouldn't focus, and so she scrambled backwards, an uncoordinated flight that was doomed to fail. He could kill her.

The only hope she had was her magic, but she couldn't concentrate enough to hold a shield. She couldn't remember how. If only she could focus, she would be OK, but that single blow had rattled her hard. The second one just might kill her.

But when the touch came, it was light and gentle. Still, she shrank away before a steady stream of reassurance came through the psychic link. Then Topaz's healing energy came coursing through her head, clearing her vision enough to see the empath standing over her.

"Thanks," said Jennifer, but the other witch was already on

the move, turning to meet a nondescript man in flannel who held a wrench over his head, ready to strike.

Jennifer twisted to her feet, looking around for a target. The bodybuilder lay unconscious on the ground, and she stepped around him, giving the body a wide berth just in case. Topaz must have really rocked his world, but the sorceress didn't have the time to be impressed. A woman in a tattered black dress struggled to her feet before her. Jennifer had just a moment to catch her breath before she'd have to engage.

She glanced around. The Ghost Rider had lashed his chain to a trapeze and climbed out of the crush of people that had held him for so long. As she watched, he dangled from the circus implement with one hand, making it look easy. He drew his shotgun with slow deliberation, careful not to bobble the weapon and lose his chance to shoot. He sighted, but he didn't fire.

Satana dangled in his way, suspended by a length of ensorcelled fabric that threatened to drop her on the ground. Jennifer unbuckled the *Tome of Zhered-Na* and flipped open the pages, skimming fast. The book contained the perfect spell, one that would encase Satana in an impermeable bubble that would carry her to the ground, out of the way of Johnny's line of fire. It would be perfect, if only Jennifer could find it.

The fabric loosened its hold. Satana fell.

# CHAPTER THIRTY-NINE

Satana fell.

"Have a nice flight!" yelled Lucifer, his voice alight with glee.

The Ghost Rider's implacable gaze swept the big top. The other witches couldn't help her. They could do nothing but shout her name as she plummeted toward the ground. Her demonic stamina could heal a lot, but falling thirty feet and landing headfirst would be too much to bear. She would die.

"No!" screamed the Ghost Rider.

The chain flicked toward her, lightning-fast, wrapping around her waist and snapping taut inches from the ground. Hellfire bit at her skin, making her shriek with agony. She swung up into the air, carried by momentum, and grabbed onto the edge of one of the platforms. Painfully, she pulled herself up to standing and gave him a grateful thumbs up. With a practiced jerk, the Ghost Rider pulled the chain free of her body. He turned his attention back to Lucifer.

But the devil wasn't alone. He held two struggling figures in Magda's wiry arms. Johnny hadn't seen them in years, but he would have recognized their cries of fear anywhere. He heard them every night in his dreams.

Emma and Craig Blaze kicked their feet as Lucifer squeezed them tight. They'd died as teens, but now they were elementary-aged again. Emma sported a missing tooth, visible as she screamed for her daddy to save her. Craig's hair was rumpled from his struggles, and one big piece stuck out in the back. His untamable cowlick had been the bane of Roxanne's existence for years.

They couldn't be real. This had to be one of Lucifer's tricks, but Johnny didn't care. He couldn't chance it. Whatever Lucifer planned for them, it couldn't be good. If he failed them again, it would break him.

"I'm coming!" he yelled.

But his body wouldn't obey him. The flames burned, brighter and brighter, as the chain whipped overhead. He couldn't make his arm stop. The tentative balance that had existed between human and spirit no longer held. Zarathos had taken control.

"I think your kids are bored, Johnny," said Lucifer, grinning his vampire grin. "Maybe I'll take them to my place. Show them the sights."

"Daddy!" Emma screamed.

The chain built up speed. Now Johnny knew what Zarathos intended, and he was powerless to stop it. But still, he struggled. He begged.

"Don't hurt them. Those are my kids, Zarathos. My kids," he said in their shared mind, over and over again.

But he heard no answer, no indication that his pleas registered at all. The Rider loosed his weapon. The chain whipped toward them despite Johnny's last-ditch effort to stop it from happening.

The burning chain whipped through empty air. Cries of fear were cut off with abrupt finality as Lucifer disappeared with his children in tow. Johnny knew he'd remember them until the end of his days; he'd replay them over and over again, desperate to figure out what else he could have done. How he could have saved them.

An agonized howl tore from his throat as the chain slid to a stop.

Satana fell.

The succubus plummeted to the ground, and Lucifer leaned over to yell, "Have a nice flight!" in a voice that suggested he hoped for the opposite.

Jennifer glanced around. No help would be coming. The Ghost Rider was still climbing out of the press of the crowd; he wouldn't make it in time. Topaz grappled with a man dressed like a killer clown. If she didn't do something, Satana would die.

There! Jennifer found the spell, running her fingers along the text and speed-reading the instructions. The words came to her mouth readily, as if she'd practiced them a million times before. Power built up inside her, a thundering pressure similar to a full-body headache but not quite. It itched.

Her chant built, increasing in volume. The magic surged inside her, desperate to be freed.

A blast of Hellfire burnt through the magical book in a flash of fire and ash and struck her in the chest. She toppled backwards, howling, as the *Tome of Zhered-Na* fell into pieces.

In the shadowy corner opposite her, Marduk grinned with satisfaction as he saw that his fireball had found its mark.

The cover crumbled to dust; the pages scattered in a sudden wind. She stared at her empty hands in shock, barely able to believe what had happened. The book should have been immune to Marduk's magic, but maybe he'd done something to it when he took it. Besides, she couldn't deny her eyes. All that knowledge, gone forever.

She had failed.

"Nooooo!" she howled in despair. After all she'd done, all she'd lost, the horror and grief threatened to tear her in two.

A portal opened in the air above her, and a distant roar of triumph announced the Hellphyr's impending arrival. The magic pounded down on her, pushing her to the floor. She gasped for breath like a beached fish, unable to form words or draw upon her power. Besides, what good was she without the book? She scrambled to her feet anyway, knowing the struggle was futile. But she'd try.

A boom of displaced air accompanied the Hellphyr's reappearance. Her ears popped as she tried to scramble out of the way, but it landed on all fours, its limbs encasing her. There was nowhere to go. The demon crouched over her, slavering with anticipation.

She held up a hand, trying to summon up her power, but the Hellfire strike and the loss of the book had rattled her hard. Pulsing purple energy wreathed her hand for only a second before it flickered and died.

The demon leaned down toward her, dripping foul, caustic drool on her face. It burned where it touched her, and she threw up her arms to protect her eyes.

*"Time to die, sister,"* it said in her brother's voice.

Satana fell.

There would be no help. No cavalry. She shouted in terror as the ground swelled beneath her, but no one answered. Her hands grasped at empty air. In desperation, she reached out through the coven's psychic link, but she couldn't feel it. Either they had left her, or they were dead.

She whistled through the air toward the ground, curling herself into a ball. She was no delicate flower, but this impact was going to hurt. For the first time in her long life, she wished she could fly. She would have even worn a cape if it would help, and capes were a major fashion faux pas. For years, she'd taunted Jennifer about her old bikini and cape combo. What kind of super hero uniform was that? Was she preparing to swim and ride a horse simultaneously?

It was a stupid thing to think about while falling, but what else did she have to do? Flailing and screaming was beneath her.

"Have a nice flight!" yelled Lucifer.

A bright orange light flared in her vision, and when she landed, it hurt, but not half as much as she'd expected. Dazed, she shook her head and tried to figure out what had happened.

The Ghost Rider had caught her.

Johnny put her down, holding onto her shoulder as she swayed. He still wore the Ghost Rider flames, and his eyeless skeleton grinned down at her.

"Thanks," she gasped.

A blast of Hellfire struck him in the chest. Normally, such things wouldn't bother the likes of the Ghost Rider, but this was no ordinary Hellfire. It seethed with Magda's magical power, increasing its intensity by a thousandfold. Not even the Rider could withstand it. The fire strengthened with every passing second, growing to laser-like ferocity.

He screamed. She'd never heard the Ghost Rider shriek like that, and she never wanted to again. She tugged at his arm, trying to pull him out of the blast radius. The hand came off, the bones scattering across her lap.

The skeleton disintegrated before her eyes. It all happened so fast. She didn't even have the time to call his name.

An alien awareness touched her mind, instantly recognizable. Zarathos. The spirit of the Rider searched for another host. Satana dropped her defenses and welcomed it in, eager for vengeance. She would stand against Lucifer in Johnny's place. He would have wanted it that way.

"*No*," said Zarathos, its jagged voice echoing in her mind. "*You are unworthy.*"

"Unworthy?" she squeaked.

The word punched her in the chest, driving her breath away once more. She'd spent years proving her worth. Zarathos was blind if he couldn't see that.

"Lucifer will get away," she begged. "You can move on to another vessel once we beat him. You can't leave us like this! Help me defeat him."

"*Despite your struggles, you are just like him, and you always will be,*" said Zarathos.

His presence faded from her mind until she couldn't feel it any longer, and no amount of screaming brought it back.

The Ghost Rider had left them to die at Lucifer's hands, and all because Satana hadn't been human enough after all.

•••

Topaz didn't see Satana fall, so Lucifer's shout took her by surprise.

"Have a nice flight!" he yelled.

Topaz disengaged a teenage boy's fingers from her hair and put her hand to his temple, sending a surge of magic through his body. He slumped, his limbs gone suddenly numb. Then someone fell on her from above, knocking her to the ground and driving the air from her lungs. The impact dizzied her, and she could do nothing for a moment but struggle for breath. Her chest stung with every gasp, a sharp pain that suggested the abrupt impact had broken something. Great. Just peachy.

The person atop her groaned. With slow, painful movements, she rolled them off her and pushed out from beneath them, ready to punch them in the face. She'd tried the peaceful solution, but she was getting sick of taking all the damage. Maybe a pop across the face would wake Lucifer's puppets up. It was worth a try. After all, nothing else had worked.

But it wasn't another of Lucifer's jumpers. It was Satana. The succubus groaned, holding a hand to her head as she struggled to sit up. She took one look at Topaz's cocked fist and scowled.

"Some kind of friend you are," she said. "I just fell out of the sky, and you want to punch me, too?"

"I think you might have cracked my rib," Topaz complained.

"Well, if you were better at catching, maybe that wouldn't have happened. I knocked my head on the floor, and you don't see me whining."

"Whining?" Topaz's voice rose an octave as her frustration boiled over. She'd had enough of the blank-minded employees who tried to tear her hair from her scalp while she was just trying to help them. Enough of the constant fear of the past few days. Enough with feeling like the most useless member of the group. Enough of being forgotten and neglected in favor of people who were louder and more useful than her quiet magic. "Let's watch you get crushed by someone from a hundred feet up and see how you like it."

"That's the point." Satana bared her teeth in an expression that pretended to be a smile but was really something more aggressive in disguise. "If you'd fallen out of the air, I would have caught you. You know, like an actual hero."

"A hero? Last time I looked, you were the opposite. What's that called? Oh, right. A demon."

"That's it."

With a snarl of fury, Satana launched herself at Topaz. The empath caught her wrists, holding them at bay with effort. But Satana's claws began to grow, lengthening by the second, their sharp edges inching toward Topaz's eyes.

"What the hell is wrong with you?" Jennifer looked down at them as they struggled on the floor. "Quit bickering and help me."

Satana hissed, her claws scratching at Topaz's cheeks. Her red eyes glittered in malicious satisfaction. Topaz relaxed, allowing the damage, and then as soon as Satana's guard was down, she slid her knee up between them, using the leverage it provided to launch the succubus into the air.

"Quit fighting!"

The toe of Jennifer's shoe nudged her in her broken ribs. Topaz snarled in pain, launching to her feet. She would have taken a swipe at Jennifer if not for the man in the sequined coat who grabbed her by the wrist and sunk his teeth into the meat of her arm. She screamed, a white-hot agony running like lightning through her body. Her free hand curled into a fist, striking at her attacker in absolute panic, but she couldn't dislodge him. His teeth worked in her flesh, sending jolts of pain through her with every movement.

Jennifer turned to look at her as she struggled. Then, without a word, she turned back towards the next approaching throng of employees and blasted them with purple energy.

The pain brought an unexpected clarity as Topaz continued to struggle against her attacker. This wasn't right at all. Jennifer would never turn her back on her coven mates like that, and while Satana could be hot-headed, she was protective to a fault. If anything, she ought to be climbing the rafters to get back at Lucifer, not crawling on the floor toward Topaz with murder in her eyes. Johnny Blaze was nowhere to be seen, and although she'd only just met him, she couldn't believe that he would abandon them to face Lucifer alone.

It was like they'd gone back to the very beginning of their coven, those first few days after Stephen Strange had brought them together, forcing them into a partnership each of them resented for different reasons. When they weren't trying to kill each other, they were at each other's throats. Although she understood the stresses that had brought each of them to that point, she still flushed with embarrassment every time she thought about it, and now it was happening again.

Topaz refused to believe that this was what they'd come to. They'd all grown up since then. They'd put the work into resolving their differences, and they'd forged a family, the first one Topaz had ever known. Family didn't treat each other like this.

Maybe she was the weakest member of the coven. Maybe her magic wasn't the flashiest. Maybe she hovered in the background while the others hogged the spotlight. But they would have her back no matter what. They wouldn't leave her to be gnawed on like a corn on the cob.

This wasn't real.

Now she knew what Magda's magic was – an illusion that wrapped each of them in their own dream world. When had it started? She wasn't sure, but she could feel the illusion tugging at her awareness, trying to lull her back into complacency. If she gave into it, she would eventually be like the circus employees – an empty body, its mind locked away in a prison of illusion and pain. She wondered what each of them saw, what loved ones they fought and tears they cried. She imagined their sorrow and fear. She knew how that felt. She could still remember how it had crushed her when she'd realized she was alone in the world and always would be.

But now she wasn't, and no one was going to take her family away from her. Not Lucifer. Not Magda. *No one.*

Her magic burst from her in a torrent of rage, grief, and furious love. It filled the room with crackling energy, freezing all the employees in place. It wound itself around her coven mates, reminding them of everything they'd shared. Every argument. Every late-night game session. Every cup of tea. It pulled the Ghost Rider out of hiding, filling his ears with the laughter of his children and the pain of losing them. It reminded them of their greatest triumphs and deepest sorrows. She would not rob them of their pain. She would heal them with it. It drew them together and reminded them of their humanity.

Her magic lashed at Lucifer, pulling images of Magda's life

from her very cells. The King of Hell had never experienced the roller coaster of human emotions, but they pelted him now. Pain and loss, ecstasy and delight assaulted him in turns. Magda's body seized, buffeted by the wave of emotions, attempting to reject its demonic occupant. But Lucifer was too strong to be dislodged. He roared in defiance.

"You are mine!" he yelled, his voice so deep it shook the walls of the big top.

"No."

Magda's voice was half the volume of his, but it had a quiet strength. Topaz could imagine what she'd been like: introverted and small, the kind of woman who hung around in the background. The kind of woman who was underestimated. Just like Topaz herself.

But Magda did not give up easily, even when possessed by the Prince of Darkness himself. With the help of Topaz's magic, she had just enough strength to reach through the veil of death and propel her body to take one last step.

Magda's foot hung over the empty air for a long moment, and then Lucifer jumped, an expression of surprise written all over his face.

# CHAPTER FORTY

Johnny didn't realize he was hallucinating until the illusion dissolved around him. He found himself crouching in the middle of an empty big top, sobbing with the intense grief of a man who had just lost his children for the second time. Later, he wouldn't be able to say what made him pause and look around. Something inexplicable shifted inside him, and he knew without a doubt that it hadn't been real.

Steady reassurance from the psychic link flooded him. Topaz's deep certainty filled him to the brim, and for a moment, he relaxed. The sight of Craig and Emma would haunt him for a long time, but at least he didn't have to carry around a double load of guilt on top of that.

A gentle yellow glow filled the room. He wiped his eyes and got a hold of himself, enjoying a moment's peace. Then he twisted on crouched legs to look for the source of the light, even though he knew without question what he would see.

Topaz shimmered with power. It coated her body, spilling from her fingertips, motes of light drifting into the air from the tips of her nails. It lifted strands of her long, black hair, winding them snakelike around her head like a benevolent Medusa. It blazed from her eyes, which were bright like the gems that shared her name. She reminded him of some ancient Indian goddess come to life, beautiful and dangerous in turn. It was a good thing he was already on his knees, because he would have fallen down before her if he'd been standing.

Movement behind her caught his eye. The empath's blinding glow made it difficult to see. He squinted, tenting a hand over his forehead in a vain attempt to screen his vision, hoping to see Jennifer or Satana emerge from the shadows. He could feel them through the link, but other than a vague direction, he couldn't tell where they were. His head was still addled from Lucifer's illusion.

The glint of light on metal caught his eye as the golden glow reflected off the sacrificial knife in Lucifer's hand. The demon raised Magda's hand, preparing to drive the blade between Topaz's shoulders. He paused, his eyes catching Johnny's. The effects of Topaz's magic had faded away, leaving the Prince of Lies in full control again.

He winked.

Johnny couldn't move fast enough. The Hellfire surged within him, but it wouldn't strike Lucifer down before he could land what was certain to be a killing blow. The wickedly curved knife would pierce her heart. Topaz wouldn't know what hit her.

Twin beams of energy blazed out of the darkness, one purple and the other red. They crackled with magical power, pinning the Prince of Darkness between them, freezing him in place just as the knife began its downward arc.

"Down!" Johnny yelled.

The light around Topaz went out like someone had flicked a switch, and she dropped to the floor in a boneless heap. Fear and fury drove the Hellfire out of Johnny's body in a concussive blast. It roared toward Lucifer like a fireball, but the King of Hell could only stand and watch as it bore down on him. The fireball hit, mingling with the witches' magic, engulfing the demon in a bubble of power that closed in on him with inexorable strength.

The bubble collapsed on itself, making Johnny's ears pop with such vigor that his jaw hurt. Ash rained down on the hard-packed ground as Magda's body returned to the earth. The shard of Lucifer's soul dissolved along with it, and Johnny could sense its slow dissolution and return to Hell where it belonged. He massaged his sore face and took a deep breath of relief.

Satana came rushing out of the shadows, falling to her knees next to Topaz. Jennifer was only a second behind her. Between the two of them, they helped the groggy empath to her feet.

"Are you OK?" Satana demanded over and over again with such urgency that Topaz couldn't get a word in to answer.

She nodded.

As soon as they'd helped her to her feet, Jennifer turned to Johnny.

"Did we get him?" she asked, worry creasing her face.

"Yeah. He's gone."

She patted her stomach as if to reassure herself that the *Tome of Zhered-Na* still sat in its carrier. Johnny's eyes tracked the movement. He knew what that haunted expression meant. He probably had one to match.

"You hallucinated too, huh?" he asked.

She blanched.

"I think we all did," said Satana. "That yob. I'd like to bring him back just so I could kill him again."

"No!" exclaimed Topaz.

"I wouldn't really do it," muttered Satana.

Jennifer held up a finger. If anything, she looked more worried than before.

"How do we know this is real, then?" she asked. "How do we know it's not like one of those nightmares where you dream you wake up, but in reality, you're still sleeping?"

They all turned to Topaz, who stood, serene if a little unsteady. The corner of her mouth quirked in a smile.

"It's real," she said. "I'm certain."

"That was some power you packed," said Satana. "I told you so. Sometimes you've just gotta let loose."

"I won't be able to do that again," Topaz replied with certainty. "Until I rest up. And practice. But that's OK. I saved my family." A grin split her lips. "You all owe me big time."

"But I saved you, too!" Satana protested.

"I wasn't exactly sitting around and twiddling my fingers," Jennifer added.

"I'm staying out of this," Johnny declared.

"Oh, no, you're not. Get over here. I need help walking, because my head wants to float away like a balloon," said Topaz.

He crossed the big top toward her and looped an arm around her waist. But to his surprise, she enveloped him in her arms. He'd never been much of a hugger, and he stiffened, not really knowing where to put his hands.

"Relax, you idiot," said Topaz, hugging him tighter.

"Aw, what the hell," said Satana, joining them. "But we'll never speak of this again, right?"

Jennifer snickered, wrapping her arms around all of them. At the center of the hug, Johnny closed his eyes and let his head fall back. For the first time in a long time, he realized it felt good to be alive.

# CHAPTER FORTY-ONE

"Food's ready!"

The thunder of feet on the stairs answered Satana's call in seconds, and Jennifer grinned as Johnny and Topaz sprinted through the living room en route to the kitchen. Johnny grabbed Topaz's arm, pulling her backwards and rushing through the door ahead of her. Topaz growled in mock anger, and Jennifer shook her head as she followed them.

"Kids," she said. "You're just like elementary school kids. Are you ever gonna grow up?"

Johnny swiped a hamburger off the platter and stuffed the entire thing into his mouth in one go. He replied, but the words were muffled, and bits of meat sprayed onto the table.

Satana snickered. "That's very mature."

Johnny threw a hot dog at her. Behind him, Topaz dissolved into a helpless bout of giggles.

Jennifer didn't begrudge them the playfulness. They were all relieved. After they'd returned to the house, they'd slept most of the day away, and now they were up, and alive, and together.

They'd faced down Lucifer and lived to tell the tale. They'd all be having nightmares for a while, but they'd escaped major injuries. Even Topaz, although when the light hit her just right, Jennifer swore that her hair still glowed. But despite all odds, they'd triumphed. No wonder everyone was feeling a little punchy. Everyone, that was, except Jennifer.

She remained quiet, listening to the steady stream of banter between the three of them as they chowed down on a wide spread of cookout delicacies. Satana had made enough food for ten people, and at first Jennifer thought they'd have leftovers for a month, but once she started eating, she realized she was famished. How long had it been since they'd last had a real meal? She couldn't remember. It seemed like it had been a lifetime since Johnny had arrived, and soon he'd have to go.

To her surprise, she found that she didn't want him to.

They had a good thing going in Salem. She was happy here. But Johnny had completed the circle in a way she hadn't even realized they needed. He needed it, too. She hadn't seen him joke around like this since they were kids.

"You OK?" he asked, studying her.

She shoveled a bite of potato salad into her mouth and nodded, trying to avoid a lengthier answer. But Satana punched her on the shoulder and scowled.

"Come on," she said. "Spill it. Who do I have to beat up?"

"I dreamed about Magda last night," Jennifer replied.

The statement fell like a brick into the middle of the conversation. Everyone stopped, their faces drawn down with seriousness.

"The real Magda or Lucifer-Magda?" asked Satana.

"The real one, I think. We sat on a swing set and talked about our childhoods, and the circus, and our families. I kept expecting some demonic creature to leap out of the woods and rush us, but it didn't happen. It was disconcertingly normal."

"So, it was just a normal dream, then," said Satana.

Jennifer shook her head. "I think it was real. At the end, she talked about her illusions, and she said she was sorry Lucifer used them against us. She never practiced her magic, I guess. She was afraid of what it would turn her into, being able to make people see whatever she wanted."

Satana winced. "Yeah. I get that."

"She wanted me to tell you all that she's OK. And thanks."

Jennifer hung her head. It didn't make sense to grieve someone she'd never truly known, but she did anyway. She would never meet Magda, not really, and no amount of triumph could erase that hurt.

After a long silence, Johnny picked up his glass and drained it. "Man, you sure know how to throw a party, Jen," he said.

"Yeah? Then stay. I don't want you to leave," said Jennifer. "I can't believe I'm saying this, but I'll miss you."

Johnny ducked his head. "Yeah. Me, too. But you know what I'm up against. The longer I wait, the worse it'll be. Although what we've done here will make the rest of it easier. Not easy, but I'll take what I can get."

"Do you need help?" asked Jennifer, unsure how she wanted him to answer.

"If I ever had any doubts, I know you're up to it. But I can't ask you to do that. It's pretty clear that Lucifer and Marduk both want to get their hands on that book." Johnny frowned. "We may have dealt them a blow, but they'll be back."

"My father holds grudges," said Satana, nodding. "Once he's licked his wounds, he'll be back to his old tricks."

"But we could take them, couldn't we?" asked Topaz.

They all exchanged silent glances. Yes, they'd proven that they could take on the big guns, but they needed time to heal. Their flesh might be whole, but some injuries couldn't be seen. That didn't make them any less real.

"I'm not saying I recommend it," said Topaz. "But we could, if we wanted."

"We could," Jennifer admitted.

"I've got it for now. What are the chances that another of those fragments has magic?" Johnny asked.

"Don't tempt fate!" Satana demanded. "What are you, stupid?"

"Yeah, yeah. I'm sorry. If I get in too deep, I'll call for help. How about that?" Johnny offered.

"I can live with that," said Jennifer.

"You could come back once you're done. Take a mini vacation?" Topaz suggested.

"A vacation?" Johnny ran his hand through his hair. "I'd probably last a day before I started hunting again."

"Yeah, but you'd be here. With family," said Jennifer.

"So, it would be a family vacation," said Topaz brightly. "Right?"

Satana groaned. "That's awful."

Topaz picked up an ear of corn on the cob and mimed whacking Satana on the head with it.

"Hush, you," she said.

Johnny pushed back from his still-full plate and looked around at all of them. His normally hard face softened, just a little. Jennifer knew he'd always be a hard case – he had to be in order to survive – but that didn't mean he didn't care. If anything, the man loved too hard. Heck, maybe that was what made him such a good Ghost Rider. His intense emotions balanced out the inhuman drive of the spirit that empowered him. She hadn't understood that until now, and she had to respect it.

"Maybe I'll swing by when I'm done. For a few days, mind you. I can't sit around and eat bonbons all day with my feet up like some people," he said.

"Was that an insult?" asked Satana. "I made this food. I can take it away, Bonehead."

He grabbed onto the plate.

"Over my dead body," he said.

They spent half the night at that dining room table, chatting and bickering as the food grew cold. None of them complained. Tomorrow, everything would be back to normal. Johnny would hit the road in search of the next fragment, and all the pain and horror that came with it. Jennifer would return to her study of the *Tome of Zhered-Na* with a new appreciation of its power. She would have to step up her game if she was going to keep it out of the hands of those who wanted to use it for ill. Satana would continue fighting against her demonic impulses, but with a new confidence in the strength of her human nature. And Topaz would return to making teas and caring for the shop, secure in her abilities and herself for the first time in her life.

Life would go on. They would win battles and make mistakes that would haunt them forever. They would fight evil and then go home to eat takeout. They'd bicker and risk their lives for each other. They would part ways and reunite. But something had changed over those few short days. Each of them had faced their personal demons – both literally and figuratively – and lived. They'd stuck by each other. In the process, they'd forged the kind of bonds that would never be broken.

Jennifer pushed her chair back from the table and held her glass aloft.

"To family!" she said.

Johnny sighed.

"Why did you wait until I drained my glass to propose a toast?" he asked. "You did it on purpose, didn't you?"

"Yes, I did," she said, and stuck her tongue out at him.

# ACKNOWLEDGMENTS

Thanks to all the folks at Aconyte Books and Marvel Entertainment for being the bomb diggity to work with. In case it's not obvious, that's a compliment. Special thanks to Charlotte Llewelyn-Wells for being the bomb diggitiest of them all. My gratitude and appreciation also goes to all of my fellow Aconyte authors, who are invariably talented and welcoming and delightful.

Suzanne Casamento, April Kirk, Paige Kirk, and Layla McMichael provided some invaluable feedback on aerial silks, and deserve all of the credit for the bits I got right. I come from a family of bikers, and Larry Rugg and Dale Lewis Sr. gave me a billion rides altogether. They deserve all the credit for the motorcycle bits I got right.

As always, special thanks go to my family: Andy, Connor, Lily, and Ryan. Thanks for humoring me every time I wanted to talk flaming skeletons at the dinner table. Special appreciation is also due to Emily Cooperider, Ali Cross, Jennifer Fick, and Sarah Ison for patiently listening to me vent about the manuscript in progress.

Last but definitely not least, I want to thank all of the Marvel fans who have reached out to geek out about my books and about these characters in general. I hope you enjoy what I've done with our favorite bonehead.

## ABOUT THE AUTHOR

CARRIE HARRIS is a geek of all trades and proud of it. She's an experienced author of tie-in fiction, former tabletop game executive and published game designer who lives in Utah.

*carrieharrisbooks.com*
*twitter.com/carrharr*

# MARVEL UNTOLD

Discover the untold tales and hidden sides of Marvel's greatest heroes and most notorious villains.

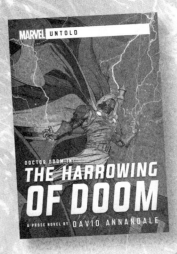

# MARVEL CRISIS PROTOCOL

Bring the action to life with the greatest heroes in the galaxy.

# MARVEL HEROINES

*Showcasing Marvel's incredible female Super Heroes in their own action-packed adventures.*

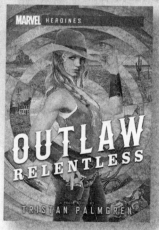

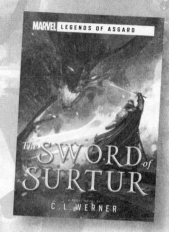

# WORLD EXPANDING FICTION

## *Do you have them all?*

### MARVEL CRISIS PROTOCOL
☐ *Target: Kree* by Stuart Moore

### MARVEL HEROINES
☐ *Domino: Strays* by Tristan Palmgren
☐ *Rogue: Untouched* by Alisa Kwitney
☐ *Elsa Bloodstone: Bequest* by Cath Lauria
☐ *Outlaw: Relentless* by Tristan Palmgren

### LEGENDS OF ASGARD
☐ *The Head of Mimir* by Richard Lee Byers
☐ *The Sword of Surtur* by C L Werner
☐ *The Serpent and the Dead* by Anna Stephens
☐ *The Rebels of Vanaheim* by Richard Lee Byers *(coming soon)*

### MARVEL UNTOLD
☐ *The Harrowing of Doom* by David Annandale
☐ *Dark Avengers: The Patriot List* by David Guymer
☑ *Witches Unleashed* by Carrie Harris
☐ *Reign of the Devourer* by David Annandale *(coming soon)*

### XAVIER'S INSTITUTE
☐ *Liberty & Justice for All* by Carrie Harris
☐ *First Team* by Robbie MacNiven
☐ *Triptych* by Jaleigh Johnson
☐ *School of X* edited by Gwendolyn Nix *(coming soon)*